RAVE REVIEWS FOR

Agatha Award-Winning Author

Katherine Hall Page

and the Faith Fairchild Mysteries

THE BODY IN THE BELFRY

"One of the best firsts in recent years, especially because of Faith Fairchild, its protagonist"

The Armchair Detective

THE BODY IN THE KELP

"Great characters, a wonderful plot and a puzzle laid out in the unfinished threads of a quilt"

Ocala Star-Banner

THE BODY IN THE BOUILLON

"Jaunty, breezy . . . **BOUILLON** tastes great!"

Boston Herald

THE BODY IN THE VESTIBULE

"Great atmosphere and a bang-up ending in the provinces"

Mystery Lovers Bookshop

Avon Books are available at special quantity discounts for bulk purchases for sales promotions, premiums, fund raising or educational use. Special books, or book excerpts, can also be created to fit specific needs.

For details write or telephone the office of the Director of Special Markets, Avon Books, Dept. FP, 1350 Avenue of the Americas, New York, NY 10019, 1-800-238-0658.

THE BODY IN THE VESTIBULE

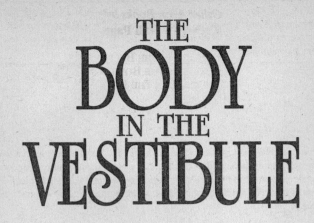

Katherine Hall Page

AVON BOOKS ◆ NEW YORK

All the characters and events of this book are fictitious, and any resemblance to living individuals or real events is strictly coincidental and unintentional. The city of Lyon and the Cévennes region are quite real, although in a few instances some slight liberties have been taken with geography and two street names.

AVON BOOKS
A division of
The Hearst Corporation
1350 Avenue of the Americas
New York, New York 10019

First Avon Books Printing: September 1993

AVON TRADEMARK REG. U.S. PAT. OFF. AND IN OTHER COUNTRIES, MARCA REGISTRADA, HECHO EN U.S.A.

Printed in the U.S.A.

RA 10 9 8 7 6 5 4 3 2 1

P.G. Humphrey

For Ruth Cavin, editor nonpareil

Acknowledgments

My thanks to the following friends and their families, who introduced me to their own particular Lyon and who keep bringing me back for more: especially François, Michèle, Barbara, and Renaud Vital-Durand, our first guides and champion correspondents; Christine Baleydier and François Maugiere; Marie-Annick Billioud; Anne, Gérard, Amélie, Marine, Alexis, and Anouck Champsaur; Madeleine and Michel Deborde; Chantal Caliendo and Pierre-Louis and Léonard Giannetti; Marc and Jacqueline Jeannerod; Françoise, Henry, and Maud Kennedy; Michèle and Michel Magnin. And to Alan and Nicholas, who are always ready to go anywhere and eat anything.

"Le mauvais goût mène au crime." "Bad taste leads to crime."
—An early French proverb or the Baron Adolphe de Mareste
(1784–1867), depending on whom you believe.

"Three men, one from Paris, one from Marseille, and one from
Lyon, are standing by the side of the road watching a girl ride
by on a horse. The Parisian says, 'Look at that horse!' The
Marseillais says, 'Look at that girl!' and the Lyonnais says,
'Whose daughter is she?'
—Anonymous

One

There are many ghosts in the city of Lyon. Some appear at twilight—on the Place Bellecour when a couple strolling across the large, open square may find the shadows suddenly deepened, the breeze cooled by the memory of the guillotine that once filled the gardens with cries for blood.

Other ghosts wait until the city is dark and different noises fill the traboules, *the long, ancient passageways snaking down from the Croix Rousse* colline *to the quais below. These are the sounds of the silk workers, hungry, exhausted, leaving the clatter of the looms to carry the richly glowing brocades to the waiting ships.*

Sometimes, the night watchman at the Musée des Beaux-Arts thinks he hears nuns chanting, looks out the window into the ancient cloister, notes the rustling leaves in the birch trees, and quickly crosses himself.

1

Then there are the ghosts that are not ghosts, the shadows that move rapidly up the steep stairs from the Place des Terreaux and vanish into the traboules. The next day, a child hastening to school may kick aside an empty syringe, stumble across some broken glass, smell the night smells, and emerge gratefully into the morning air.

To know the city is to know all the ghosts.

Faith Sibley Fairchild waited impatiently for the light to change on the Quai St. Antoine so she could get to the open-air market on the other side of the street. Several times, she was tempted to dart across the traffic, yet after a week in Lyon, she had not only learned which baker had the best bread but that French drivers would not hesitate to mow you down if you put so much as a toe in the way of their Renaults and Peugeots—respectable-looking individuals hurling quite unrespectable phrases out the window in the process. It was just like Boston, in fact.

She swung her empty straw market basket, her *panier*, idly back and forth. Despite the delay, she felt a lovely sense of well-being. Her husband, the Reverend Thomas Fairchild, was happily engaged in work; her three-year-old son, Benjamin, was happily playing at nursery school; she'd happily made it through four enervating months of pregnancy and still wanted to have a baby; and—most important of all—she was in France for a month. It had been a wonderful incentive for getting over morning sickness, which in Faith's case came like clockwork at dinnertime. The idea of passing up the fabled food of Lyon was unthinkable. Whatever the reason, this pregnancy had been better than the first, or rather less worse, and now all her appetites were back.

And at four months, she did not have the sensation of two bodies occupying the same and equal amount of space at one time, which was contrary to somebody's law, and, recalling the experience now, Faith felt, should surely be against whoever's it was. Four months was a little gift from nature, a hiatus of sorts, to allow prospective parents to paint the nursery, read thirty or forty books of baby names, and, if so gifted or inclined—Faith was neither—knit a bootie or two before settling in for the long stretch. It was a time when you thought of soft little bottoms and tiny kissable fingers, not dirty diapers or sleepless nights. *Well-being* was exactly right. She felt well right down to her toenails and even slightly mellow, edges blurred. This was a very different Faith from the one normally known to her near and dear. That Faith's crisp judgments about the world and its inhabitants were swiftly uttered more often than not. Now they were hidden in some warm, fluffy corner of her brain. She was enjoying this kinder, gentler state for the moment, secure in the knowledge that it wouldn't last long and soon she'd be back in full form.

It was a long light and the traffic continued to stream by. Faith's mind wandered back to the February afternoon when Tom had come home with the news that he had an opportunity to spend a month in France working on his dissertation. She'd been huddled on the living room sofa, wrapped in a down comforter, trying to convince herself that she had made a wise choice when she left a glittering career as one of Manhattan's most successful caterers to be a parson's wife and mother of one and two-ninths children in the small (and at present very cold) village of Aleford, Massachusetts. Tom, rosy-cheeked from the frosty air, his thick reddish brown hair hatless, his coat unbuttoned, had come bounding through the front door, lustily singing "La Marseillaise" at the top of his voice. The sight of all that energy was so galling, Faith had wanted to throw something at him. But there had been nothing at hand and it would have required too much effort to get up.

He'd grabbed her and cried, "Faith, *ma chérie,* we're going to France! Soon! April, if I can swing it!"

Tom had spent an undergraduate year in Paris, developing a fluency in the language and a permanent love affair with the country. He'd also acquired a number of friends, and if he was currently no longer in touch with a certain Simone, he was with Paul Leblanc, a graduate student who'd lived in the same pension. It was a letter from Paul, now in the history department at the Université de Lyon, that Tom was waving ecstatically as he told Faith of the proposal. Paul had learned he could bring in visiting scholars to give a lecture or two, offering them a small honorarium and the chance to do research at the university in return. He'd known Tom had been struggling to finish his work on the effects of the Albigensian heresy in twelfth-century France on subsequent Christian practice and he thought his old friend might want to make use of the university's famous library. Tom most certainly did.

"I've checked the calendar and you know Easter is early this year. I'd have to be here then, of course, but we could leave by the middle of April. I can get people to cover the pulpit for a month. Lord knows, I've done it often enough myself for others."

"I'm sure He does," Faith agreed, her mind—and body—in a whirl. "But, darling, what about the rest—all the meetings, the hand-holdings, not to mention the serious stuff?"

Tom had been momentarily perturbed. "I've been wrestling with that all afternoon. The opportunity to finish my doctoral work is important to the parish, certainly, except I know I want to go just for the fun of it, too. Maybe even mostly. I'm sure First Parish could survive for a month without me, probably a whole lot longer, but—"

Faith had interrupted him there. Lyon was in the southern part of France. It would be warm. Her way was clear.

As it turned out, the congregation was unanimous in its support and in typical Yankee fashion seemed to be looking forward to coping on its own in novel and ingenious ways. The lone nay-sayer was Millicent Revere McKinley, better known in the Fairchild household as a strong contender for the world semiprofessional meddler title. Millicent kept an eye on things from her strategically located clapboard house across from the village green, as well as an ear firmly directed toward whatever ground she happened to be treading. And Millicent covered a lot of territory. The sole reason Faith characterized her as "semi-professional" was because of Millicent's oft-stated aversion to paid employment as being, well, slightly déclassé. There was no question that she was a pro.

"We've always been Congregationalists, of course," Millicent would announce to all and sundry in the check-out line at the Shop and Save, or wherever else she could find a captive audience. Her tone clearly indicated that none of the men of *her* cloth would do such a quixotic thing. The only legitimate reason for a minister to abandon his flock was missionary work, and although she believed the French were no better than they should be, and might well qualify, she doubted that was what the Fairchilds—especially Faith, she'd added to a select few—had planned. "Mind you," she'd told Hattie Johnston, the ex-postmistress, whose former position and generous attitude toward what someone wrote on a postcard—if it was meant to be private, they'd have written a letter—had cemented the friendship between the two women. "Mind you, I'm not criticizing Faith, but you *know* she's only going there to buy more clothes, and somehow she's convinced poor Tom to go along. Research, my eye. Doesn't he have the Boston Public Library right here?"

For once in her life, Millicent was wrong. Faith was also going to eat French food.

But everything had worked out and the plane had left Logan Airport as a light snow was falling. Faith had contentedly watched the lights of Boston harbor and the expressways grow dimmer and dimmer until they disappeared

5

altogether. "Good-bye Boston. Good-bye Aleford." Ben and she had waved out the tiny window, filled with a swirl of snowflakes. "Good-bye goldfish-bowl life," Faith had added in a whisper. As the date for departure had drawn closer, she'd been filled with an even greater than usual longing for anonymity.

Faith was no stranger to parish life. Her grandfather and father had both been ministers, and despite having lived in a parsonage that was a duplex on New York's Upper East Side and enjoying relative privacy, she'd decided by the time she was twelve there was no way she'd ever marry a minister. But at twelve, she hadn't yet met Tom.

Brakes were squealing. She was jerked back into sun-drenched Lyon—miles and worlds away. She looked at the people on either side of her. The wonderful thing about travel was that on a certain level you ceased to exist. Nobody knew her name—or that she hated baked beans, and sometimes took a Judith Krantz out of the library, or directed meaningful glances at her abdomen, or . . .

It was great.

The light changed and Faith crossed the street. She'd been to *le marché* St. Antoine almost every day since she'd arrived and still got excited when she looked down the seemingly endless array of stalls that stretched along the river Saône. She started walking, passing the flower sellers first, who called out, *"Bonjour,* Madame Fairsheeld" to her. She'd be back later. It was a pleasure, almost an honor, *not* to be anonymous here. Then past the old lady sitting behind a small card table with her cartons of fresh eggs, a few onions, some herbs, and today some bunches of flowers stuck into ancient tin cans of water. As usual, she was wearing two sweaters under her apron and a black kerchief on her head. She sat quietly, patiently, in contrast to the noise and crowds around her—the cries of other vendors piercing through the din—*"Un kilo, dix francs! Super! Un kilo, un kilo . . ."*

Faith squeezed by an elegant Lyonnaise ruthlessly bargaining at a fruit stall for a flat of clementines, her chunky gold bracelets glittering as brightly as the shiny fruit. The lettuce man was next. He had a large beet-red face and wore bright blue workers' overalls. He'd been the first to tell Faith the old chestnut about there being three rivers running through Lyon: the Rhône, the Saône, and the Beaujolais. The veins on his nose attested to his familiarity with the latter at least. He greeted her warmly. 'Ah, *mon chou*, what will it be today?" Then he deftly mixed the varieties she indicated, weighed them, and wrapped them in a square of brown paper.

Most of the vendors had umbrellas over their tables, which rested on trestles, or, in the case of the larger motorized stalls stocked inside with goods, the side of the truck lifted up to shade the wares. The rows of *platane* trees lining the river on both sides arched into another awning higher up. Through them all, the strong April sun still managed to find an opening and shone in bright spots on the asphalt strewn with debris—vegetable peel, flower stems, crusts of bread, stubs of the yellow cigarettes favored by the farmers.

Faith headed for the cheeses. She didn't have time to go over to Fromagerie Richard in Les Halles de Lyon, the large indoor market on the other side of the Rhône. There was no question, mother and daughter Richard, both attractive blondes with unfailing smiles, were the queen and crown princess of cheesemongers. Still, Faith's mouth watered as she looked at the array before her at the quai. If she could get St. Marcellin, perfectly runny as it was today, back in Aleford, she'd never complain about living there again.

She tucked the package into her *panier* and moved on. It was too late for the sport of chef-spotting. Other days, she'd been delighted by the regal procession of the area's famous *cuisiniers*—Bocuse, Lacombe, Chavent—usually in spotless, starched white jackets with names discreetly embroidered over the pocket, selecting just the right melon or string bean. They caressed the fruit, snapped the vegetables for freshness, and moved on with an entourage of kitchen help trailing along to load the purchases into large carts and settle the accounts.

On the way back through the market, she was distracted by a display of mushrooms. There were so many varieties, it took several minutes to decide—cèpes, chanterelles, mousserons, pleurotes, on and on. They had names with music in them. She'd make an omelet for a first course tonight, or pile them up on a sliver of toasted *pain de campagne,* a dense, crusty, chewy loaf.

With a final hasty stop for flowers, she walked quickly back toward the apartment the Leblancs had found for them, pausing at the bakery on Place d'Albon to pick up bread for dinner and a baguette that Ben and she would probably finish for lunch. Staff of life, she told herself, and looked down at her rounded abdomen. She could see her shoes, and would for some months—unless they stayed in Lyon. The pregnant French women she saw did not look any different from their American counterparts, except for the style of maternity garb that proudly emphasized with belts and sashes what still tended to be kept under wraps in the States. But with all this food, why didn't they gain a ton? she wondered.

And with that thought clearly in place, she headed for her butcher, Monsieur Veaux, to buy some of the incomparable chicken from Bresse. Monsieur and Madame Veaux's establishment was located a few steps from the apartment and seemed to function as the information center for the neighborhood. It wasn't just the little three-by-five cards that covered one wall, offering apartments for *louer* or university *étudiants* to tutor the *garçons* and *jeune filles* of the district. Several chairs had also been thoughtfully placed against the wall for weary customers and were usually occupied by one or more of the local residents. They had stopped talking at her approach when Faith first started going there, but now after a week of observation during which it became clear that here was a young woman who knew her *côtelettes,* she was hailed with great familiarity whenever she passed by, and Benjamin had become a favorite.

"I don't understand!" Clément Veaux had exclaimed as he stood in front of a cheerful poster issued by the butchers association of France, proclaiming: MON BOUCHER —IL EST UN ARTISTE! His white apron with the red streaks from the day's work stretched tightly across his round body. "You Americans throw away all the parts we like best."

"Not this American," Faith had assured him as she scooped up brains, *boudin*—blood sausage—and even *tête de veau*—although she still had not acquired a taste for the calf's eyeballs.

Veaux's wife, Delphine, sat at the cash register all day. She was less round than her husband and wore her dark black hair in a neat Dutch bob, the thick fringe of her bangs reaching the top of the frames of her glasses. The whole effect was of *une femme sérieuse*—until she smiled. She asked Faith endless questions. What did they eat for dinner? Was it true they sold ice cream for dogs in the United States? It was tempting to answer nettles and peanut butter to the first query—Delphine would not have blinked. It would also have been nice to say, "No, of course not!" to the second. But she stuck to the truth.

After finishing at the Veaux's, Faith walked quickly to the small square in front of her venerable building and went into the dark, cool, sometimes pungent vestibule. The huge dumpsters, *poubelles,* for the building were at the rear of the narrow hallway.

The apartment had been a surprise. It belonged to a

relative of the Leblancs, both of whom were from old Lyonnais families, and the cousin—a generic term for all kin outside the immediate family—was willing to let the Fairchilds use it because he did not dare to rent it. Since the Napoleonic Code, a sitting tenant has had such inalienable rights that it often took years to get rid of one, no matter what the lease said. Paul's cousin planned to move to this apartment in another year; until then, it was virtually empty. There were a bed, two tables, a few lamps, and some chairs. There was also a phone, since to disconnect service could mean never getting it restored. The Leblancs had produced a child's cot for Ben, some plates, cutlery, and kitchen equipment, and it would suffice for a month.

When Faith and Tom had struggled with Ben and their suitcases up the five flights of dizzying circular stone stairs to open the heavy oak door, using three separate keys, they had walked into an immense apartment with high ceilings adorned with intricate plaster bas reliefs and moldings, the walls beautifully painted and papered, ornate fireplaces with carved marble mantels in most rooms, and small balconies outside the almost floor-to-ceiling windows. The windows were tied shut now after Ben had exuberantly flung one open and managed to take a heart-stopping step outside onto the balcony.

Tom had walked about slowly, then let out a whoop. "Pinch me, Faith—it's like camping out in some corner of Fontainebleau!" he'd exclaimed.

The room with the bed in it faced the immense fifteenth-century church of St. Nizier directly across the square, and the clock face on one of the steeples seemed close enough to touch, especially at night when it loomed through the windows they were loath to cover with the inside shutters. The statuary on the façade seemed to come alive when illuminated at dusk, the babe in the Madonna's arms wriggling slightly, high above the street.

After their first enthusiastic impressions, the Fairchilds

began to take note of the antique plumbing—the toilet in a closet so tiny that one's knees grazed the shut door once enthroned, and with a chain pull so high that Faith, not a small woman, had to stretch to reach it, producing a cascade of water that threatened never to stop. The bathtub—at the far end of the apartment from the w.c.—had lion's-paw feet and was large enough for all three of them. Faith found it handy for laundry.

The kitchen had a stone slab of a sink and a doll-sized refrigerator and stove. To get hot water, there were two Victorian contraptions, one in the kitchen, one in the bath, that required a great many pressings of buttons, lightings of matches, and prayers.

Faith loved the apartment more than any place she had ever lived.

They'd immediately gone to Mammouth, a sort of combination supermarket, department store, and hardware store in a building the size of an airplane hangar, and bought a tricycle for Ben and other essentials. He careened recklessly from room to room. There was nothing to worry about: no furniture, no heirlooms, hardly any possessions at all. Faith filled the rooms with flowers from the market, arranged in some pitchers and vases from Mammouth. She covered the table in the dining room with a few yards of paisley fabric, from the Monday nonfood market, the *marché forain*, and that was the extent of her decorating. She didn't miss her home, the parsonage with all their things. The feelings possessions bring seemed to depend on immediacy. Or, as she put it to herself in her current euphoria, the whole place could sink into the earth and she'd merely say, "Too bad."

The first night, savoring the cheese course, still suffering from *décalage horaire,* jet lag, and feeling slightly drunk—Tom on the excellent Côte du Rhône he'd discovered he could buy in bulk at the *vinotheque* nearby and Faith on the grape juice she'd found at Malleval, a fancy *épic-*

erie—they'd watched the sun set and asked themselves how they were ever going to be able to leave.

And now after she put the food from the market away, this was how Faith started a long-overdue letter to her younger sister and only sibling, Hope. Their parents had stopped short at Charity. Hope was a newlywed, living and working in New York City with her husband, Quentin, and their yours, mine, and ours Filofaxes.

I can't remember ever being so happy. Tom says it's my hormones, but he's grinning, too. Even the job of switching from winter to summer clothes early—you know how boring that is, and in New England, you no sooner drag all the stuff out than the season has changed again. This year it was easy, because nothing fit Ben or me and I decided to wait to get things here. You must be wondering what it's like in Lyon. Very different from Paris. No place is like Paris, but I think it's more livable here. The Leblancs have been sweethearts. I liked them immediately. We've been there twice for meals *en famille* and sit and laugh and talk for hours. They have two children: Stéphanie, who's thirteen and can seem thirty, as well as seven when she plays with Ben, and her nine-year-old brother, Pierre. He's very solemn and like all these French children, so perfect in their long Bermudas and polo shirts, Chipie, the hot brand and very *branché,* of course. The small children in Benjamin's school, the *garderie,* look as if they are going to a birthday party every day. But the *marque* with the greatest cachet for the preschool set is—Oshkosh! Very expensive and treated like gold.

We've also met some of the other people in our building. The d'Amberts live directly below us and their apartment stretches from Place d'Albon to Place St. Nizier, so they look out at the church on one end and the river on the other. The Saône, that is. I've finally gotten them straight. We're in Presqu'île, the center of the city, which extends like a finger between the Saône and the Rhône. Lyon is a very walkable city and Ben and I go exploring every day. He's changing so fast. You won't recognize your grown-up nephew when you see him next, and I miss my little two-year-old. I think this is how kids get their parents to produce siblings for them to play with.

It's hard to describe our apartment's location. Two buildings back onto and around a kind of courtyard, except no court—more like a large, open elevator shaft. Everyone uses the deep sills for plants, small laundry lines, and for cooling pots. The windows are all discreetly curtained, of course, but not always closed, and I'm becoming dangerously voyeuristic—or whatever it is when you eavesdrop, too. I can see the Saône if the windows in the apartment across from us are open and at the right angle. I can also see the photos of their ancestors hanging on the wall—Grand-père looks remarkably like Lenin, or maybe it isn't Grand-père at all. It's a bit strange to know so much about your neighbors—what they're having to eat, the state of their lingerie—without knowing who they are or what they look like in some cases. By the way, the French really *do* say "ooh la la" or "ooh la" for short. They also say *merde* a lot, and I don't think it's as bad as saying "shit" at home. Anyway, back to the travelogue.

Vieux Lyon, the medieval part of the city, is on the other side of the Saône and I haven't been there much yet. The best cheese, cakes, chocolate, and sausages are all on the other side of the Rhône. I know this may not fascinate you as much as it does me, but it tells you how I'm spending my days. (Citibank, you'll be happy to hear, has an office on the next block. So we are not totally devoid of amenities.)

Not getting much done on *Have Faith in Your Kitchen,* but I plan to incorporate lots of Lyonnais recipes into it and so this all falls under the category of research.

Faith looked up from the letter and out the window to the square below. Another thing that was making it difficult to work on the cookbook she was writing was the noise. Not the traffic, or occasional siren, but the music from the *clochard*'s radio. *Clochard* was the word for "tramp," she'd learned, and the literal translation did not take into account the kind of romanticism these men—and a few women—of the roads had been invested with by their more prosaic compatriots. She wouldn't have minded a little Edith Piaf or Charles Aznavour for atmosphere, but this *clochard* had other tastes—the French equivalent of elevator music and loud.

He arrived each morning quite punctually, spread out a small tattered blanket, took a couple of bottles of wine from the battered attaché case he carried like a proper *homme d'affaires,* then positioned his animals—an old mutt and a rabbit in a cage—and sat down. Just in time for the first mass. He took a small brass bowl from his case, set it down, and placed a ten-franc piece dead center. By the end of the day when he reversed the proceedings, his bowl runneth over. Faith wasn't too sure what the animals were intended to convey—a latent sense of responsibility or simply colorful window dressing. He was often joined by other *clochards* and frequently by non-*clochards,* especially teen-agers, all of whom appeared to invest him with some special kind of wisdom. The court of the bearded philosopher beggar. The large, greasy-looking cap, *casquette,* he always wore—his crown. She resumed writing.

So, there are the d'Amberts. They need a big apartment because they have five children. I see them on the stairs, very polite, very BCBG, *"bon chic, bon genre,"* Stéphanie Leblanc told me. It's some sort of French version of a well-born Yuppie. Stéphanie did not seem to be all that impressed. Tom told me the other version he'd heard from Paul, *"bon cul, bon genre,"* considerably cruder and roughly translates as "nice ass, may be underused." I don't know the d'Amberts well enough yet to know to which, if any, category they belong. They do have a very elegant card on their mailbox and a fancy, highly polished brass nameplate on their door, though.

Then above us are the Joliets. He's also at the university and always to be found at the forefront of whatever anyone is protesting, Paul told us. Madame is Italian, Valentina, and owns a small art gallery a few blocks away. She has invited us to a *vernissage,* an opening, Saturday night. She's very lively, very pretty. No kids. She told me her husband was enough.

On the top floor, there are some students and, in a closet-sized apartment, Madame Yvette Vincent, the widow of another *professeur*—it's quite an academic building. Madame is over eighty and climbs up and down the stairs several times a day to do her marketing or take her little dog out. (Everybody seems to have dogs here, if the streets are any evidence. We even saw a couple bring their dog into a restaurant we ate at the other night, and order for him. When the food came, it was garnished with parsley, just like ours. *Bonne préparation,* as if FiFi would notice!) Back to Madame Vincent. Besides being agile, she's extremely elegant— well coiffed and very à la mode suits. I had a chance to see her apartment when she invited me for a cup of tea. The main room was filled with armoires, commodes, tables, fragile little chairs all from Louis somethingth. Her bed was behind a silk drape, which she proudly pulled to one side. Ben's crib was bigger. We drank from Sèvres cups, of course, or I should say, *bien sûr*. My French is improving dramatically, but not as fast as Ben's. He rattles on about *le petit lapin*—named Peter Rabbit!—at school and his *bon ami* Léonard."

Faith looked at her watch. She'd have to finish the letter later. It was time to get said child. She glanced in the tiny mirror over the bathroom sink and put on some lip gloss and blush. French mothers, at least in Lyon, never appeared in the streets in untidy clothes or without makeup. They didn't have the kind of style Faith saw in Paris or even elsewhere in Lyon, on rues Victor Hugo or Emile Zola, where skirts were very short, and agnés b. or Clementine supplied them, yet the mothers still had that seemingly unconscious ability of most French women to look good—no matter how homely they were. She thought of her neighbors back in Aleford in their ubiquitous jogging suits, jeans, or, in the case of the older women, ensembles from Johnny Appleseed's. Informality was easier, but it didn't look as chic.

She raced down the stairs, paused almost at the bottom until the walls stopped spinning around, then opened a door and took Ben's stroller out. She'd been lugging this up and down the stairs with Ben and usually a full *panier* in tow until, happily, Madame d'Ambert pointed out that one of Faith's keys opened up what had formerly been living space for a concierge and was now a storage area for bicycles, etc. As she grabbed the stroller, she was struck as always that the good old days hadn't been so lovely for all concerned. The Belle Epoque in this case meant a low ceiling, a single interior round window, so dirty that little light passed through, and narrow rooms extending the length of the building. She locked the closet again and went out the door into the square, hoping Ben would consent to be pushed in his *poussette* and not demand to push it, as usual.

It was close to noon and everything in Lyon had come

to a halt for the sacred hour, sometimes longer, for lunch—or almost everything.

Faith and Tom had been amused to discover that St. Nizier and the small, narrow surrounding streets composed one of Lyon's red-light districts. At lunchtime, the prostitutes were out in full force, as men put aside work for the pleasures of the table, and perhaps the bed, as well. Every day to and from school, Faith passed the same three women who stood casually a half block down from the butcher's. One had a small, fluffy dog that Ben adored and it wasn't long before they had entered into conversation. The dog's name was Whiskey, she told them. Faith realized that as an outsider, and a transient one, as well, she had the freedom to break the conventions people like the d'Amberts, and even the Leblancs, followed whether they wanted to or not. So she was fast becoming close friends with her butcher and his wife and could stop and shoot the breeze with the ladies at the corner. Their names were Marilyn, Monique, and Marie. Marilyn appeared considerably younger than the other two and wore glasses, which she pulled off whenever a car slowed at the curb, then called discreetly, *"Tu viens mon minet?"* The little dog was hers.

Monique appeared to be about Faith's mother's age and had the largest bust Faith had ever seen. She favored tube tops in a variety of neon colors, miniskirts in black, and patent leather go-go boots—a kind of universal outfit, as much at home over the years in Boston's Combat Zone or Paris's Pigalle as here.

Marie could have been twenty or forty. She smoked constantly—how constantly was a question that crossed Faith's mind—and had a mane of bright red hair to her waist. It was when Marie had told Faith one day last week to hurry upstairs, her husband had come home for lunch, that she'd begun to suspect Lyon was a village, too.

It was always difficult to get Ben to leave school, especially when he'd been playing with the riding toys in the big

17

room, and today was no exception. It ended the same way as usual, too. The teacher, Jeanne, watched Faith cajole, speak firmly, start to leave in the blind hope he would follow; then, with a smile, she stepped in and said firmly, *"À demain, Benjamin. Dit 'au revoir.' "* And Ben kissed her, said good-bye, and left. Of course, it was one of life's perverse truths that children will always behave better for anyone else than a parent, but Faith was convinced Jeanne possessed some hidden powers. Mesmerism, or something she sprinkled in their milk.

The *garderie* was a godsend. Faith was afraid she might get a little boring about how wonderfully the French arranged their lives when she got back to Aleford, but the government-sponsored child care *was* truly wonderful. And the public transportation. And the health care. And the . . .

Benjamin was in high spirits and raced out to the street with Faith in swift pursuit, awkwardly lugging his stroller. She called, "Stop" at the top of her voice, then switched to *"Arrêt,"* and he did. Miraculously, he also allowed himself to be strapped into the stroller. Ben's blond hair was losing its curls with each haircut, although hot weather and exercise produced the damp that restored them and his face was framed with tendrils. He gave her an angelic smile. It didn't fool her for a moment, but it was a nice moment.

They made their way slowly back to the apartment. Ben was fascinated by a barge on the river, crying, to Faith's delight, *"Bateau!* Mom! *Bateau!"* They crossed the street to the bridge to stand and watch it pass underneath. It was a houseboat, a *péniche,* with a small, bright green square of AstroTurf, complete with lawn chairs, on the deck. From the bridge they were standing on, they could look down the river to the other spans arching gracefully across the Saône. On one side, old Lyon sloped from the medieval cathedral of St. Jean and the Palais de Justice up the mountain to Fourvière, a nineteeth-century basilica with Byzantine leanings that dominated the skyline. Then,

18

on the other side, the shops and apartments of Presqu'île crowded close to the quais, row upon row of brightly painted exteriors—rose, ocher, yellow—their balconies filled with pots of flowers. Once, Paul Leblanc had told her, Lyon was completely gray, matching the rains that fell for weeks in the winter. Louis Pradel, the mayor during the sixties and early seventies, had started the restoration back to the original colors. Paul was convinced this was when the city began to shed some of its reputation for bourgeois correctness and provincial snobbishness. He swore it began to rain less, too. Faith looked up at the brilliant sun. For whatever reason, the weather had been perfect so far.

When they got back to their block, Ben saw Marilyn and ran to her. As Faith drew near, she noticed the dog was cradled in Marilyn's arms, instead of at her feet as usual, and she had buried her face in its fur. Her stiff, slightly pink blond hair contrasted oddly with the puppy's fluffy brown fur. The other two women were nowhere in sight. Ben was trying to pet the puppy. Marilyn lifted her head toward them and Faith said, "Another time, Ben," and pulled him away.

Marilyn did not look like *une fille de joie*. She was crying her eyes out.

Two

Faith and Tom had been to two French dinner parties, not counting the familial gatherings at the Leblancs, and on the basis of these experiences, Faith, never one to shy away from sweeping generalizations, declared that they were the easiest parties in the world to give. And naturally, she was giving one, too.

"You don't have to worry about the food," she'd explained to Tom. "If you don't have the time or inclination to cook, you simply go to Chorliet the *traiteur,* pick up say some blinis and smoked salmon for the first course, maybe a nice duck with green peppercorns for the next or veal stuffed with sweetbreads, a few hundred of those yummy puffed-up soufflé potatoes, salad, cheese. Then off to Tourtillier for some incredible *gateaux*. Light a candle or two, pour a great deal of wine, and you're in business. Plus, you never have to worry about people not going with other people or a lack of conversation. Even if they don't like each other, the French will always talk. Then, of course, they look so nice and come prepared to have a good time."

"I think your sample is a bit small and contaminated by bias, but I agree with you. There is that tendency in Aleford to view a dinner invitation with fear and loathing."

Faith laughed. "That's because of two things. One is the weather. In the winter—roughly October to May—once you're in your own warm house, you don't want to go anywhere. The rest of the year, you don't want to go inside, because you'd miss those few fleeting moments of heat."

"And what's the other?"

"That if you go, you'll have to invite your host and hostess back to your house someday, and since I'm not back in business yet, this means cooking your own mess o'porridge."

"So *that's* what I had at the Forbeses' when I first arrived in Aleford! You can't imagine what I had to eat before I met you, darling."

"Poor thing, but let's not give ourselves nightmares."

As minister's spouse, Faith had herself consumed enough portions of mystery meats and chicken drenched with every Campbell soup sauce known to woman to want to push these memories back into her dark unconscious.

Tom was getting in the mood. "I think a party is a great idea. Who should we invite? And what'll we do about chairs? We can't ask people to stand around balancing plates for hours. Speaking of which, what will we do about plates? We only have four."

"All this is true, but the people in the building can bring their own chairs and maybe one or two extra. We'll ask the Leblancs for some more plates and accoutrements. Ghislaine keeps telling me to let her know if we need anything. It may not be the usual kind of dinner party, but we're Americans. We can be as eccentric as we please."

They settled on the Leblancs, d'Amberts, Joliets, Madame Vincent, the Veaux, and the Duclos, one of the couples from the university who had invited them last week. The Duclos couldn't make it, nor could the Picots, the other couple. Faith figured she'd be doing another party soon. She might have to invest in some plates. It left a guest list of eleven, and by putting in the leaves she'd found in one of the closets, they could all sit around the table.

Thursday, Faith was busy getting ready. She bought a roll of gift wrap that looked like malachite to cover the table, paper napkins, candles, and inexpensive holders, all at Monoprix, her favorite store in Lyon. It was even better than an old-fashioned five-and-ten, because it had great clothes for Ben, turned out to be the most reasonably priced place for sexy underwear for herself—she'd tried to seduce Tom into the brief briefs Frenchmen wore, but he was stolidly clinging to his boxer shorts—*and* sold food upstairs, but not *marché* or Chorliet food. She rarely bought anything from the shelves of canned cassoulet and a *frigo* section complete with frozen *pommes frites,* the original French fries, yet she liked knowing it was there.

She returned to the apartment with a full basket, which she set down while she opened the mailbox in the vestibule. She heard someone come in behind her, and looked up, expecting the pharmacist's wife from the shop located on the street floor of the building.

Madame Boiron was, curiously enough, an Anglophile, unlike most of the French Faith had met, who seemed to regard their hereditary enemies as ready to pull the same kind of fast one Wellington had at Waterloo. Then there was that distressing tendency the British had of referring to their friends Jacques and Marie across the water as "frogs." That the embers still smoldered and the water was wide was dramatically illustrated one morning in the *marché* when

Faith heard a large, pink English lady say loudly to her companion, "Mind your purse, Daphne." Shoppers around her froze for a moment, then moved conspicuously away. It was a wonder the Channel tunnel had ever been approved.

But it was not Madame Boiron calling, "Good morning, Mrs. Fairsheeld" in her beautifully accented English, hastening over for a practice chat. It was Christophe, the eldest d'Ambert, who nodded his head and said, *"Bonjour, madame. Ça va?"* Christophe was at *lycée,* high school, and probably returning home for lunch, although usually students this age filled the bars and small bistros near their schools during the hour or more break.

"Yes, thank you. And you?" Faith answered, still chary of her accent. Christophe spoke excellent English, due, he had told her, to his parents' desire for reducing the numbers in the apartment whenever possible. Faith knew that, in fact, his parents were doing what all the other parents of their class did, which was to send their children off at a tender age to another country to perfect their language skills during the *vacances.*

Christophe picked up her basket and gave a small courtly wave of the hand. "After you, please." Like the other French teenagers she'd observed, he seemed impossibly grown-up. Maybe it was that impossible exam, *le bac,* the *baccalauréat,* looming up at the end of their schooling that made them so somber. They sat at small sidewalk tables, chain-smoking Gauloises, or American cigarettes when they could afford them, and drinking cup after cup of *café noir.* But then she would also see them chasing each other over the playground equipment at Place Lyautey, eating cakes like happy preschoolers.

Christophe, however, at eighteen did seem to have taken a final giant step across the line between childhood and early adulthood. Somehow she couldn't picture him climbing a jungle gym. He was very good-looking—thick dark blond hair that waved conveniently back from his brow, deep blue eyes. He wore his 501 jeans with shirts and cashmere sweaters from Façonnable, a fashionable men's store whose prices left Faith gasping. She'd seen sale signs in store windows advertising, *PRIX CHOC!* and she'd told Tom that "Price Shock" was a more apt description for the physical condition you felt when looking at the tags. She'd ventured into one children's clothing store and realized an outfit for Ben was more than her new winter coat had cost last year. And this from a woman who walked fearlessly into Barney's, New York.

She knew Monsieur d'Ambert was a lawyer—his offices were on the floor above the pharmacy—and he must be doing very well, indeed. To be sure, all those clothes could be passed down to the younger d'Amberts, but still. Faith thanked Christophe for his help and said good-bye. He leaned over and casually kissed her on either cheek. All this kissing was becoming such a reflex with Faith that she was sure she'd find it hard to stop in Aleford and would stun the community by kissing everyone from the beggar at Shop and Save to Charley MacIsaac, the chief of police. Maybe even Millicent. And maybe not.

Faith turned to open the door and had the distinct impression that Christophe was lingering on the stairs. When she looked over her shoulder, he was gazing with appreciation at what Tom called her *"bon cul,"* accentuated today by a short checked skirt. Christophe did not appear at all embarrassed, nodded, and clattered down the stairs to his *déjeuner.* Faith was amused—and pleased. But teenage boys, even one who had obviously been shaving for years, did not attract her. Except, of course, in the purely aesthetic sense, she told herself.

She unloaded the *panier* and decided to finish her letter to Hope. She'd mail it on her way to get Ben.

Municipal workers were planting begonias in symmetrical circles around the lamppost in the middle of the square. She felt a little sad she wouldn't be here gazing down on them when they came into full bloom and covered the bare earth.

The *clochard* had been joined by two others. One was the man Ben called the "party man," after watching Faith, Tom, and others in the building repeatedly chase him from his refuge behind the *poubelles* in the vestibule with cries of *"Va-t'en, parti, parti!"* The other was younger, dressed in a long woolen coat tied around the waist with string. He had long hair that might be blond when washed but was a curious gray color and matted close to his head. The three were companionably sharing a bottle of wine and calling out to passersby to join them. The radio was blessedly silent.

Faith had almost finished the letter when she heard the sound of crashing glass and loud shouts through the open window. The younger man was running across the square toward the river, the *clochard* of St. Nizier in pursuit. He stopped and menacingly waved the broken bottle by the neck at the departing figure, shouting *"Ta gueule, salaud!"* followed by a gesture that made the meaning clear in any language. Then he stumbled unsteadily back to the church, still shouting. The "party man" was creeping slowly away, his back pressed against the stone façade of the church, holding his bright yellow Prisunic shopping bag close to his chest with both hands. His eyes were filled with fear. The *clochard* whirled around, saw him, and in one swift motion slashed his cheek with the bottle. Blood poured down his face and he collapsed on the ground.

A group of people had gathered outside the pharmacy, avoiding the normally crowded walk outside the church. No one moved for an instant, then as the *clochard* viciously began to kick the fallen man, who feebly tried to protect his head with the bag, several people ran across the square to stop him. Faith, like the crowd, had also stood motionless, stunned by the swift change from conviviality to violence. But when he started to kick the helpless figure, she yelled

25

from the window, *"Arrêtez! Arrêtez! Je telephonerai la police!"* The *clochard* looked confusedly toward the sky and appeared not to know where the voice was coming from. He dropped the neck of the bottle and returned to his spot by the door to the church. Two men grabbed him. There was a wail of sirens, yet he did not appear to notice, nor did he offer any resistance. Three police cars screeched to a stop. Several *gardiens de la paix* jumped out, pulled notebooks from their pockets, spoke to a few people, then dispersed the crowd and took both *clochards* and the animals away.

Five minutes later, all that was left was the broken glass, spilled wine, and a large boodstain on the empty sidewalk.

Faith realized she was shaking. It was time to get Ben and she had to force herself to walk past the church.

The next morning, the *clochard* was back, looking slightly cleaner. Same animals, same radio, same *casquette*.

"Ah, Tom, you have put your finger exactly on the problem. What will happen to us poor French in 1992 when all Europe will be homogenized into one community? We will be flooded with Spanish and Italian wines and, *quelle horreur,* perhaps English cheeses." Everyone laughed at Georges Joliet's gloomy prognostications, then proceeded to all talk at once. It remained for Madame Vincent's softer, yet more pronounced voice to rise above the rest as, slightly flushed from the white Côtes du Rhône, she declared, "France will always be France. It has nothing to do with wine or cheese, but who we are. Whether you live in Paris, Lyon, the countryside—*'la France profonde,'* we French share something that politics and economics cannot destroy. It is our destiny to be French." The rest cheered. It was a wonderful party.

The room was filled with a glow produced by the warmth of the food, the people crowded around the table, and the candles Faith had placed wherever she could find room. Everyone had brought flowers and she'd had to put the last bunch—beautiful arum lilies—in the teakettle and prop them up on the mantel. They looked perfectly at home.

They'd started with champagne and *feuilletés salés*— assorted small crunchy bits of puff pastry wrapped around an olive, flavored with cheese, or forming the base for a bite-sized pizza—the French answer to cocktail peanuts. At the table, she'd served the first asparagus of the season from the Luberon in Provence, delicate pale green stalks, steamed with a lemony mousseline sauce. Then bouillabaisse. She'd toyed with the idea of trying to create a real American meal—chicken and dumplings, baked country ham, but she had neither the ingredients nor the *batteries de cuisine*. With only one rather small frying pan, it would have taken a long time to fry chicken for eleven. She did have a big pot, though, and having walked past the seafood, artfully displayed on crushed ice day after day in the market, she'd longed for the chance to cook as many varieties as possible—which meant bouillabaisse. The only departure from her usual recipe—more a fish stew than a soup—was to remove the meat from the lobster and shrimp shells before serving. There wasn't enough elbow room at the table for the guests to do the dissections themselves, nor space for a bowl for the shells. There *was* room for a platter of slightly toasted bread liberally spread with rouille—the garlic and saffron mayonnaise, which is so delectable when dipped in the *jus*.

She'd been a bit worried that no one would want cheese after the first courses, but when she'd produced the platter from Richard, where admittedly she'd gone a little wild—charollais, epoisses, picodon, bleu de Bresse, reblochon, and more St. Marcellin, there was a murmur of appreciation. Paul Leblanc had eyed the *fromages* with delight. "Cheese. You can always find room for cheese. It's like salad."

Now they were all finding room for the cold compote of blood oranges with crème anglaise Faith had made the day before and the assortment of dark chocolates Tom had picked up at Bernachon—the correct answer on the analogy section of the SATs to the question "Richard is to cheese as _____ is to chocolate."

Faith gazed happily at Tom, who was busy pouring a Sauterne to go with the dessert. He was a good host back in Aleford, yet France seemed to inspire him to new heights. He was off the leash—or rather without the collar—and enjoying every minute of it. She knew his sense of humor and general joie de vivre were a surprise to some of the people they were meeting. Protestants, correctly or incorrectly, were regarded as a solemn, rather dour bunch, and Tom behaved more like a priest.

Throughout the meal, the talk had ranged from new movies to politics to gardens. Paul Leblanc and Clément Veaux had discovered they shared a passion for growing things, waxing lyrical about the taste of a certain pear, poire William, plucked straight from the tree.

They were continuing to talk quietly to each other about pruning, while Georges Joliet again bemoaned the creation of the European Community.

"But you are a Communist, Georges," Ghislaine Leblanc said. "Surely you are in favor of doing away with these artificial borders created by capitalistic wars?" Ghislaine wore her dark hair pulled back from her face, which emphasized her high cheekbones and the large full mouth that punctuated her question with a slightly mocking smile.

"Yes, it is true I am a Communist, but I am a Frenchman first—" he started to elaborate.

Valentina interrupted him. "You just don't want to be under the same flag as your Italiano in-laws."

She addressed the group, "Georges is a Communist, but he draws the line at my family."

Georges's face, under an untidy beard in classic anarchistic style, was crossed by an expression of intense irritation. Then he apparently decided to treat his wife's remarks as a joke and forced a laugh.

The talk ambled on. Solange d'Ambert—a feminine and very slightly older-looking version of Christophe, despite five children—lit a cigarette. Her hair was shorter on one side than the other, and when she swept the chin-length side back across her head, only to have it tumble back in a silken curtain, the gesture looked so sexy and so fashionable that Faith instantly decided to find a coiffeur to duplicate the cut with her own thick blond hair.

"Were you here during the fight between the *clochards* yesterday?" she asked Faith.

"Yes, I watched from the window. Do you know what it was about?"

She shrugged. "Not really. I was watching from the street and the old one was shouting about money. I think the young one had taken some coins from the bowl to get more wine and the old one thought he was stealing them. Or maybe he was stealing."

"Does this happen often?" Tom asked.

"Oh no," Solange reassured him. "This is a very safe area."

"Except for cars," Delphine Veaux interjected. "Lyon is noted for car theft, but with our Renault Five, we don't worry. Now if we could afford a BMW or Peugeot Six-oh-five, that would be something else. We would be lucky to have it a week."

"Cars *and* jewels, which we also do not have in abundance and so have been spared," her husband added. "There has been a rash of burglaries around here, in Ainay, and a few across the river in the Brotteaux area. However, the thieves are not greedy. They leave stereos, TV, even cash and take only jewelry and occasionally a small and valuable bibelot."

"Perhaps it's not greed but good taste," Solange offered. "In the Brotteaux, they find expensive new toys, in Ainay, all the valuables *tout Lyon* has passed down from generation to generation, and here—perhaps a mélange."

"This is a serious matter, *chérie.*" Jean-François d'Ambert appeared surprised at his wife's flippancy. "I can't understand why the *flics* have not been able to be a stop to it. What are we paying them for? To put tickets on our cars? Yes, they are very proficient at that, but when it comes to real crime, they have not a clue. Just last week, our friends the Fateuils were out of town for her mother's funeral and when they came back, pouf! All their good silver—*disparu!*"

Faith was happy to have the opportunity to use one of her favorite French words: "Do you think it is the work of one *cambrioleur*—or *cambrioleuse*—or a gang?" Immediately, her mind was filled with scenes from *To Catch a Thief*—the female cat burglar being chased across the roof tiles of Monte Carlo by Cary Grant, roof tiles like the ones she could see from the apartment windows.

"There has been some speculation on both sides in the press. I myself think it is a well-organized gang, probably operating outside our borders. Are you interested in things of this nature, Faith? I would imagine you have a great deal of crime in your area. You are near to New York City, yes?"

The French whom Faith had met so far, unless they had traveled to the United States, had a very sketchy idea of distance. "I have a cousin in Milwaukee. Perhaps you know the family?" someone at the Duclos' last week had asked her in all seriousness. But everyone knew two things—the location of Disney World and New York. They also assumed one had to have the equivalent of the Croix de Guerre to venture a visit to the latter and it was close to achieving such a dream to visit the former. Faith was beginning to think she should get the key to the Big Apple for all the public-relations work she was doing. She was about to answer Jean-François when Tom beat her to it.

"The place we live, Aleford, is a *petit village* near Boston, about four hours' drive from New York City and, *oui,* my wife does seem to have an interest in crime, in addition to a particular knack for discovering dead bodies."

Everyone laughed, assuming it was some sort of American joke, a *blague, très drôle*. Faith did not correct them and shot Tom a look to *fermer* his *bouche*. Yes, she had been involved in some investigations—a bit difficult to explain, especially in the midst of a dinner party and in a language for which she had a large vocabulary but unreliable grammatical skills. Jean-François seemed to find the joke particularly funny. Like the rest of his family, he was good-looking, but perhaps on the verge of carrying too much weight.

"Since you are interested in crime, you will enjoy meeting our friend, Inspector Michel Ravier. He will be at the *vernissage* tomorrow night, unless he is called away. I will introduce you. You can ask him about the break-ins, but"—Valentina Joliet's piercing dark eyes swept the room—"I do not think you have to worry."

"Could the *clochards* be responsible?" Faith asked, thinking to steer the conversation away from her own personal history.

There was more laughter. "A *clochard* would take the wine and maybe the TV or something like that—if he could figure out how to get into an apartment," Paul said. "These men have been drinking so long, their mental state is not very clear. Additionally, in some cases they are schizophrenic or have some other form of mental or physical illness."

"But you seem to admire them so much. I see well-dressed people sit and talk with this *clochard* all the time."

"Of course, we admire them. They are free. We envy them their lack of responsibilities. They never have to stand at the *guichet* at the post office and arrive at the front of the line, only to be told by the cretin in power to go to another window. Or produce the birth certificate of their grandmother's second cousin once removed in order to get permission to buy a car. They don't mail letters, pay bills. They don't care about birth certificates, or passing the *bac,* or any other worries."

It did not make a whole lot of sense to Faith, but she supposed it was all part of the incredibly complex nature of the French, which was even now being vividly illustrated at her dinner table. Envy of the *clochards* was part and parcel of the same impulses compelling the French to drive like maniacs when set free on the autoroutes. Tom had told her highway deaths were twice the kilometer rate as those in the United States. All that pent-up frustration had to go somewhere.

"*I* do not admire these *clochards,*" Madame Vincent said. "They are filthy and disgusting. They prey on people to get money for drink. You see them sitting so pathetically with little signs, *J'ai faim. Bien,* just try to give them food instead of money. I offered the one in front of the church a sandwich from the baker one day and he threw it at me! They are sick people, perhaps. I am sure this one is not so old. The drink has aged him, but he has no business on this earth. As far as I'm concerned, Lyon would be a better place if he and his friends were eliminated."

Faith was a bit surprised at the vehemence of Madame Vincent's remarks.

Jean-François agreed. "I am with you, madame. It does not do to become sentimental about these people. The police should round them up and make them go to the shelters. They cost us precious tax money better spent on things like catching criminals."

It was yet again time to turn the conversation in another direction and Faith hastily searched her mind for a topic. She needn't have worried. Tom stretched his arms back and said, "I need a little exercise after all this. Why don't we walk into the next room and have some cognac." The somewhat askance looks that had greeted the first part of his statement—Americans were known to jog at unseemly hours—gave way to laughter and general movement. There were offers to help Faith clean up—offers from the women, she observed—but she refused, saying she would do it later.

The party drifted into different parts of the apartment. Ben was sound asleep in his small room. Amélie d'Ambert, age fourteen, had come to take care of him during the earlier part of the evening and also put him to bed before going back downstairs to her own apartment. She was very shy, very dark, unlike the others in her family, and Faith hoped to enlist her as a baby-sitter for the duration of their visit.

Faith joined the Leblancs, who were gazing at the Eglise St. Nizier, which was illuminated at night, the steeples and statuary silhouetted against the dark sky. The bright lights shone only on the front of the church, flattening it in a curious way that suggested one might walk around to the side and see wooden props holding up a stage set, rather than the ancient, massive stones of the church.

"I prefer the Gothic brick steeple," Paul said, pushing away the strands of light brown hair continually falling across his forehead. He was losing hair from the top of his head and seemed to want to keep whatever was left, however inconvenient. "The new one is an atrocity. So much damage was done in the nineteenth century by all the Viollet-le-Duc fanatics seeking to harmonize and restore what was best left alone."

"Here we go," Ghislaine said, laughing. "Paul is a fanatic himself on the subject."

But Faith was interested, and Paul promised to take the Fairchilds on a tour of his Lyon, *"le vrai Lyon,"* he added. She liked both of them so much and understood why Tom had become friends with these newlyweds, and newly parents, years ago. Ghislaine worked at a travel agency on rue de la République and seemed happy to take time off to shop or just to meet Faith for a coffee. Faith felt as if she had known her for years.

Clément Veaux came up behind them. "Everyone has a different Lyon. I will show you mine someday. Not, as you may suspect, the abattoirs, but the gardens and greenhouses in Parc de la Tête d'Or."

"We took Ben to ride the carousel there last weekend and didn't have time to explore any further. We'd love to go."

"*Bien,* it's done. We can go on a Sunday after we close the shop at noon and eat *pommes frites* and *saucisson* while we stroll. Benjamin can bring his *vélo* and join all the other children who ride like madmen on the paths—as I did at his age."

So that's where it starts, Faith reflected. *Vélos* in the park, then Renault 5's on the autoroutes. She looked down into the Place St. Nizier. It was late, but there was still a great deal of activity and noise. Cars were parked everywhere—on the sidewalks, in small streets—in total disregard of regulations and, in fact, they wouldn't be ticketed. It was after six o'clock and anything went. She saw someone enter the building and wondered who it was. It seemed everyone in residence was here. The door was locked after the pharmacy closed each night, so it must be someone who lived here, someone with a key—probably one of the students from the top floor. She saw Marilyn walk by, arm in arm with a young man, her hair iridescent in the orange haze of the sodium vapor streetlight. Something about the way she was looking up at him suggested he wasn't a client, but a boyfriend—or her pimp? Ghislaine had told her the French word was *macquereau, mac* for short—so much slang seemed to involve food, she'd noticed—the national passion. Ghislaine had also told her the penalties for pimping were extremely severe—lengthy prison terms—whereas, although against the law, prostitutes were viewed as victims and rarely arrested. Faith sighed. Marilyn looked about eighteen. She hoped it was a boyfriend and they were off to the cinema.

She went into the next room. People had brought in the chairs from the dining room. Valentina was sitting on her husband's lap and whatever she was whispering in his ear was evidently promising. His face was raptly expectant and he was stroking her long black hair. It was hard to imagine him at the barricades. Now he looked like a rumpled, slightly balding middle-aged man whose sole concern was whether to take another sip of cognac and possibly impair his projected performance—or not.

Solange d'Ambert had lit another cigarette and was talking to Delphine Veaux about children. The surgeon general or whatever the equivalent was in France had not made much headway in changing the smoking habits of the French, and Faith worried about the effects of secondary smoke on the baby. The baby! She was feeling so well these days and was so busy, she occasionally forgot she was pregnant—sometimes for as long as ten minutes.

Tom came over and put his arms around her. "Tired, sweetheart?"

"A little, but it's such a nice party."

It was Madame Vincent who decided that nice as it was, it was time to go, and her departure started a general exodus. The d'Amberts and Joliets took their chairs. The Leblancs insisted on taking home their hastily rinsed plates, glasses, and cutlery over Faith's protestations. "We have a *machine à laver, chérie.*" There were many kisses and Tom went down with the Veaux and Leblancs to unlock the door to let them out.

By the time he came back, Faith had cleaned up what remained, bundled it into several garbage bags, and was ready for bed.

Tom joined her and they spent a happy half hour or so discussing the party—the food, the people.

"I'm not too sure about Jean-François. Seems a little too sure of himself and *très* conservative."

"Well, you could say that about Madame Vincent, too," Tom said.

"Different packaging and more to my taste. Besides, he seems a little too willing to let Solange carry all the domestic burdens. Did you notice when anything about the kids came up, he laughed and said it was her department? I'll bet Jean-François never changed a diaper in his life."

Tom held his nose. "Lucky man. It's not the part of fatherhood one rejoices in, Faith. Or the spitup on my cassock, either."

Ben the infant had had an uncanny ability to recognize newly washed and ironed or expensive, fragile clothes and preferred these as targets for his projectile vomiting—the baby-book name for the phenomenon—which always suggested to Faith and Tom that NASA was monitoring the stage. In Ben's case, the agency might have been surprised by the data. He never seemed to be in the mood when his parents were in jeans and old shirts—and his range and accuracy were amazing. Faith figured with this second baby, it would now be close to the turn of the century before she could safely wear white or silk again in the presence of said offspring. After spitup came sticky fingers, then muddy sneakers, climbing into your lap—on and on until college.

"Imagine having five children," Faith said, yawning. "Think of the dry-cleaning bills. And how could you talk to that many people in a day?"

"Maybe you don't, and how about not talking ourselves for a while, *ma poule?*" Tom liked these culinary French endearments. Calling your wife a "hen" or a "little cabbage" in English could kill the moment.

Faith, very much alive, wrapped her arms around Tom's neck. "But of course, Monsieur Fairsheeld."

Despite the relaxing nature of the night's final events and her fatigue, Faith couldn't sleep.

It wasn't Tom's slight snoring, although she had rolled him over twice to stop it and did so again with success.

It wasn't Ben. She'd already slipped out of bed once to check him. He'd kicked off the blanket, but the night was warm and he didn't really need it. Still, she tucked it firmly back around him. It felt like the maternal thing to do.

It wasn't that she needed to pee, though this month had seen a drastic increase in her number of trips to the w.c., revealing aspects of Lyon few visitors, fortunately, were forced to encounter.

She punched her pillow into a more comfortable shape, pulled the covers up around her shoulders, and listened to the darkness—an old trick for putting herself to sleep. It was completely quiet. She closed her eyes and prepared to drift off.

Maybe she should go to the bathroom one more time and then when she did get to sleep, she wouldn't be awakened. It was a good idea.

She got up, went down the hall, and afterward decided since she was so near the kitchen, she might as well have a little piece of the *pain aux noix,* walnut bread, she'd gotten to go with the fresh chèvre. Maybe she'd have a little of the cheese, too. She cut a slice of bread and spread it with the soft white cheese. As she sank her teeth into it, she realized the kitchen smelled like the lobsterman Sonny Prescott's bait shack back home up in Maine. It was the bouillabaisse debris. She wrinkled her nose and went back to the bedroom. The smell followed her, but she finished her bread and climbed back into bed, determined to sleep.

Pillow plumped, covers up, eyes closed.

And her brain promptly resumed its feverish activity. She would have been in France two weeks on Monday. It seemed both that she had been here forever and not long at all. They'd met so many people, eaten so much good food, and things happened every day. Not like Aleford, where one dawn blended effortlessly into the next and suddenly it was Sunday again, time for church. She patted her stomach. Whoever was waiting there was going to be going to work with Mommy. Lyon had put the final seal on her decision to go back into catering. Infants were delightful to cuddle and watch for varying amounts of time, but as companions they tended to pall rapidly, and this time Faith had no intention of remaining parsonage-bound. She was beginning to get sleepy. Coming to Lyon had been such a good idea. Think of the wonderful diet this little person was getting. He or she would have a head start in the gourmet department. There would be no cries of "Do I have to eat this?" but instead, "Mom, what great spinach soufflé." It was a soothing image. Ben had been developing a scary preference for macaroni and cheese lately.

Outside, a car horn sounded. Combative even in the middle of the night, she thought. Combative. That reminded her of the *clochard*. She tried to erase the image from her mind. He was nothing but an old drunk in need of help, like the man he had attacked. There must be organizations working with the *clochards*. Paul would know. He knew everything about Lyon. *Le Tout Lyon,* no, that was the group that put out the Who's Who list—everyone who mattered, supposedly. Paul had told her he did not care to be in it. Faith bet the d'Amberts were, though. Marilyn, Marie, and Monique were probably not. Maybe that's why Marilyn had been crying. She would never be a member of *Le Tout Lyon,* or *Tout Paris,* for that matter. But really, why had she been crying? Faith turned over on her other side to try to get more comfortable. As soon as she did, the odor from the kitchen assailed her again. *Dégueulasse,* disgusting. It would stink to high heaven by morning. She should have had Tom take it down when he went to let everyone out. He was breathing quietly now, deeply asleep.

Suddenly, she knew she'd never get to sleep if she didn't get rid of the smell. It might be three o'clock in the morning, but she had to take out the trash.

She put on her bathrobe and dropped the keys into the pocket, then slipped on a pair of espadrilles. She didn't want to make any noise going down the stairs and possibly awaken someone. Footsteps on the stone sounded like a cannon barrage. She took the two plastic sacks, bright blue and tied shut with an orange plastic cord—even in matters of debris, the French were chic—and let herself out. Peering over the edge of the railing, she wished she could just drop them. If the *poubelle* had been open, she might seriously have considered it, but there was nothing to do but go down—and then back up again: 121 steps. She and Ben had counted them. She pushed the switch in the stairwell. The lights were on timers and you had to be pretty nimble going from floor to floor or the dim light from the naked bulb would go out before you reached the next one. Whether this originated from ecological or economical motives, Faith did not know, but she suspected the latter in a country that regarded nuclear power as the best thing since sliced *pain*. She spun her way rapidly down the spiral stairs, praying the bags would not break and send their contents flying all over.

She was close to the bottom now. As far as she was concerned, she had no fear of heights, but when she was with Ben, it was another matter—she held on to his hand like Super Glue when they made the ascent or descent. She'd been plagued with visions of his climbing over the railing to see the bottom—he had begged to do that the first day—and then plummeting to the stone floor below. She gulped. She was at the bottom.

She pushed the light switch hastily as the one above her went out and then went back up a few stairs to reach the top of the large dumpster, which, with its twin, was wheeled in and out of the building every other day with great rapidity by men in bright coveralls—the Departement de Propreté, literally, the Department of Cleanliness. The container was so large, it was difficult to stand next to it and reach the lid. You couldn't even see into it unless you were on the stairs. Faith had noted that both Solange and Madame Vincent used her method. She'd never seen anyone else put out trash.

She put the bags down, then leaned over and flung the lid back.

Someone had been getting rid of some old clothes, she noted. Anything reusable was left to the side of the trash bin. These looked very worn. She picked up her bags and started to drop them in, and drop them she did, but not in the trash. Fish heads, bones, lobster and shrimp shells, orange rinds splayed out on the stairs as Faith screamed. She screamed again.

It wasn't old clothes. It was the *clochard*.

And he was dead.

The *clochard* of St. Nizier—his mouth hideously slack, eyes rolled back, and one hand grasping the filthy *casquette*, still in place on his head.

The lights went out. Faith was alone with the corpse.

Three

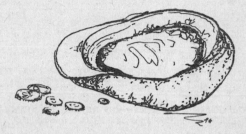

Faith stumbled down the few stairs to the vestibule and frantically pushed the button to turn on the lights. She intended to turn right around and run as fast as she could up those 121 steps to Tom and a phone.

But she knew she had to do something first. She had to make sure he was dead.

The thought was nauseating and she could hardly bring herself to approach the trash again. Slowly, she crept around to the side of the large container and groped for his hand. She could feel the slick plastic of the garbage bags surrounding him, then the rough wool of his coat. The stench of the rotting garbage made her feel faint. She followed the arm down to his naked wrist and tried to find a pulse. She did not even want to think about what she might have to do if she did.

There was no pulse. It wasn't just the smell of the trash. It was the smell of death that filled the hall.

Faith instantly dropped the lifeless hand and went up the stairs, pausing to close the lid of the *poubelle* that was now a casket. It didn't seem right to leave it open. Besides, she didn't like the idea of looking down on the body as she went up the stairs—and she knew she would look, no matter how much she told herself not to.

As she started to close the lid, she wondered what death throes had caused that convulsive grasping for his cap. His hand was like a leathery claw—the skin in folds, crossed on the back by a deep scratch, perhaps inflicted during yesterday's fight. She let the top come down and it slammed shut. She shuddered and quickly started to climb the stairs, hitting the light switch at each landing in terror at being left alone in the dark again. The cold from the stone stairs traveled through the thin rope soles of her shoes and she clutched her robe closer to her body.

How had the *clochard* gotten into the building and why had he climbed into the trash? *Clochards* slept wherever they wanted—in the parks or under the bridges of the Sâone and Rhône in good weather; in shelters or the silk workers' tunnels, the *traboules,* in bad. If they could get into a building, they'd sleep in halls, but even *clochards* wouldn't sleep in dustbins, especially with the lid down. And the door to Place St. Nizier had been locked.

One more flight. She raced up and arrived at the door, panting for breath. It was only while she was fumbling with the keys that she realized no one had responded to her screams. Were the walls that thick?

"Tom!" She ran into the room and jumped on the bed, shaking him. "Wake up, Tom!"

Tom did not make the transition from deep sleep to consciousness easily even in the best of circumstances and it took a moment for him to sit up and ask, "What the hell is the matter?" In another moment, he was out of bed, "Ben? Is it Ben?"

"No, Ben's fine!" Faith grabbed Tom's arm and pulled him back to the bed. She sat down next to him. "We've got to call the police. I don't know how it happened, but that *clochard* who's always outside the church is in the trash downstairs, and he's dead."

Tom shook his head and rubbed his eyes—hard. He knew that pregnant women had fancies, and during Ben's gestation, Faith had been fanciful indeed, yet it had usually taken the form of cravings for certain delicacies from New York restaurants and delicatessens that there was no way he could find at the Store 24 in Byford, the only source of food at ungodly hours. This hallucination was definitely something new—and one for the books.

"Darling, calm down and get back into bed. I think you've had a very powerful nightmare, but everything's fine. I'm here."

Faith reached over and put on the light.

"I'm *not* dreaming! I wish I were! I couldn't sleep and the smell of all that fish was bothering me, so I took the trash down to the *poubelle*. And when I opened it, he was there. Dead. I even took his pulse." At the recollection, she immediately got up to wash her hands. "Go look for yourself if you like, but we've got to call the police. I mean you've got to. They'd never understand me."

Tom followed Faith into the bathroom, where she started to scrub her entire arm thoroughly with Roger & Gallet's sandalwood soap.

"All right. I do believe you. It just seems so improbable."

Faith briskly dried off and they went to the phone.

After telling the beginning of the story several times to what was apparently the wrong branch of the Police Nationale, Tom managed to explain the entire situation and was told they would be there *immédiatement*.

"I'll have to let them in. Are you sure you're all right here?"

"Yes—and I certainly don't want to go with you."

Tom left with the key and Faith stood by the windows overlooking the street. In what seemed like only seconds, two police cars pulled up. She was impressed.

They approached the door and gave three resounding knocks with the heavy iron door knocker. The sound filled the night and Faith saw several lights go on in the buildings surrounding the square. Presumably, screams were normal nocturnal sounds in this part of the city. Such knocks on the door were not.

Tom must not have reached the vestibule. They knocked again. Faith opened the window and stepped out onto the small balcony. She was intending to tell them he was coming when she saw the door open. Several more lights went on at the neighbors'.

She stepped back and closed the window, then went into the living room to wait. After a few minutes, she decided to make some tea. She was freezing and maybe if she did something, she wouldn't keep seeing the *clochard*'s face in front of her everywhere she looked.

The water had just come to a boil when she heard the keys in the locks and dashed down the hall to open the door. Tom stepped in first, followed by two policemen, *gardiens de la paix* in the city, she'd learned, not *gendarmes,* but they all wore those hats that made them look like children's book illustrations.

Tom appeared—what? Worried, embarrassed, tired— he was panting slightly and the *gardiens,* although trim, were winded. They were both tall, with dark hair. Their cheeks were flushed and so smooth, it wasn't clear whether they'd both recently shaved or hadn't started to grow beards yet. The greatest difference between them was that there was a thin film of sweat on one's forehead, causing the dark hair that grazed it to curl slightly.

Faith stood contemplating the group for a moment, then asked, "What is it? What's happening?" No one seemed to be rushing forward to tell her anything.

"Why don't we sit down, sweetheart," Tom said, and led her to one of the chairs left in the living room after the party. The police glanced around in some surprise at the lack of furniture and remained standing.

"Faith, honey," Tom said gently, "There wasn't anything except trash in either of the *poubelles.*"

"What!"

"This is not to say you didn't see the *clochard,*" Tom started to explain, but then the younger of the two policemen interrupted.

"If I may, Monsieur Fairsheeld? I have some English, madame," he explained, and pulled a chair next to hers and sat down, but not before glancing over his shoulder toward his partner. Madame was in a fetching white *chemise de nuit* insufficiently covered by a robe of the same material, her blond hair was delightfully disarranged, and her blue eyes, perhaps even larger than usual at the odd events of the evening, were striking. Madame Fairsheeld had been in bed no doubt and would soon return—it was a prospect with much appeal.

He pulled his chair a bit closer. "First permit me to introduce myself. I am Sergeant Louis Martin and this is Sergeant Didier Pollet." He paused for emphasis. "Madame, what we believe has occurred is of course deeply upsetting. Occasionally, one of these men of the street—we call them *clochards*—will wander into a building and sleep there. Yes, even in the dustbins," he added as she seemed to protest. "Your presence most certainly awakened him, but he was afraid you would berate him, or worse, so he pretended to be asleep and as soon as you left, *phhtt"*—he made one of those French noises impossible to reproduce, accompanied by appropriate gestures with his hands—"out the door. So when we arrive, we find nothing."

45

"But I felt his pulse! He didn't have one! And his face! I know he was dead!"

Both police looked troubled. This *Américaine*—so lovely, so young, and perhaps so crazy.

"Besides, how could he have gotten into or out of the hallway without a key?" Faith's voice was triumphant.

"Ah." Louis Martin looked slightly chagrined. "To be perfectly honest, you can get into most of these old Lyonnais apartment buildings with the same kind of key. Some, especially, have the knack—you give a little turn and press hard, then *voilà.*"

Faith reached for the keys on the table. "You mean I could get into any of the apartments around here with this key?" She held up the largest one, an ornate, ancient key four to five inches long that looked like the one the man in the iron mask would have greeted with whoops of joy.

"But yes. However, only the front doors, madame. Not the apartments themselves."

"What a relief," Faith replied, fully aware that her sarcasm was being totally wasted.

"So you see, he came here to sleep. We did, in fact, find some empty bottles, so he was perhaps not even aware where he was. They also explain his very slow pulse. Then, like *Princesse Charmante,* you awaken him and he leaves." Sergeant Martin stood up, shared a congratulatory look with Didier at his *petite blague,* and prepared to leave.

"Tom, what do you think?" Faith was not going down without a fight—even if that fight was going to be with her husband.

In the vain hope of avoiding further discussion and possibly getting some more sleep, Tom chose to be circumspect. "I don't really know what happened. All I know is that there was no one in either one of the *poubelles.* We searched through the garbage and the only carcasses were the lobsters we consumed this evening—or I should say, last." He was very, very tired.

It was hopeless. Faith knew what she had seen and no one, not even her own husband, believed her. She would have cried in frustration, except it would simply have added to the already-damning picture of instability that had been created—the word for crazy in French is *fou,* and she felt like an utter one. She hoped Tom hadn't told them she was pregnant. There were enough stereotypes floating around.

But, of course, he had.

They stood by the door, an uneasy parting. What does one say, particularly after the inevitable little black notebooks had come out and information back to childhood solemnly recorded? Tom thanked them for coming. Not at all, not at all. Anytime, and enjoy your stay in France. Didier was from Burgundy, he revealed in a rush of sudden intimacy. He hoped they would visit the vineyards, although perhaps madame was not drinking wine. He directed his eyes significantly below, but not too far below, her waist. . . .

That was enough. Faith said, *"Au revoir. Merci,"* and firmly shut the door—yet not before she heard their voices as they circled down the stairs, wondering whether it was a custom for American women to dispose of their garbage at such an hour. Certainly, one has heard about their fetish for showers and baths, but it was strange, *non?*

It was very strange, indeed.

Faith woke up in a fog the next morning. It was a moment before she comprehended that she was in Lyon and not her bed in Aleford, a bed fast acquiring a certain allure. She groped for Tom, but his side of the bed was empty. She sat up. Her head ached and her whole body felt heavy and cumbersome, more like the ninth month than the fourth. The events of the night before crowded her consciousness and the fog didn't get any clearer.

She got out of bed and walked slowly to the window overlooking Place St. Nizier. She could hear Tom and Benjamin in the kitchen. As she got closer to the window, she suddenly realized she had been hearing something else, too. Music. Loud.

It was the *clochard*. Same place. Same pets. Same *casquette*.

Faith ran to the kitchen.

"Tom, come to the window! The *clochard* is back!"

Tom came to the doorway and gathered his wife in his arms.

"I know, darling, he was there when I got up."

"But I know what I saw! I'm not going crazy! He was dead!"

Tom clearly didn't know what to say, but Ben did.

"Who is dead, Mommy? Can Ben see?" He pulled vigorously on her nightgown. They'd explained that she was growing a brother or sister for him and he was hopeful the whole idea had been scrapped by a providential grim reaper.

"No one is dead, lovey. No one you know. Mommy was just saying something to Daddy."

Faith and Tom exchanged looks that spoke whole encyclopedias. It was difficult at times to remember that Ben understood everything they said these days. And there'd be two of them eventually. Until Ben had been born, Faith had never fully realized that when you had a child, the child was there for good. God evened things up to some extent by arranging for children—small ones, anyway—to go to sleep earlier.

"Why don't we all go to the market together and after lunch we can take the funicular up to the top of Fourvière?" The last thing Faith felt like doing was going out. Every cell in her body was sensibly advising her to get back into bed and sleep for a very long time. Unfortunately, neither husband nor son heard them.

"Great idea, honey. It's a beautiful day. Let's see how fast you can get dressed, Ben."

"Superfast. I'm Super Ben. Watch how fast," and he sped down the hall to the closet where they kept their clothes. By the time Faith caught up with him, he was pulling garments off the shelves and there was a pile on the floor.

"Ben!" she shouted angrily. He stopped, startled, then started to cry.

"I'm losing it, Tom," Faith said. "You get him dressed and let's get out of here."

The stairwell of the apartment was always dim and it seemed to Faith as they descended half an hour later that it was dimmer than usual. The garbage she had spilled had been cleaned up, but the odor of fish remained. She stopped and looked at the two *poubelles*. Tom took her arm and pulled her toward the door. The sun was streaming in from outside.

"You don't believe me, do you?" It was said, what had continued to nag at her since the police had departed.

"I believe you saw him, but how can I believe he was dead when he's sitting over there collecting a fortune in *monnaie* and blasting us all with his horrible music? And you must admit he seems an unusual choice for the miracle of Resurrection, even though the Lord does work in mysterious ways."

Faith sighed. At the moment, she wasn't sure she believed herself. She remembered Ben's pregnancy as often a kind of out-of-body experience—not merely trouble concentrating but a real sense of floating away in all directions. She hadn't felt like that with this one. Maybe it was hitting her all at once. It was the only logical explanation. She sighed again.

The man had been dead. There had been no pulse.

For once, the market failed to entrance her, and she quickly bought smoked sausages and *choucroute* sold by one of the butchers with a market truck. *Fait à la maison,* homemade, he swore. Melons were beginning to come from Spain. They'd have that first—Tom's with a little port poured in the middle. She still had salad and cheese from the party, so all they needed was bread. Ben and Tom walked along behind her, munching what Ben called "air cookies," small sponge cakes sold from a patisserie truck by a lady Faith had never seen without a smile. She couldn't decide whether the smell of the *choucroute* was making her hungry or nauseated.

"Let's get a coffee," she proposed. There was a café she liked near the market. Early in the morning, the market vendors and farmers stopped there for a *petit mâchon,* first breakfast with coffee—or a glass of *vin rouge*—before opening their stalls. Tom had christened it "Café Sport du Commerce de France," paying homage to its brethren throughout the country. An old-fashioned café, no glitz, no phony Belle Epoque repros. At this time of day, it was crowded with shoppers. They found a place and Faith sat down thankfully. Her ankles hurt. She was facing the wall, which was covered with large mirrors reflecting the pedestrians outside. Her face looked the same as it had the night before, maybe a little pale and wan, but she was still Faith. The waiter set down large steaming cups of *café crème* in front of Tom and Faith, and an Orangina for a delighted Ben, who immediately began repeating "Orangina, tina, nina" over and over until they stopped him.

The coffee smelled wonderful. In what Faith was beginning to appreciate as typical French directness, the term for decaffeinated coffee was *café faux.* She took a large sip from her cup. It was real, all right. The café was warm and the noise level increased as more customers pushed their way in. The mirror began to get a bit fogged from the heat of the coffee and the swirling smoke from all the cigarettes. Faith took another appreciative sip from her cup and started to look forward to lunch. As she put the cup down, she saw Marilyn strolling with her dog in the clear part of the mirror. As she passed by the window, Marilyn looked in and their eyes met for an instant. Faith started to turn around to wave a greeting but was astonished instead to see a look of intense fear cross Marilyn's face before she ran across the street and walked swiftly in the other direction.

She started to tell Tom about it. One more odd thing in a sea of oddities. Maybe another time. Besides, Ben was there, now vigorously searching out the last drops of soda with his straw.

"Anybody hungry?" she asked in what she hoped was a bright, untroubled voice.

The sidewalks were emptying and stores closing, as was usual at lunchtime. They paused at one end of the market so Ben could watch the commotion as the stalls were dismantled, trucks packed up, and the street cleaners took over with their hoses and brooms, still made of twigs, only plastic ones now.

As they approached Place St. Nizier, Faith looked for Marilyn and the other two, but they were not at their corner. Ghislaine Leblanc, acting as a member of what Faith was beginning to term the Leblanc-Lyon Fundamental Information Service, had told her that Saturdays and Sundays were big days for the *filles de joie*. Days of leisure for their clients, they meant busy times for the girls. Faith had been a bit surprised at the openness of the trade, but Ghislaine had told her that it had always been this way, and besides, it prevented rape and helped to keep peace in the house, *"paix des ménages."* The one time the police had cracked down on the trade in the mid-seventies, the prostitutes had sought sanctuary in the Eglise St. Nizier, to the slight embarrassment of the priests, who nonetheless allowed them to remain for a week or two in protest—restriction of free trade. After all, they paid their taxes like any other citizens! They had been more or less left alone after that; and their dramatic leader, a Germanic prostitute named Ulla, later made a sharp turn and became involved in trying to get women *out* of prostitution, and for some, *into* a drug-rehabilitation program.

Faith had a sudden flash, picturing the ladies from Boston's Combat Zone seeking refuge in Aleford's First Parish, with some sort of Valkyrie at the fore, and wondered what the community would do. Probably try to adopt as many as they could. Whenever they were downtown, her friend and neighbor Pix Miller repeatedly averred to Faith as they walked by, "That one could be saved, I'm sure." It was spoken in her usual audible voice, trained since childhood to speak up and speak clearly.

The *clochard* was still at his post and she tried to think of a reason she could tell Tom for going over and looking more closely at what she still thought of as her corpse—perhaps a sudden need for prayer—but Tom was already hustling her in through the front door. They picked up the mail. Two epistles from home. One was a postcard of the White House from Hope and Quentin, on which they had written that they were spending a delightful weekend with old business school cronies. Faith debated whether the choice of card carried any implications other than being the nearest to hand on the rack. It could well be that Quentin had political aspirations, yet somehow he struck her as a behind-the-scenes man. But you never knew with Hope. Last summer, she had said pointedly to Faith, "When everyone is always saying what a great president the president's spouse would make—Betty, Barbara—don't you think voters are ready for a woman?" Faith didn't. However, if anyone could convince first the Republican party and then the nation, it was her sister.

The other mail was a letter from her mother—a brief, succinct report of the weather in Manhattan and their activities of the last week, closing with the lines, "I do hope you are taking care of yourself, darling Faith, and getting plenty of rest. You know how you tend to overdo." With that understatement ringing in her ears, Faith started up the stairs.

After lunch, which was consumed down to the last crispy, artery-blocking bite of *grattons,* those delectable fried pieces of pork, duck, or goose skin not to be mentioned in the same breath as pork rinds, Faith's fatigue became apparent to both husband and son.

"Ben, why don't we let Mommy have a little nap and we'll go up the funicular by ourselves?"

Faith started to make a feeble protest. She loved the view from the top of Fourvière. It wasn't just the panoramic view of all of Lyon. On a clear day, you could see all the surrounding mountains, the Monts d'Or, such a lovely name, and occasionally as far as Mont Blanc to the east. But at least mountains stayed put and she could see them another day.

Faith stretched out on the bed. Ben had patted her brow. "Poor Mommy," he said before running gleefully down the hall and out the door with Daddy. Was the glorious Oedipal phase over so soon, Faith wondered drowsily, wherein she had been loved so primitively, so totally?

Her eyes started to close and she fought sleep desperately. She had plans, but Ben and Tom had to be well away first. Her eyes were closed. She tried to open them, except the lids weighed more than the Arc de Triomphe and refused to budge. She slept.

A while later, she rolled over and blinked. Again it took a moment to orient herself. Perhaps it was the way the church seemed to occupy the whole room that startled her so often upon waking. She sat up slowly. She hadn't been inclined, or increasingly able, to make sudden movements these days. She looked at the clock on the façade of the church. She'd been asleep for almost an hour. Tom and Ben would be coming back soon. The afternoon shadows were beginning to lengthen. She'd have to be quick.

Since this morning, there had been one overriding

thought in her mind. She *had* to get a closer look at the *clochard*. Quickly, she slipped on her shoes and went to the window. The music had stopped and she had a dreadful thought.

It was true. He was gone. She was furious at herself.

"Great going, Faith," she muttered aloud. "Sleep your life away." She'd have to wait until tomorrow to see him. Why it was so important, she wasn't sure. She could see him perfectly well from the window, but she wanted to touch him to see if he was real or if her hand would pass through his body like some projected image. She tried to think how she could have done things differently last night. Stayed with the body and screamed her head off was the only alternative that seemed possible. After a while, someone would have responded. However, the idea that the body would disappear was one that quite naturally had not occurred to her, and she wasn't a screamer by nature.

She was still tired. She crept back into bed. They were going to the opening of a show at Valentina's gallery, then out to dinner with the Leblancs and some of their friends. It was the last thing she felt like doing.

"Hello, darling, did you have a good sleep?" Tom was kissing her awake. She wanted to snarl at him that she had slept all too well and would have to wait until the morning for further *clochard* investigation, but she didn't want him to know what she was planning. The Reverend Fairchild took a dim view of his wife's sleuthful proclivities.

She managed to wrest a smile from somewhere and realized she did feel better. Oh sleep that knits . . .

Two hours later, she was feeling even better, as who could not in the jovial atmosphere of Valentina's gallery. The exhibit was called "Lyon Aujourd'hui"—four artists' views of contemporary Lyon. Faith wandered contentedly through the brightly lighted rooms. The crowd spilled out onto the sidewalk, wineglasses in hand, catching up on the news. Everyone seemed to know everyone else. The rapidity with which the French language is spoken increases in proportion to the number of people speaking it, and Faith was aware only of a word or two in the conversational swirl around her. Tom was in the thick of it and seemed to have picked up several new hand gestures since their arrival, as well as a distinctive shrugging of the shoulders and pursing of the lips. She'd get him a beret before they left, even though they were not so universally worn anymore. He'd look wonderful wearing it with his vestments.

Solange d'Ambert came over to Faith. She was wearing white linen Bermuda shorts and a gauzy chocolate brown blouse that complimented the tan she still had from *le ski*. She smelled of Hermès and smoke.

"You must think we are terrible. No one is looking at the paintings, but a *vernissage* is really a social event and to show support for Valentina. She has been incredible to make such a success of this place."

"This is exactly like a New York opening," Faith assured her. "Everyone comes back later to look at the paintings instead of the people. I certainly want to come back to see these again, especially the ones in this room."

"Ah, Truphémus. You have very good taste, I think. He is one of our best and most famous painters. He paints us just as we are."

The painting Faith was standing in front of was the interior of a café, one lone patron seated at a table by the window, gazing out to vague suggestions of the street and buildings beyond. Looking at the painting was like looking through layers of netting; the colors were muted and outlines blurred, but the powerful image of loneliness was not obscured.

Valentina Joliet joined them and linked her arm through Faith's. "My favorite painting in the show and, as you see, already sold. Let me show you his others. He is not here tonight, but if you like, you can meet him another time, here or at his studio."

Faith allowed herself to be steered and listened to Valentina's subtle sales pitch, which flowed effortlessly and sounded unrehearsed despite, Faith was sure, its constant repetition. All the while, Valentina's dark eyes darted about the room, canvassing the crowd, and seemed to take in even those behind her.

When they entered the next room, Faith noticed some other people who also seemed to be interested in the paintings. They were studying the works of art with care and making only an occasional comment to one another. They were teenagers and *très serieux*. Christophe d'Ambert was one, and he broke away from his friends to come over to greet them.

"Bonsoir, Madame Fairsheeld, it is an excellent show, no?" He leaned forward and swept his lips over both sides of her face, then repeated the gesture with Valentina. "You are to be congratulated, Madame Joliet. May I introduce my friends?"

"Of course. I'm glad you could come," Valentina replied as two girls and a boy approached at a wave from Christophe. Like Christophe, the other boy, Benoît something, was wearing a Chevignon jacket, neatly pressed American jeans, and a crisp shirt. One girl wore a short black dress with white polka dots and bright red tights. She had a black fedora adorned with all sorts of pins—advertising logos, characters from popular *bandes dessinées,* comic strips, which in France are considered an art form. The other girl had shiny straight blond hair, cut shorter than the boys', and wore a man's dinner jacket from the thirties over a lacy white bustier. She completed the outfit with a short ballerina skirt, black pipe-stem pants and gold leather tennis shoes. They were wonderful to look at, these *adolescentes*—all of them so beautiful—and Faith was drawn to them immediately. She also registered the fact that like

Christophe, their *pères,* and *mères,* too, these days, must be bringing home *beaucoup* the bacon, one of Tom's favorite Franglais phrases. All those shopping trips to the *branché,* or as the teenagers say in Verlan—a kind of reverse language like the old pig latin—*chebran* stores with names in English: Graffiti, Casual, Imperial Classic. The two girls, Dominique and Berthille, nodded gravely at being introduced, then the whole group drifted back to the pictures—the sole reason they were here, unlike their elders.

Valentina lowered her voice as they passed behind Christophe and the others. "I was like that at their age, too. Adults were so shallow and only my friends and I could understand the meaning of life and art."

As they passed though the door, they almost collided with someone. Madame Joliet gave a small cry of delight or surprise.

"Mon ami, I am so happy you could come. This is my wonderful new neighbor from America who is here for a month, is it not? Madame Fairsheeld, Michel Ravier. He is the one I mentioned last night, the *inspecteur divisionnaire* of our *police judiciaire*—I think in English you say chief inspector of crimes."

Inspector Ravier was of medium height for a Frenchman but would have been termed somewhat short in the States. He had dark, slightly thinning hair, the rather distinctive nose of many of his forefathers, and a dazzling smile. Oddly enough, everything combined to produce one of the sexiest-looking men Faith had seen in a long time. Sadly, he did not kiss her hand, this custom being apparently passé, and she had to be content with a decorous handshake.

"Your name is familiar to me, Madame Fairsheeld." He seemed amused.

Faith blushed. The room was terribly warm. She tried to think of a witty reply, or any reply at all. Valentina beat her to it and her laugh was loud enough to arrest the conversations of those closest to them. *"Bien sûr!* You must have heard about the corpse she found in our *poubelle*—a corpse that walks!"

Faith's fondness for Valentina began to ebb slightly.

"Oh, *chérie,* it is wrong to tease you. We have all had the unpleasant experience of coming upon the *clochards* engaged in all manner of dirty activities in our hall." Faith was a bit mollified.

Georges Joliet interrupted them. "Valentina," he said excitedly, "someone wants to buy the Fusaro. You are needed."

"Excuse me," Valentina said, and followed her husband into the other room, her bright yellow silk dress cutting a swath through the gallery.

"Georges is like a child about all this. When his wife sells a painting, it is like found money to him, and there is no question he is living in a way he never dreamed because of it. Valentina is a very good businesswoman. Now"—Inspector Ravier cupped Faith's elbow in the palm of his hand and gently moved her away from the others to a secluded corner by the door to Valentina's storeroom—"tell me about this body in the vestibule."

Faith was tingling. There was the possibility that someone—and someone official—would actually give some credence to her story. Then there was that delicious closeness. The French, the French.

"I know it sounds as if I imagined the whole thing—"

He cut her off. "Please, no apologies. I would like to hear what happened last night just as you experienced it."

Faith obeyed. "I was having trouble sleeping and the trash smelled bad. We had had a dinner party where I served bouillabaisse. I realized it was this smell that was keeping me awake, so I decided to take it down to the dustbins, which, you understand, I would never ordinarily do at such an hour." She hoped he would relay this tidbit back to the guys at the station, or whatever it was called in

France, and dispel the notion of a nation of anal retentives. Lunacy was bad enough.

"But of course, *la bouillabaisse.* The remains are *plus fort,"* he murmured close to her ear.

"When I opened the top, there he was—the *clochard."* Faith instinctively made a face of disgust and unconsciously took a step closer to the inspector.

"He appeared dead, but I felt I had to check in case the poor man could possibly be resuscitated." She made the face again, moved closer, then stepped back as she realized what she was doing. At this rate, by the time her grisly tale was over, she'd be in his lap. She knew she was blushing again. It had to be her condition, she reflected. Ordinarily, Faith's blush came in a compact.

"I went around to the side of the container and found his hand. There was definitely no pulse. He was absolutely still. You can tell when someone is dead."

"Yes, this is a good way to describe it—the stillness of death. You have seen many corpses then?" He looked into her eyes. His were very brown, with little flecks of gold. She took a deep breath.

"Not so very many." She didn't think it was the moment to reveal her previous involvements with several mortal remains.

"Please, finish your story. I find it very interesting."

"After I checked for the pulse, I closed the lid and returned to my apartment to call the police. Then, as you must have heard, by the time they arrived, he was gone."

Inspector Ravier ran his finger over his chin. He did not need a shave.

"It is strange. Very strange. If, as you say, he was dead. How did someone get him out and dispose of him so quickly?"

"Exactly. And who is that out in Place St. Nizier?"

"Pardon?"

"The *clochard* was back at his place this morning. You haven't heard yet?"

The brown eyes changed expression ever so slightly. But Faith knew what it meant.

"No, he replied cautiously, "I have not heard that part of the story."

"That's what makes it so strange." Faith knew she had lost an ally, and what splendid comrades in arms they would have made. She sighed.

He responded immediately, "But, madame—Faith, if you will permit—do not be dispirited. I am sure there is an explanation and you must not allow this unpleasantness to spoil your stay in Lyon."

"It won't. That would be impossible," she answered, and was aware it was true.

"Now, here is my card. You see, 'Michel Ravier,' *c'est moi,* and you must call whenever you like." He took out a small silver pen; not for the inspector the Bic-type *stylos* of Sergeants Pollet and Martin. "On the back, I give you my home telephone."

He handed her the card and she thanked him. They moved out of their corner and stood in front of a small charcoal sketch, also by Truphémus, of the Place Bellecour. Faith made an appreciative murmur.

"So you like Jacques's work. We will go have lunch at the restaurant Henry, which is decorated with murals by Truphémus. And the food is not at all bad, a very nice *homard breton*—they do a *salade* with the meat from the lobster's tails and claws, since you seem to favor it." His smile almost made up for the implication. "Of course, Monsieur can come, too, if he likes."

Monsieur was walking toward them and introduced himself. When he heard Michel's profession, an anxious look crossed his face. Faith hastened to direct the conversation. She'd had enough for one night.

"Are you a native Lyonnais, Inspector Ravier?" she

asked. It was her stock-in-trade, guaranteed to evoke from the individual paeans of praise if he was from Lyon or a passionate defense of his own region if he wasn't. Inspector Ravier wasn't.

"I am not Lyonnais, no," he said with pride, "and you must call me Michel. Although I was here in my school years living with my grandparents, we are from the Gascogne. Tell me, do you like foie gras?" He obviously considered the question answered. "You must take some time to go. I can tell you where to find the best you have ever tasted and the countryside is also *magnifique.*"

All this talk was making Faith hungry. She wondered where they were going for dinner. It was almost nine o'clock, but that was still early for Saturday-night supper.

Paul and Ghislaine swooped down upon them. "There you are. We have been looking for you everywhere. You will excuse us, Michel?" This was all accomplished with such ease and much kissing of cheeks that one would have assumed it an honor to be so interrupted.

"Please remember," Inspector Ravier said in a low voice as he followed suit and kissed Faith carefully first on one side of her face, then the other, "call me if you are troubled."

As she left and made her adieus to the Joliets and others, the idiotic adage "Don't trouble trouble till trouble troubles you" repeated itself over and over in her head, like Ben's current maddening practice with certain words and phrases, until she wasn't sure *what* she wanted.

Whether it was because of her fatigue, the baby, or their dinner at Leon de Lyon, Faith fell asleep shortly after crawling into bed. First, she took a moment to savor the meal over again in her mind. It had progressed from one mouth-watering course to another—*terrine de foie gras* layered on top of an artichoke heart with a light hazelnut oil dressing and followed by *rouget,* filets of red mullet in a buttery cream sauce that enhanced their rich, fresh flavor, so fresh they seemed to have been scooped from the nets in the bay off the rocky shores of Cassis minutes before cooking; then cheeses from Richard; and a plate of desserts of the season—not a biteful of which she skipped.

She slept soundly, dreamlessly, awakening to the peal of church bells. Mass. Her annoyance at falling asleep the day before vanished. Of course, she would see the *clochard* at mass!

The Fairchilds had adopted St. Nizier as their neighborhood church, despite their own religious affiliation. Or, as Faith said, "God is God." They'd taken Ben last Sunday and he had been so intrigued by the service movingly led by the brothers in their dramatic white robes and deep purple stoles and the interior of the church that he had sat still as a church mouse throughout the mass. Faith had not had to take out any of the books or small toys she'd brought for his distraction. The only rough moment had come early when he'd tried to blow out some votive candles on his way in.

The *boulangeries* were all closed on Sunday, so there was no fresh bread. They really were getting spoiled, Faith told Tom. She'd bought a large brioche the day before and it had kept nicely. All three of them dipped wedges of it in their bowls of coffee and hot chocolate for Ben, then hastened to wash their drippy chins for church.

The *clochard* was there, receiving alms and doing quite nicely. Madame Boiron had told Faith that he often came to the pharmacy to exchange his coins for bills and she was too frightened of him to refuse. On a good day, she said, he could make three hundred francs or more, around sixty dollars—not bad for nontaxable nonwork.

As they approached the door of the church, there were several people in front of them and Faith had a good chance to look at the *clochard* as they waited. There was no question. Same clothes, same filthy *casquette,* pulled over his eyes. Same matted beard on his red, somewhat bloated face.

She reached into her purse for some change and leaned closer to him, placing a five-franc piece in the bowl he was pushing toward her. She looked at his hand, then quickly at the other one resting on his knee. Filthy hands, the dirt ground into the folds of the skin. She stood up and walked into the church behind Tom and Benjamin.

Filthy hands—but unscathed. There wasn't even the suggestion of a scratch on the back of either one. No one healed that miraculously, even when sitting all day in the shadow of the Lord's temple.

She wasn't crazy.

It wasn't the same *clochard*.

Four

At the end of the mass, Faith guided Tom and Ben rapidly down the aisle and out into Place St. Nizier.

"What's your hurry?" Tom asked. "We're not due at Paul's mother's for an hour."

"I know, but we're certain to get lost and I want to get some flowers in the market to give her, and they'll be closing soon. Why don't you take Ben upstairs and get him ready while I *cherchez les fleurs,* and we'll meet here in twenty minutes?"

"I want to go with Mommy," Ben complained.

"Not now, sweetie, go with Daddy and *faire pi pi,* then pick out a toy to show Stéphanie and Pierre."

Ben's face brightened at the prospect of seeing the Leblanc children, but Faith could still hear him patiently pointing out to Tom, "But Daddy, I don't *need* to *faire pee pee*," all the way across the square.

She raced to the market and had a bouquet of blue delphinium, white roses, and pale pink ranunculus arranged. She liked this system: You pointed to the flowers you wanted, then greens were added and the final product wrapped in stiff, clear plastic trimmed with cascading curls of ribbon swiftly achieved with the flick of a scissor blade. The treatment made even the humblest daisy look like a treasure.

When she returned, Tom and Ben were not down from the apartment yet, as she had planned, and she started across to the church, where the *clochard* was still sitting in hopes of a franc or two from worshippers lingering inside after the mass. Madame Vincent was one of these and had apparently softened her attitude of the other evening. She dropped a coin in the *clochard*'s bowl, then leaned over to exchange a few words with him before straightening up and crossing the square. She waved to Faith in passing and called out, "Tea tomorrow? I'll speak with you in the morning," before disappearing into the building.

Faith stopped directly in front of the *clochard* and said in the careful French she had been rehearsing since entering the church an hour earlier, "How are you? You did not seem to be feeling very well the other night in my hallway."

She had no idea what to expect, but she wanted to see what he would say and also get a better look at his face, obscured as it was by the cap. She looked at his hands again. One held a cigarette and the other possessively clutched a liter of wine—*Le Cep Vermeil*, The Silver Vine— its low price and wide availability belying its elegant name.

She stared at his hands. Not even a trace of a scar, but there was a trace of a ring on his right ring finger—a very definite place that had escaped the sun. Her *clochard*, as Faith had come to think of him, hadn't been wearing a ring.

Nor did she recall that his nails had been bitten to the bloody quick as this one's were.

She repeated her question, since the man had made no reply and had, in fact, not moved at all.

This time, he answered. "Get away, *putain,*" he hissed in a low voice without looking up. "Get away!"

Shaken, she hastily moved into the church and walked down the darkened nave to the small chapel of St. Expedit, patron of lost causes. It was always cool inside St. Nizier and at the moment the only sound was the soft shuffling of the priests as they went about their work. One passed close to her and when she turned to look at him, he nodded and smiled. He was carrying an armful of baguettes and wearing white Nikes under his robes. She stepped up into the chapel, dropped some francs in the box and lighted a candle. The sun shone through the stained-glass window, dappling the statue of the boyish-looking saint in greens, blues, and gold. Faith bowed her head and got down on her knees. The position was surprisingly comfortable, whether from an easing of the soul or of baby fatigue, she wasn't sure. She took a deep breath and let it out slowly.

It was certainly a different man. And that could only mean the other *clochard* was dead. There was no other reason to go to all the trouble of impersonating him. But this poor wreck outside hardly seemed capable of engineering such a switch, let alone committing a murder.

Murder. She'd said it finally—or rather thought it and knew it was what she had believed ever since hearing the body was gone. Someone had killed the *clochard,* put the body in the *poubelle,* then removed it before the police arrived. It would have to have been done quickly. A car waiting outside? But she had been at the window like Sister Anne in the tower and she hadn't heard a sound until the police pulled up. And why kill the *clochard* in the first place. Who was he? There had been no trace of violence and presumably the police had checked for obvious bloodstains in the trash. Given the man's nature, he might have been killed in a fight with another *clochard* who then panicked and dumped him in the bin, yet that left the charade of the last two days.

And what about the man outside? Who was *he?* She hadn't expected the frighteningly venomous response—it wasn't every day she was called a whore—but then, what had she expected? That he would tell her what was going on?

She got quickly to her feet. Ben and Tom would be waiting.

When she went back outside, the *clochard* was gone.

The Leblancs had come up with an old but perfectly reliable Citroën Deux Chevaux for the Fairchilds' use. It had a canvas roof that folded back, windows one pushed open and clicked into place on the exterior, and something akin to park benches as seats. It was bright red and they had all come to love it, especially Ben. Now they chugged their way up a steep hill to St. Didier-au-Mont-d'Or, where Paul's parents lived. They found the address after only a few wrong turns and pulled into the gravel-covered courtyard. It was a beautiful old stone house with a magnificent garden. Large hydrangea bushes on either side of the front door spilled their puffy flowers out into the sunshine and filled the air with their soft scent.

Sunday dinner in the country—straight out of a French movie, and after struggling to keep up with sisters, cousins, cousins' sisters, Faith gave up on pairing names with faces and let the infectious good humor of the day sweep over her. It was a relief. She resolutely switched her mind to automatic pilot, put a smile on her face, and decided to live in the moment. There was nothing she could do just now, anyway.

Ben was immediately claimed by the Leblanc children and their kin. When she went to check on him, he was happily seated in the driver's seat of a vintage pedal car, zooming around a smaller garden, complete with vine-covered playhouse. The older children were busy setting places at a picnic table under a tree and assured her she was completely unnecessary for Ben's well-being and happiness. Well, she had eyes, too. Not sure whether to be delighted or rebuffed, she returned to the adults, and it wasn't long before delight won out—easily.

It was just like all the other parties and dinners she had attended. People came to have a good time. There was a great bustling to and fro from the kitchen. The adults were also eating outside at a table set up under a grape arbor adjacent to the house. Faith tried to help and was firmly placed in a canvas lawn chair next to Paul's father, who told her in slow, very precise English that he was a great admirer of the United States and did she know Philip Roth. "We like his books here very much. I try to read them in English, but I have to look at the French sometimes to be sure. You must have the same problem when you read French."

Faith gave what she hoped was a noncommittal reply, her reading in French being limited to the French editions of *Elle* and *Vogue,* with an occasional glance these days at *Le Monde,* and quickly asked about his family, which took them away from Molière, Colette, and whomever to the table. He was continuing to list various relatives and telling stories as they sat down.

"You see that beautiful statue there?" Faith nodded as he pointed to an Italian marble garden statue of some female deity. "My grandfather brought it back from Tuscany and that naughty girl there"—he moved his arm from in-dicating the statue to a very pretty dark-haired woman bringing a bowl to the table—"that girl, *ma fille,* my own daughter," he continued in a slightly louder voice now that everyone was listening, "painted it bright blue when she was a child. You can still see traces of the color," he told Faith as the group exploded in laughter, as if hearing the story for the first time.

"And it looked much better, too," his daughter, Michèle, rejoined.

Paul's mother apologized for the *picque-nique* and Faith immediately insisted, truthfully, that it was all the food she loved the most. There was a large platter of *oeufs en gelée*—perfect three-minute eggs taken out of their shells and placed in a small mold, then covered with gelatin. These also had tiny shrimp set on top and a flower cut from a carrot slice and parsley, so the unmolded result both looked and tasted delicious. The eggs were surrounded by fresh tomatoes. Another platter held slices of cold veal that had been stuffed with pistachio nuts. Then there were several large bowls—*saladiers*—of tabouleh; potatoes with herring and a vinagrette sauce; the tiny lentils from the town of Le Puy, the so-called caviar of Le Puy, mixed with bits of bacon, shallots, and a mustardy vinaigrette; a large green salad with several lettuces; and *salade museau,* something that appeared to be thin slices of some kind of ham in a light mayonnaise. It went down better with some English-speaking people if it wasn't translated, Paul told them. Pig's snouts did not sound as good as they tasted. In addition, there were all sorts of the famous Lyonnais sausages—*rosettes, cervelas, sabodet*—and plenty of bread—crusty baguettes and large round country loaves. The board groaned. It was a feast. Pitchers of Côte du Rhône and water were passed around and the noise got louder. Paul was sitting next to Faith.

"We are a bit crazy on the weekends. There's always this dinner at my mother's. She has the largest house and whoever is around comes."

"I like it," Faith responded. "And you certainly seem to be a close family."

"Oh, we are. We may hate each other, but we are close."

She looked surprised.

He laughed. "It would be impossible to be with this many people without some friction, and from time to time we won't see someone for a while. Eventually, he or she comes back. No one is ever turned away, no matter what."

Faith wondered if this was a universal French custom. It certainly wasn't something she'd observed often in the States. But families there tended to be more spread out and that had to account for some of it. She was on the point of asking him more when he told her how much he had enjoyed the dinner party at her apartment.

"Even though we are both at the university, I seldom see Georges, and Valentina never, unless she has an opening. Georges and I were at school together in the dark ages. With the Marists on the Fourvière Colline. Before they were admitting girls and getting soft. Believe me, we were *taught.*"

"How did Georges like that? He doesn't strike me as someone who would take to strict discipline easily."

"Oh, he hated it, of course. We all hated and loved it, but perhaps he did not love it so much. He was already quite political and thought the whole business very *facho,* you know, fascistic. It was the sixties, remember, and he went on to play a big role in Paris as a student in the events of May in '68. Used to live in those blue cotton overalls workmen and farmers wear. Sometimes I think his life since then has been a bit disappointing to him. All the real excitement of youth is over, even though he still gets out there whenever there's a need—SOS Racism, the group fighting discrimination, the Barbie trial demonstrations. I admire him for sticking to his guns."

"And Valentina? Is she also political?"

"Oh no, Valentina only wants to make money. She has been amazingly successful—partly because of her connections in Italy. She has become known as a source for contemporary French art and much of her business is selling to

Italian customers. Her brothers handle things in Rome. She has also discovered some Italian artists and represents them in France. It's a bit of a dilemma for poor Georges. She gave him a fancy new car last year, a BMW, and the way he sneaks into the parking lot with it, you'd have thought it was stolen. However, I notice he keeps it immaculate. I've even seen him flick dust off it with his handkerchief—and he has an alarm system. Ah, how easily we are seduced."

It was but the leap of an instant to Inspector Ravier.

"You seemed to know their friend Inspector Ravier. Was he also at the Marists?"

"But of course, we all were. A very serious, dark little boy, Michel. Perhaps it was living with his grandparents. Still, the hot-blooded Gascogne is there, too. Never had trouble attracting women."

"Is he married, then?"

"No. We tease him and you can be sure my wife has married him off innumerable times, yet nothing ever happened. He has girlfriends, *bien sûr,* but Michel is too set in his profession for a wife and family. I can't imagine him in this way."

"Inspector Maigret has a wife."

"Ah yes, Madame Maigret, a rare woman. Perhaps that is what Michel seeks. But in any case, Michel is not Maigret. And he is a reader of history and politics, not the *roman policier.*"

New plates appeared for the cheese, brought to the long table on round, flat baskets. Tom had tried to get up to help clear but had been pulled back to his place. None of the other men offered.

Faith eyed the chèvres—blues, St. Marcellins, morbiers, all sorts of triple crèmes, temptingly set upon fans of deep green grape leaves—and realized it was true, you could always eat cheese. Madame Leblanc placed a large earthenware bowl before her. "This is a Lyonnais specialty, *cervelle de canut*—we take a fresh *fromage blanc* and add salt, pepper, a little white wine, a soupçon of oil and vinegar, some chives, and, of course, garlic. Please try some."

Faith knew what *fromage blanc* was—a superior cottage cheese that was served with heavy cream and sugar. She was doing a quick translation. *Cervelle de canut.* Could she be right? She looked over to Tom, who was watching her with evident enjoyment. "The brain of a silk worker?" she said aloud. The table burst into laughter.

Paul said, "Again, it doesn't work to translate these things; just enjoy it."

"I intend to," she answered, and did. It was delicious.

Dessert was fruit, two enormous cherry *tartes* someone had brought and a plate piled high with those delicate beignets called *pets-de-nonne,* nun's farts, provided by Paul and Ghislaine for the fun of the name as much as the enjoyment of the pastry. Then they all took their coffee out into the garden and collapsed into the lawn chairs. It had been a *bon repas.* Monsieur Leblanc was soon asleep, with a large handkerchief knotted at each corner covering his balding head. Faith felt her own eyelids drooping. The sun was warm and the buzz of conversation soporific. She made no attempt to try to understand what they were saying and let the words simply drift around her.

But despite the calm of the afternoon, her mind was filled with all those questions that would not go away. She'd been focused on the food and ambience, yet it was impossible to block out the events of the morning any longer.

She had to tell Tom it was not the same *clochard* and what that implied, but she knew it would upset him—to put it mildly. She didn't doubt he would believe her this time when she told him about the scratch, but where did they go from there? He was accomplishing so much at the university and was sure he would be able to finish his thesis with the notes he was taking. As she glanced over at him good-humoredly arguing with Paul's relations about the merits of the French political system versus that of the United States, she hated to be the one to rain on his parade. But they never kept things from each other—well, he didn't and she hardly ever did. Was this one of those times?

If so, then what should she do? The obvious answer was to call Michel Ravier and tell him, but would *he* believe her? After all, he wasn't married to her. Of course, it would be nice to see him again. . . .

Then there was another choice.

Forget the whole thing and enjoy herself. It was no doubt something involving the *clochard* community, a kind of underclass, and as such had little effect on other people. This certainly seemed the path of least resistance. But she knew her feet weren't going to be following it. Murder was murder, no matter whether you had a home address or not.

Monsieur Leblanc was snoring gently. Others were strolling about the garden and she could hear the children's shouts from the tennis court. She got up and went into the house in search of Ghislaine. Faith suddenly felt the need of conversation.

Inside the house, she followed the direction of the laughter she heard and emerged from the long hall to step down into the large sunny kitchen, where it appeared most of the women had gathered. Some were still cleaning up; others sat with coffee and cigarettes around the table. The kitchen was what some Aleford ladies of her acquaintance were striving desperately to replicate in Pierre Deux, Ethan Allen, or whatever they could afford—Country French. Here pewter chargers, pitchers, and faïence plates from Gien were displayed on the shelves of antique cupboards. Carved mahogany chests for linens and cutlery, a towering armoire for staple goods, and mismatched chairs with rush seats lined the walls. There were worn rust-colored tiles on the floor and more decorative ones on the wall behind the stove. This *cuisine* was the real thing.

"Faith!" Ghislaine called from a small pantry where

the sink was located. "We thought you were taking a *petite sieste* with my father-in-law. No, that doesn't sound right, although I'm sure Henri would not mind." Everyone laughed. "We should have come to get you. Come sit with us," she finished. "I'll join you in a moment."

Faith went into the pantry and picked up a dish towel, over Ghislaine's protestations, and started to dry the silverware.

"I did think I might nod off," Faith said, "all the lovely food and the sunshine, but somehow sleep evaded me."

Ghislaine paused in her work and looked at Faith searchingly.

"You do not seem to be the same cheerful *fille* we knew when you first came. Is it still this business with the *clochard?* It's not the baby, is it?"

Tom and Faith had told them at dinner Saturday night about the whole strange experience. The Leblancs had expressed concern for the unpleasantness and hoped it would not spoil the visit. Faith was so busy reassuring them it wouldn't that she had almost convinced herself. But this was Sunday now and there was no reassurance anymore.

"Oh, the baby is a dream so far. Much easier than the first time. It's not that," Faith hastened to say. "But you're right, I am upset about the *clochard.* It doesn't seem so simple as it did at first and I am wondering what to do."

Ghislaine looked puzzled. "You mean something else has happened?"

"Yes, in a way," Faith replied. She wasn't sure she ought to involve Ghislaine when she hadn't even told Tom yet, but certainly Ghislaine knew more about Lyon and its inhabitants.

"About these *clochards.* Where do they go to get help, or for food? Surely there must be some who cannot support themselves on the street." Faith had decided that the key to it all must be with the *clochards* and their way of life, something she knew very little about. "In the United States, we have shelters where they can go for food and a place to sleep, though they are still inadequate for the numbers."

Ghislaine appeared relieved. Apparently, Madame Fairchild—who was, to be sure, a minister's wife—was simply concerned about these poor unfortunates, nothing more.

"Of course, we have them here, as well. The Armée du Salut, Secours Catholique, Emmaus, and the Restaurants du Coeur. But most prefer the street and the trash bins, as you have seen only too clearly."

"Then there must be one of these shelters close to us." Faith was thinking out loud.

"Oh yes, there's a Soupe Populaire in rue Millet. Although Paul would scold me for calling it that, even though everyone does. Soupes Populaires existed in the twenties and after the war for poverty-stricken and jobless people, not *clochards.*"

A soup kitchen was a soup kitchen as far as Faith was concerned and she was sure she could find out more there about the two *clochards*—if indeed the man sitting outside St. Nizier now *was* a *clochard.* It wasn't certain, but it seemed logical that whoever they were, they would go to the nearest place for free food.

The dishes were all dried and they joined the other women around the table, who seemed in no hurry to get back to their respective mates. Faith settled in comfortably and listened to the gossip, talk of offspring, and speculation on hemlines with a familiar feeling—the company of women.

One *femme* was busy stitching together small triangles of bright calico, and seeing Faith's glance, she said, *"Le patchwork.* Just like you American women do. It is quite the rage here. We are all busy making—what is your word?— quilts." Faith did not want to disillusion the woman, but her own forays into quilt making had consisted of getting others to do it for her, especially in the case of a quilt top she'd purchased at a house auction in Maine, which had led to a treasure hunt and more. "Oh yes, it's very popular where I live, also," she said. Her friend and neighbor Pix Miller, whose car sported a bumper sticker that read I'M A QUILTER AND MY HOUSE IS IN PIECES, kept telling Faith that if she could do a running stitch, she could quilt. But it was the *number* of running stitches one had to do, Faith reminded her. She was glad to meet a French quilt maker and it would be something to write to Pix about. Perhaps the two women could start to exchange patterns and eventually their children would meet and marry, and all because of a few scraps of cloth. Life could be like that, Faith believed.

"How is Dominique?" Michèle asked a woman across the table. "Is she worried about the *bac?*" She turned to Faith in explanation. "The *baccalauréat* is a very difficult, perhaps even ridiculous, exam French teenagers must take to get their diplomas."

The woman sighed and put her cup down. "Who can tell? Whenever we ask her, she just says not to nag so much and everything is fine. That is her answer for everything. 'Where are you going?' 'Where were you?' It is as if she has a secret life. And the way she dresses—like the circus!"

Everyone laughed and Michèle reassured her, "They are all like her, these *adolescentes,* secretive and so very serious. Not like us. *We* were perfect."

A slight feeling of nausea came over Faith, which she knew had nothing to do with either food or fetus. It arrived whenever she contemplated "Ben, the Teenage Years." And now, foolishly, she had signed up for a sequel.

Ghislaine was talking. "We are never satisfied. I get worried because Stéphanie seems too good. The only thing she ever criticizes is my accent when I speak English to Faith!"

Faith loved Ghislaine's delightfully accented English and much preferred it to Stéphanie's more correct British version, learned at school. She doubted that her own attempts at speaking French carried the same charm as Ghislaine's phrases: "You have learned me so much," she had told Faith and Tom Saturday night.

She continued to extol her daughter's virtues with a mixture of pride and concern. "She still talks to us, is polite, and does what we ask. It's not natural. When I think of what my poor mother endured!"

"Yes, I know all this," said Dominique's mother. "And"—she looked skeptically at Ghislaine—"Stéphanie is only thirteen, yes? Wait, *chérie,* a few more years. It's so hard to understand. Martin and I are good parents. We are not wardens who insist Dominique stay by our side or even that she go to *rallyes,* where she might be with some nice children."

"Rallyes! Those ancient elephants!" Michèle exclaimed. "Cécile, think how bored you were when Tante Louise made you go, and besides, what seventeen-year-old girl wants to meet 'nice children'? She wants to meet the opposite, then maybe later she will settle down and marry someone you wanted her to meet in the first place."

"What are these *'rallyes'?"* Faith asked, images of antique cars racing incongruously to mind.

"They are very correct little gatherings arranged by a particular sector of Lyonnais parents for more years than anyone remembers, so little Marie or little Louis will meet a suitable mate. In the winter, there are dances and in the warmer months, tennis or pool parties. I hesitate to say *parties,* because all this is sans alcohol and under the eyes of the parents. There used to be more of them, and of course nice boys like my Paul were always invited, but I'm happy to say we met normally—on the metro," Ghislaine explained.

"I know *rallyes* are old-fashioned," Cécile said, "yet at least our parents knew where we were."

A few eyebrows went up, but no one said anything, although Faith could see Michèle's mouth was twitching. It was obvious that Cécile was very upset about her daughter's behavior. Faith's stomach gave another lurch. She'd been hoping for a daughter of her own. Yet it was true—she'd heard girls were tougher in their teens. Maybe there was a good convent school near Aleford.

It was growing late and, a few at a time, the women slipped out of the kitchen into the garden to fetch a child or remind a husband of tomorrow's busy schedule, until only Faith, Ghislaine, and Michèle were left.

"Do you think Cécile is overreacting about her daughter, or is Dominique really difficult?" Faith asked Ghislaine.

"I see the girl at Christmas and Easter, perhaps a Sunday here or there in between when her father has been feeling the need to flex some parental muscles and make her come, so it's hard for me to say what she is like. She was always very bright and did well in school. If she messes up her *bac,* then there will be some cause for alarm. Actually, you saw her the other night. She was at Valentina's gallery with Christophe d'Ambert and some other friends. She was wearing gold—what do you call them?—sneakers."

"But she looked great in them, a very pretty girl."

"I agree; however, Cécile would prefer her in a long navy pleated skirt and flower-print blouse from Cacharel—a slightly different uniform. Now I would love Stéphanie to dress a little more like Dominique. My own daughter, and not interested in what she puts on her back. Pierre is the opposite—not only a certain *marque* but it has to be from the right shop."

"Oh, boys are much worse than girls about these things," Michèle agreed. "Patrice is barely eight and if his Floriane Bermudas or shirt are from the warehouse and not some place in the Brotteaux, he is ashamed. Of course, I don't pay any attention to him," she added proudly.

The clock in the hall struck and Faith looked about in surprise. She'd had no idea it was so late and realized, too, that her mind had moved far away from the dark preoccupations of an hour or so ago. Now her main concern was to get the address of the Floriane outlet from Michèle.

Ben cried when they left and everyone tried to comfort him, which only made it worse, because they were so nice and that was why he didn't want to leave in the first place. The lure of riding in the Deux Chevaux soon worked its magic, he cheered up, and they finally got him in the car. Such is the fickleness of youth.

"Did you have a good time, darling?" Tom asked as they drove down the hill toward the city, beginning to sparkle as lights went on against the twilight.

"Wonderful. The longer I'm here, the more I love it."

"Me, too. You know we should get together with our families more. Go down to Mother and Dad's, see my brothers and sister."

"But Sundays are your busy day."

"Well, a Saturday then. Big families are nice," he added, looking pointedly at Faith's abdomen. He had obviously been struck by the togetherness of the Leblanc clan, as she had, too; but manufacturing their own seemed a bit drastic.

She shot him a look. "We'll go down to Norwell as soon as we get back. I'll talk to your mother. This isn't touch-football season, is it?"

The Fairchilds, scattered among various towns south of Boston, were a game-playing family—outdoors if the weather was good, and sometimes if it wasn't—and indoor board games for torrential downpours or blizzards. They had tried in vain to enlist Faith on whatever the team of the moment was. She was glad of her condition for an excuse this time. She liked his family—in small doses. Maybe if they spoke French . . .

By the time they reached the apartment, it was dark and Ben had fallen asleep in his car seat.

"Why don't you carry him up and I'll park the car." Faith offered.

"Good idea. With luck, he won't wake up until morning."

They pulled in front of the building. Tom got out and Faith moved into the driver's seat. She drove slowly down the block, looking for a space, and was lucky enough to grab one not too far away. As she was about to get out, she was startled by someone opening the passenger-side door. It was Marie, the *fille de joie,* and she swiftly got in.

"Drive to Perrache, the train station, you know it?" she ordered Faith.

"I'm happy to take you if you need a ride," Faith started to say, slightly piqued at the abruptness of the request.

"I don't need a ride. Just drive in that direction—*vite!"*

Faith started to pull out onto rue du Brest when, as quickly as she had jumped in, Marie cried, "Stop!" and got out of the car. Thoroughly confused, Faith backed into the space again and tried to see where Marie had gone. There were several people passing on the sidewalk, but the girl had vanished.

She walked slowly back to the apartment and up the stairs. Obviously, Marie had wanted to tell her something. And obviously, something, or more likely someone, had frightened her away. Faith would have to try to speak with her alone tomorrow, which wouldn't be easy. The three graces seemed to be on the same timers. They were either all on the corner or all otherwise occupied.

She opened the apartment door, determined to tell Tom during the course of the evening some of what had been happening. False *clochards,* prostitutes jumping in and out of her car like "Pop Goes the Weasel"—it was getting too strange.

Ben was indeed asleep and even though they had insisted they wouldn't want another thing to eat that day, nine o'clock found the Fairchilds sitting at the table with some tomatoes, radishes and butter, cheese, and yesterday's very crusty bread between them.

"Tom," Faith started hesitantly, "you know I can't get the business with the *clochard* out of my head and there is one explanation we haven't explored."

"What's that?" he asked through a mouthful of Camembert. He'd heard the European Community was proposing to limit the bacteria levels in cheese and had told Faith it was their sworn duty to eat as much real Camembert as possible before it was a distant memory.

"What if the man outside the church is in disguise—impersonating the dead *clochard?*"

"You've been reading too many mysteries, honey. We went to church this morning. It was definitely the same guy as far as I could tell. Didn't you think so?"

"The *clochard* I found had a scratch on the back of his hand. This one doesn't."

Tom looked surprised. "Are you positive? Was it a deep scratch?"

"Of course, the light was poor, but it did look pretty deep."

"It couldn't have been a thread of some sort from the trash, red string from a sausage casing?"

She looked at her husband. He believed her, yet his desperate search for possible alternatives showed he really didn't want to. For if he did, it would mean the end of their idyllic sojourn.

She couldn't do it to him.

Faith gave Tom what she hoped was a reassuring smile, passed him some more Camembert, and said, "There could have been a thread or something like that in there."

Not yet. Not until she was absolutely positive.

Five

They were greeted by the sound of a steady rain when they awoke on Monday morning.

Tom looked out the window gloomily. "You know it can rain for weeks like this in Lyon."

Faith had noted the abundance of umbrella shops and figured there had to be a reason.

"Solange d'Ambert told me it rains more in the winter and early spring. They call it suicide weather—*le temps de suicide*. So I'm sure this will pass. It's the wrong time of year."

"I prefer the other expression Paul taught me years ago. Rain like *une vache qui pisse.*"

Faith had never taken the opportunity to observe a cow engaged in this particular activity, and in any case, it was overly suggestive of her own frequent journeys to the w.c. these days.

She felt depressed. The inclemency made it that much harder to get in touch with Marie. She didn't imagine the girls got enough business during weather like this to make it worth while to stand in the freezing rain.

She stared out the window at the passersby huddled under umbrellas and hurrying down the street. The *faux clochard,* as she had come to call him, was not braving the downpour.

As she was helping Ben get dressed, the plans, which had been floating about her head since the night before, crystalized. First, she'd look for Marie at the corner on the way back from taking Ben to school. If the girl was by some chance alone, they could arrange a time and place to meet. If the others were there, she could ask Marie to help her find a particular address, necessitating stepping inside someplace for shelter while they looked at the street map of Lyon. It was all she had been able to come up with, apart from simply hiring her for an hour in order to find out why she'd made her hasty entry and exit the night before. But Lyon was not unlike Aleford, she suspected, and Faith had no doubt she'd see headlines involving minister's wife and solicitation before the day was out. Probably "hallucinatory minister's wife," if anyone consulted Sergeants Martin and Pollet.

Once outside, she discovered the rain was indeed as cold and drenching as it had looked from inside. She had her sturdy Burberry and an umbrella big enough for several Mary Poppinses, but Faith still felt wet to the bone. The whole city looked gray and the water in the gutters swirled about, churning up a mixture of filthy refuse. No one was at the corner. In fact, there was almost no one anywhere.

Faith hurriedly deposited Ben at the *garderie,* where he quickly joined an eager group at the window who were watching an enormous garbage truck empty the bins with appropriate gear-stripping sounds. Heartrending, Faith thought, as she passed the truck out in the rain once more, her course set for hot tea and crawling back into bed. She got as far as the vestibule when she made the fatal mistake of turning around to gaze at the leaden Eglise St. Nizier opposite her. *Clochards,* like others, would be seeking warm food and shelter on a day like today. It was the perfect time to check out the kitchen *de soupe,* or whatever it was called, on rue Millet. She braced herself and walked back out into the storm.

Rue Millet turned out to be a short street between the pedestrian street rue de la République and the Rhône. It wasn't hard to find the shelter. Most of the buildings were old warehouses. The shelter was the only noncommercial building in evidence. There was also a sign. She opened the door and found herself in an open courtyard that would be a pleasant place to linger on a sunny day. It had benches and several large containers filled with pansies, their bright blooms beaten flat by the rainfall today. Crossing swiftly, she entered a passageway on the other side and followed the sounds and appetizing smells to a large reception area. She could see a low-ceilinged refectory beyond it. A young man, tall and thin, with a long ponytail turned from a bulletin board where he had been stapling a notice and asked if he could help.

Although Faith was in desperate need of something hot to drink, this was not her top priority, even with soup close at hand. On the way, she'd decided the best thing to do was tell a relatively straightforward and honest story.

"I wonder if you might—" she started in French.

"Are you English, American?" he interrupted in English.

So much for all the time she'd been spending practicing rolling her *R*'s, Faith thought, slightly chagrined.

"Yes, I'm American. My name is Faith Fairchild and—"

Again he interrupted her, this time with considerably more enthusiasm. "Ah, America. I love the États-Unis. Jack Kerouac, John Gregory Dunne. Big Sur. And Route Sixty-six. It's my dream—to follow it. Where are you from?"

"Originally, New York City, but I—" She was ready for the next interruption.

"New York! The Large Apple. I dream of it. But why are you here, mademoiselle? Are you lost? This is an agency that helps some of those in Lyon who have had bad times and need a meal, a bed. You—"

It was her turn. She cut him off. "I know what this is. I'm not lost. You see I am married to a minister and we are very interested in the ways other countries are dealing with the problems of the homeless and I thought perhaps someone here could tell me something."

He became positively radiant, so radiant that she knew she would feel guilty and end up sending him a Christmas card every year or some such thing. It was too late to bear a child for him.

"I am Lucien Thibidaut and at your service. Perhaps we can start with a *petit tour* and then you may ask away your questions."

It was what she had hoped. He led her straight into the room where volunteers were busy setting steaming bowls of stew and baskets of bread in front of the individuals seated at the long tables. Some appeared not to notice, while others virtually dove into the food. There was a vast range in cleanliness, age, and attire; yet everyone had a shopping bag or two close at hand. These contained whatever they possessed, or had collected. One's whole life in a paper sack from Galleries Lafayette. A *clochard* without a bag would look naked. She tried to pay attention to Lucien's monologue while scrutinizing each face and hands. No luck.

"Is there another room? Another place where people

can eat?" It was possible either of the *clochards* might be somewhere else.

Lucien appeared surprised, as well he might. The room they were standing in was enormous and the tables were by no means full.

"No, this is sufficient," he answered.

"I'm sorry," Faith apologized, "I meant sleep. Is there a place for beds?"

The glow returned. "But of course, let me show you. We have separate facilities for men and women, with beds and showers. Also a small separate apartment for mothers with children, equipped with a playroom. It is surprising and sad to note the increase in their numbers."

Faith followed him up the stairs and walked politely beside him as he showed her the sleeping quarters—clean, comfortable-looking—and completely empty.

Neither man was there.

It was unlikely either would be in the family quarters, but she obediently followed her guide and made appropriate noises of approval, which were genuine. It was an excellent arrangement.

They returned to the reception area and Faith asked some more questions about who sponsored the shelter, how it was administered, and how many were served. It really was a model shelter and she felt less guilty as she took a card and promised to return with her husband. She knew Tom would want to see it.

Then a last try: "We are living in Place St. Nizier. Not far, of course, and we seem to have a resident *clochard* at the church."

"Oh yes, Bernard. Quite a character. I think he was in the army, then became alcoholic, couldn't work. It is a familiar story. When he is not drunk, he can be very sensitive. People tell him their problems. And he is quite intelligent. Doesn't miss much. But when he is drunk, it's another story."

"Yes, I know. I saw him attack another *clochard* last week."

Lucien shook his head and sighed audibly. "We are here to help them—find work, take care of their *Sécurité Sociale,* get them to the doctor, but so many like Bernard do not want to change. We have not seen him for some days. He must be on the road again. They all do this from time to time."

"Does he have a brother or relative who is also on the streets? I saw someone who looked very much like him."

"No, not that I have heard. Certainly he never came here. But after a time, many of them do come to look like each other—the reddened face, the unwashed hair. If I told you the ages of some of the people in there, you would not believe it."

Faith said good-bye, thanked him, and over his protests gave him a donation. She wanted to do it—and it made her feel a little better about using him. She crossed back through the courtyard, thinking how much the world needed Luciens, and pulled open the door to the street. She gasped and stepped back.

It was the "party man." The rain had loosened his bandage, which hung off the side of his face, revealing the ugly wound. He still clutched his shopping bag and he stank. His vacant eyes swept her face and he appeared not even to register that there was another person standing there. He stumbled by and she stepped thankfully into the street. There was no point in trying to question him as to anyone's whereabouts. He didn't even know his own.

Despite this encounter, she felt slightly elated. She hadn't located either *clochard,* but then, had that really been her object? Wasn't it to find out who wasn't there? And the *clochard* she'd found in the trash bin hadn't been seen at the shelter for some days. It could mean, as Lucien suggested, that it was ho for the open road, yet Faith believed otherwise.

It was too early to get Ben, but there wasn't time to put her original cup of tea and nap plan into effect, so Faith decided to walk to the café in her neighborhood and order a big cup of steaming chocolate. If there were any croissants left from the breakfast crowd, she'd have one of those, too. She was starving. As she was about to enter the café, someone darted out from the alley next to it and grabbed her arm, pulling her back into the narrow passage.

It was Marie, of course. Faith was relieved but hungry.

"In here, quickly." Here was the back entrance to one of the buildings on rue Chavanne. It had space for the inevitable *poubelles,* the two women, and not much else. Marie banged the door shut.

"This is the only way I can talk to you and I pray no one saw us," Marie said as she lighted a cigarette.

It was no time to protest secondary smoke, and as the pungent Gaulois fumes enveloped them, Faith asked, "What is this all about? What's wrong?"

"I don't have much time, so be quiet and listen. The others are too frightened to tell you and you mustn't mention what I say to anyone, not even your husband."

"All right," Faith agreed. Marie was definitely agitated. She was smoking in quick, jerky motions, inhaling deeply and forcefully exhaling, almost at the same time. Her raincoat had fallen open, revealing her work clothes, tight black jeans and a neon chartreuse halter. She must be freezing.

"What you found in the trash was what you thought. So now it is not safe for you to be in Lyon. These people would think nothing of putting you there, too. For them, it is just part of business." She spoke so quickly, it took Faith a moment to translate. And when she did, she could scarcely believe it. She said the first thing that came into her mind.

"What people?"

Marie looked at her in annoyance. "Just leave Lyon, okay? Go back to the U.S."

"But what excuse can I make to my husband? We're supposed to be here for two more weeks."

"Tell him you want to be near your mother or your doctor. You will think of something. Men always listen to their wives when they are *enceinte*, you know, even if they didn't before. Now, I will leave first and *don't* speak to me when you see me."

Faith put her hand on Marie's arm to stop her. She was so thin, it felt as if the coat was still on a hanger. "Please, I'm sure we should go to the police. I know someone who would keep it completely confidential." Somehow she felt confident promising for Ravier.

"A *flic* like that does not exist and would not believe someone like me in any case. Now I have done what I have to. Take care of yourself."

Faith tried to thank her, but Marie dashed out the door. After counting to one hundred, Faith followed and was in time to see her farther down the street, teetering on her high heels, her long red teased hair blowing about her head. She went into a hotel near the river, definitely not a Michelin four star.

On the way to get Ben, she tried to figure out what she was feeling. Oddly enough, she wasn't scared. It was too bizarre. No, what she was feeling wasn't fright—at least not yet. What she was feeling was vindication. There *had* been a *clochard* in the *poubelle*—a very dead *clochard*. And the man collecting alms by the church *was* a fake. Marie—and presumably Marilyn and Monique—knew she wasn't out of her mind.

But then, so did someone else—or more than one.

Tom called to say he would be late so Faith fed Ben first, the French way. Papa came home, said good night to the children, then the adults sat down to a civilized meal. While heartily applauding the idea in theory, Faith didn't always put it into practice. It meant Ben and Tom didn't see each other much and also two meal preparations, unless she wanted Ben to subsist on bread, cheese, and fruit.

Ben was sitting in his bed drowsily looking at books when Faith heard the first key turn in the lock and went down the hall to greet her husband. She realized she had been longing for his steady presence all day and opened the door just as he did. His arms were filled with nosegays of lilies of the valley—*muguet des bois*.

"It's the first of May!" he told her. "I almost forgot, but Paul reminded me, and at lunch the Boy Scouts came into the university cafeteria selling these. You're supposed to give them to the woman you love, my love." He set the flowers on a card table someone had loaned them, which had become a repository for all sorts of things from mail to Ben's toys, and drew Faith close. The delicate smell of the flowers and the comfort of his embrace brought tears to Faith's eyes. "I am really getting sentimental in my old age," she thought, having crossed, to her, that great divide into the unknown thirties.

Tom was still talking. "You should have seen the kids. They looked so cute in their uniforms, carrying these huge baskets of flowers. I love the way the French say scouts, 'scoots.' Anyway, better late than never, and even if we didn't say it this morning, 'rabbit, rabbit.'"

Saying *rabbit rabbit* upon awakening on the first of each month for good luck was an old New England custom to which Tom adhered religiously. Faith had never been able to ferret out a reason for it and it was prominent on her ever-expanding list of endearing regional incomprehensibles.

While they were eating, Faith went through what was beginning to be an alarmingly familiar debate with herself about what to tell Tom. She ended up shelving the whole thing out of the happy mood of the moment, as well as weariness and indecision. Tomorrow morning, she'd write a note arranging a rendezvous with Marie and she would try harder to persuade her that the safest thing for all concerned would be to go to Michel Ravier and tell him what was going on. Marie's panic had convinced Faith the woman believed the danger was real—from the underworld, *le milieu* as it was called, or some other source. But Faith was an American citizen, after all, and she couldn't imagine whoever they were would think she knew enough to endanger them—which she didn't. She would tell Marie that she would not have to go to Inspector Ravier with Faith, only provide her with a bit more information. Faith would keep her out of it, never mentioning her name at all.

That night, she had trouble sleeping again. Her body was suddenly becoming uncooperative and she found it difficult to get comfortable. As she'd told Ghislaine, baby number two had been remarkably considerate so far and Faith's occasional heartburn was probably due to her rich diet. However, the fact that her T-shirts were getting tighter across the chest was not. She'd have to pick up some new ones, she thought drowsily, cheered by the idea of shopping. Maybe some of those striped ones from agnès b. or the white ones that looked like men's Hanes undershirts, also a current rage, but with CLEMENTINE PASSION written on the front—or another designer's name.

The rain was still coming down. She could hear the sound on the roof tiles and the cars made a swishing noise as they drove by. This time in France had taken a totally unexpected character, not unlike the mood swings she found herself experiencing during her pregnancy. It was like being on a seesaw. Give a wonderful dinner party—you're up. Shortly after, find a dead body—*swack,* your feet hit the ground. Go to a convivial family Sunday in the country. Come back and have a prostitute jump into your car, subsequently warning you to get out of town. Up and down, up and down. She fell asleep vaguely conscious that her toes were poised to push off.

The next morning, the rain was continuing. Looking out, it seemed there was no space between the drops, just one solid wetness descending upon the city like a boulder. It was hard to believe Marie would be out in this. Faith was also dismayed about the rain because it was the day of the *garderie* mothers' tour of the *hôtel de ville,* the city hall—a fabulous seventeenth-century building facing Place des Terreaux. Most of it was not open to the general public, and since Faith's arrival, everyone had told her how lucky she was to go.

After breakfast, she wrote a note to Marie telling her it was urgent that they meet and suggesting noon inside the front door of the *hôtel de ville.* There was a large entry hall, which served as a location for various commercial or art exhibitions and also as a pass-through from Place de la Comedie to Place des Terreaux. They could figure out where to go from there or she might agree it was an inconspicuous place to talk. The tour was bound to be over by then and she did not have to pick Ben up until 12:30.

Feeling more relaxed now that she had a plan of action, Faith took Ben downstairs. He was in a particularly sunny mood, in contrast to the day. "Will you play with me at school?" he asked.

"Not today, lovey, but we'll play when you get home."

"Forever?"

"As close as we can get," she assured him, wondering when and where he had picked up this concept. Children were a constant source of amazement to Faith. They seemed to bring themselves up as much as be brought. Perhaps she needn't feel so guilty about not continuously playing all those imported educational games with Ben or starting phonics in the playpen as some mothers she knew did.

Contrary to her expectations, yet in accord with her hopes, the girls were out in full force. Marilyn had a minuscule shiny plastic hooded white raincoat that matched the one the dog wore. Marie and Monique wore short somber black trench coats and carried umbrellas. All three looked morose and unwelcoming. It would have to be an *homme* in dire need to approach the three, who today looked like caricatures of *Macbeth*'s three weird sisters, Faith thought.

But then again, it just could have been her. Nobody was saying *Bonjour,* not even to Ben. Definitely not a glad-to-meet-you crowd.

Faith walked over to them, anyway, commented on the weather, then said to Marie, "Have you lost this? We found it near here yesterday." She handed a small change purse to Marie. When Marie gave it back, saying, "No, madame," Faith swiftly pressed the note she had palmed into the young woman's hand. "Perhaps it belongs to one of you?" Faith asked. They also denied ownership, which was, of course, no surprise, since Faith had taken it from her own drawer a few minutes earlier.

"Too bad," said Faith as she gave a slight shrug. Tom was not the only one adopting French gestures. "It's a pretty one. Well, we must be off to school and the *hôtel de ville*—a tour for the mothers." She glanced with what she hoped was nonchalance at Marie.

"How nice for you, madame," she said in an affectless voice, appearing to speak for them all.

Faith trudged off into the rain and hoped Marie would come, although given the woman's fear it was unlikely. If she didn't show up, Faith would get in touch with Ravier herself and tell him—what exactly? That the *clochard* was a fake, the real one probably murdered, and that she had received a warning from a prostitute? These were the facts, but they were pretty murky—at least to Faith—and she hated to be kept in the dark.

The *hôtel de ville* was as splendid on the inside as the

outside. The mothers reverently climbed the *grand escalier d'honneur* to the second floor, dwarfed by the statues and paintings on the walls, ceiling, and balustrade, then gasped audibly upon entering the *grande salle des fêtes*—twenty-six meters long and twelve and a half meters wide, the guide told the awestruck group. Faith looked around her. It seemed so incongruous for them to be there in their twentieth-century garb, albeit neat and in the mode—a single strand of pearls at virtually every neck—when the huge, ornate gold-framed mirrors, gilded intricate parquet, and deep rose silk draperies called out for ball gowns, diamonds, powdered wigs, and perhaps intrigue. Intrigue! There was enough of that. She wondered again whether Marie would be downstairs after the tour. The group trailed obediently after the enthusiastic guide, who almost wept when describing the fire of 1674 that had destroyed so much of the building, including irreplaceable allegorical murals by Blanchet, which she then proceeded to describe in such intricate detail that Faith gave a passing thought to a belief in reincarnation.

They entered a room overlooking the Place de la Comedie and the Rhône. Faith walked over to the long window at the rear and stood next to a door. The woodwork was darker in this chamber and she listened as the guide once again flung herself into an impassioned recital of the building's history. This, it appeared, had been used during the revolution for trials. Lyon had been a Royalist city and paid dearly. The guide walked over to Faith and with somewhat ghoulish relish flung open the door to reveal a large closet with another smaller door in the wall. It was locked, she told them in a slightly muted whisper, and concealed a stairway to a tunnel that led straight to the river. Often after the Jacobins found the defendant guilty, as they invariably did, justice was meted out swiftly and efficiently—the body disposed of down this series of chutes. Faith gave a shudder and moved away as the guide went on to bewail the destruction to property done by the revolutionaries—*"les statues, les peintures, les meubles,"* she intoned. There was no question whose side she was on.

It was just past noon and the guide quickly wrapped things up, reminding the mothers what a signal honor had been accorded them. They filed past her, murmuring thanks and pressing a small token into her hand, which she did not refuse. It was still raining and Faith hastened back from the open courtyard, where the tour had ended, into the entrance hall. There was no sign of Marie. Faith stood by the door, then decided it would be better to pretend to look at the exhibit, which had something to do with hydroelectrics.

At twenty after, she began to get anxious. Had Marie come and left, not seeing her there at the dot of twelve? She doubted this. Most of the French she knew were notoriously late and expected the same from others. She was forced to admit that the prostitute was too frightened to risk a meeting—and maybe she was right.

At 12:30, Faith was late herself and rushed across the Place des Terreaux, past the Bartholdi fountain, and toward the *garderie*. She gathered Ben up, and after lunch, they both took naps. She was exhausted.

They spent the afternoon indoors, playing Legos to Ben's heart's content. He made little cars and Faith made houses—or, rather, garages, as far as Ben was concerned. She was trying very hard to avoid stereotypes, but Ben had consistently picked anything with wheels since birth and she had reluctantly become convinced that there was a vehicle gene.

By the following day, the rain was a mere drizzle and a faint glow indicated the sun was struggling to burn through. Tom took Ben to school and Faith headed for the market. She was hungry and decided to prepare a special dinner that evening.

One of the first things she saw was an array of small

paper boxes filled with *fraise des bois,* wild strawberries, sitting on the old lady's card table. The boxes were lined with strawberry leaves and the red fruit glistened against their dark green. Faith scooped up two containers. She took their presence, with its promise of all the lush summer fruit to come, as a good sign, and Lord knows, that's what she was in the market for. As she thought this, fragments of a collect came almost to her lips:

O Lord . . . , who hast safely brought us to the beginning of this day; Defend us in the same . . . and grant that we fall into no sin, neither run into any kind of danger . . .

She looked over her shoulder at the housewives with their baskets, some pushing strollers, occasionally with a toddler in tow. One of the chefs was selecting pineapples at the next stall. It was all so normal—and all so menacing. She was alone and she was frightened.

After that, she swiftly put her meal together, feeling a sudden compulsion to get out of the market—almost as if all the friendly faces of the vendors she'd come to know might instantly turn to those of hostile strangers. Scenes of sudden violence like the *clochard* fight pushed into her mind—the tables overturned, fruit rolling down the walk, someone chasing her. She blinked and found herself standing at the lettuce seller. He smiled and winked at her. What did madame want today? Madame wished she knew. She did know one thing, though. She'd make a *salade Lyonnaise*—several kinds of lettuce, including plenty of curly endive and dandelion greens, dressed with a strong vinaigrette, small crisp pieces of bacon, croutons, and crowned with an egg somewhere between soft- and hard-boiled that broke deliciously over the mixture when you ate it. The traditional Lyonnais recipe called for herring, as well, but she thought the flavor would be too strong for the *caille,* the quail, that she was going to roast to follow.

Faith tucked a bouquet of anemones into her loaded *panier* as she left the market, even though the apartment was filled with Tom's flowers. They'd add some color and it seemed important to seize some brightness.

Marie, Monique, and Marilyn were nowhere to be seen and she decided to call Michel Ravier. As she walked, she wondered if all the indecision she'd been experiencing over the last few days was due to her unfamiliarity with the country or her relative unfamiliarity with pregnancy. She had a nagging feeling that if she'd been home and/or not with child, she would have been more resolute by now—probing around more herself or prodding police chief MacIsaac to get on the stick.

She headed for the *boucherie* to get the *caille.* The sun had broken through the clouds and the rain had stopped. Good signs.

As soon as she walked through the shop door, she knew something was wrong. All the chairs were occupied and everyone was speaking in hushed tones. Alarmed, she looked around quickly for Clément and Delphine. She was relieved to see them at their usual posts—he behind the counter, she in front at the cash register.

She asked for the *caille* and walked over to Delphine. "Has something happened? Everyone seems very quiet."

"It's that poor girl, you know the one. They are always standing there." Delphine gestured toward the corner. "The one with the red hair. She's dead; she has suicided. They found her in the river near the confluence."

"But that's impossible!" Faith exclaimed.

One of the regulars, an elderly man, said, "No, madame, unfortunately not. Many of these women are very depressed. They drink too much or use drugs and life can sometimes be too much for them. It is sad but not unheard of."

Faith felt ill. The shop began to swim before her eyes and she was aware that someone had given her a seat.

"It's all right," she said, "I'm fine now." The Veaux wanted to call Tom or at least get her a restorative coffee, but she finally convinced them it had been a momentary giddiness due to her interesting condition. She took her package and walked back toward the apartment. Marilyn and Monique were not at the corner.

She mounted the stairs, dropped the basket by the door as soon as she was inside the apartment, and went straight to the phone. She took Michel Ravier's card from her purse and dialed the number.

She was not fine at all. She was sick. Sick with overwhelming guilt. If Marie had stayed away from her, Marie might still be alive.

Ravier was out and they would not tell her when the Chief Inspector was expected back. She tried his home number. A woman answered after several rings. The voice did not sound like that of a young woman. His mother? The cleaning woman? Michel was not home. After Faith identified herself, it appeared the woman *was* his mother and she began to chat volubly. She related that Michel, such a wonderful son, was in Marseille working. Who was this calling again? Faith left her name and hung up, sorry that the appendage of *Madame* when she repeated her name seemed to dash the good lady's hopes. Faith's own hopes were dashed, as well. She didn't know what to do now.

Marie had not committed suicide. She had been murdered, and apart from Marilyn, Monique, and the killers, Faith was the only one who knew it. She couldn't imagine the other two prostitutes going to the police after what had happened to Marie. It was up to her and she did not hesitate. She dialed again, 17—the police emergency number—and told the individual who answered that she had some information regarding the suicide of the young woman, Marie, found in the river that morning. She was swiftly transferred to another individual who switched to English as soon as he heard her speak. More proof that her accent had not achieved the level she was aiming for, Faith reflected dismally. He told her he would be there as soon as possible.

She put the food away, although the idea of cooking the meal, not to mention eating it, made her feel ill. The doorbell rang and she ran to answer it.

She opened the door and her heart sank. It was Didier Pollet and Louis Martin—or Dum and Dee, as she thought of them. Come to placate the crazy Yank again.

"Madame Fairsheeld, a pleasure to see you. Inspector Moreau asked us to speak with you, as he is occupied."

Sure, sure, thought Faith, occupied with urgent police business like hoisting a *pastis* or two at one of the cafés near the *commissariat*. She was seriously annoyed.

They went into the dining room and sat around the table. Didier had his notebook out, at least that was something.

Sergeant Martin smiled at her. "You have of course seen the *clochard,* quite well, or as well as he ever was." It wasn't a question.

"Yes," answered Faith slowly. The mood was set, but they were her only hope at the moment. She told them the whole story—the scratch that disappeared, Marie's warning, and the missed meeting. They were incredulous.

"But this is an amazing!" said Sergeant Martin, *if true,* his voice clearly indicated.

Faith was feeling desperate. She had heard it said in jest that the French police tended to view those reporting a crime with as much suspicion as those committing one, and if her experience was anything to go by, it wasn't such a joke. They proceeded to quiz her about the shape and depth of the scratch and whether there were any other differences. Then they asked what time had Marie come to the car, where had Faith parked, what kind of car was it, which alleyway, and so on. Grandmother's maiden name was coming next. She became angry.

"I'm *sure* Marie has been murdered. She was on her way to meet me at noon and somehow she was abducted, killed, and thrown into the river."

"A bit hard to do in the middle of a busy city, wouldn't you agree, madame? Besides, her death was by drowning, according to the autopsy. Very *triste,* but no question of anything else."

Faith sighed. There was nothing to be gained by all of this and she thanked them for coming. At the door, they assured her they would make a full report, again hoped she would put these unpleasantnesses out of her head and enjoy *la belle France.* She managed to dredge up a smile, then went off to collect Ben. She'd have to wait until Michel returned from Marseille. She hoped it wouldn't be long.

All through lunch, she listened to Ben prattle on about the super *velo* his friend Léonard had and could he come to play and ride Ben's bike? Ben's bike was not a big boy's bike, except it was a good one too and so on and so on. Faith agreed absentmindedly, as she would have to anything, then put Ben firmly down for a nap. He thought he was too old for naps now, but Faith had told him he would be taking them until further notice—much further notice— say, college.

She could hear him talking to the Paddington Bear they had brought with them, and after a while that stopped, replaced by Ben's steady breathing. She took her shoes off and stretched out on her bed. When he woke up, she had plans.

Maybe Marie had decided to meet her after all. It had been a rainy, miserable day and she might have assumed she wouldn't be noticed slipping off to the *hôtel de ville.* The woman certainly had had guts. She'd taken an enormous risk in warning Faith in the first place. Maybe she'd had enough and wanted to get at the people controlling her life.

The people who caused all the *filles de joie* to walk the streets in fear. But they got to her first. She never made it to the rendezvous. Which meant she was stopped before she got there or after she arrived. The entire building had been emptying out for lunch. Not too difficult to find a secluded spot, even when the building was occupied. Faith's eyes drifted shut. She had to find out. She had to do this for Marie.

In what seemed like a few minutes later, Ben and Paddington bounced onto her bed, announcing, "I'm awake!" Faith sat up and gave him a big hug.

"Let's go get some nice cakes for supper."

"And Ben wants one now," he insisted.

"And so does Mommy," Faith agreed. She might be involved in an investigation, but one thing was clear—the French know how to make cake.

Marilyn and Monique were at the corner. Both women's eyes were red and their attire somewhat subdued. The two women were grieving. They were also clearly afraid.

Faith went past them hurriedly, resolved not to speak to them lest it imperil them, too. She was plagued by the awareness that it may have been by warning her that Marie had gone to her death.

She stopped at the Veaux's and bought a package of juicy Agen prunes—sold at the *boucheries* for some reason, along with other items to go in or outside the meat, such as jars of olives and pickles. The prunes were for Ben's snacks, since to Ben's dismay, his parents hadn't adopted the French *goûter* custom for children of a slab of chocolate between two pieces of buttered bread. As she paid Delphine, she asked casually, "When did you see Marie last? Did she seem depressed?"

"She said hello yesterday morning as usual when she passed and I saw her again on the corner when I went for a coffee later in the morning, but she didn't come back after lunch. *Pauvre petite*. She seemed the same as usual. We never know how another feels."

So Marie had not been seen after noon, at least not in the neighborhood. And where else would she be? Faith thought she knew and walked up rue Chenavard to the Place des Terreaux and back into the *hôtel de ville*. She went to the information office and told them she had left her glasses on the windowsill in one of the rooms during the tour yesterday. Had they been found? No, perhaps she herself could take a quick look. She smiled winningly. She knew exactly where they were, she added. The man behind the desk did not resist. He took them into the courtyard and indicated the door from which Faith had emerged the day before.

"My pleasure, madame, but please do not take much time and let me know when you leave. We do not usually permit this."

"I understand and I appreciate it very much."

Faith went up the stairs as rapidly as she could with Ben in tow. She was very aware that either the baby was intent on making his or her presence known or else all the monarch butterflies west of the Rockies had decided to winter in her stomach instead of Pacific Grove, California. She turned and went straight into the room of the tribunals. Yesterday, it had been empty when the tour entered and it was empty now. She closed the door and went to the rear of the room where the windows overlooked the Rhône. She sat Ben on the floor and gave him her purse to explore. "There could be a sweetie in there for my sweetie," she told him shamelessly. Then she pulled on the gloves she had shoved into her pocket and opened the door that concealed the entrance to the tunnel into the river.

She'd brought along a pocket flashlight and she shone it on the other opening. It was a long shot, but not impossible. She steadied the beam of light. Not impossible at all.

Caught in the smaller door, down near the floor where the head of a body might have rested briefly before being carried down the stairs and into the tunnel to the river, were several long bright red hairs.

Six

Benoît stood tentatively on the fire escape outside the kitchen window of an apartment on rue Sully. Dominique had assured him she had unlocked it when she went to say good-bye to her friend who was leaving with her parents for a week at their house in Ramatuelle.

It was very dark and although he was not cold, he shivered. Why did it seem that he was the one to draw the short straw so often? The scene in the children's playground near school where they held their meeting yesterday was as clear in his mind as if it had just occurred. It was a repetition of all the previous ones. They had joked about some fellow classmates and decided to go to a concert at La Cigale. Le Voyage de Noz was the group playing and Berthille knew one of the band members. He remembered asking how well and was surprised at the intensity of her denial. "You boys are all alike. You think everything is sex. Your minds are never anywhere else!" He apologized and they got down to business and when the straws were presented, one by one they drew long ones. He was last and it was inevitable—la courte paille again. He'd made a vague protest and they'd immediately asked him if he was afraid. He'd denied it.

Now standing outside the window dressed in black, complete to his gloves, he admitted he was afraid and the fear was part of the thrill.

He raised the window without any trouble and stepped over the sill. The room was completely dark, but he could see perfectly well from the light outside. Switching on a flashlight, he walked softly down the hallway, opening doors randomly. It was true. No one was home.

He went into the master bedroom and looked through several drawers before he found what he was looking for. Madame had not taken all her jewelry to the Côte d'Azur. He put a diamond-studded watch and several brooches in the bottom of the shopping bag he carried, first removing several layers of old clothes. There were some nice rings and he added them to the collection, hesitating over her engagement ring, her bague de fiançailles, the traditional sapphire surrounded by diamonds. No doubt it had a great deal of sentimental value. Though, reflecting on his own parents' marriage, perhaps it was in the drawer because the owner no longer valued it much. And, he reminded himself, others had a greater need.

He wandered about the bedroom, found a nice Rolex and some old coins in a small leather box on monsieur's commode. On impulse, he threw the box in, as well.

In the salon, there were some ornate snuffboxes in a glass case. The key was in the lock. Too simple. They deserved to be taken. He wrapped them in an old shirt and added them to the bag. He tested the weight. It wasn't too heavy. They had been warned to stick to light things. In one of the other bedrooms, he found some more jewelry—a gold necklace and *bracelets. Totally at ease, he lay down on the bed. It was a girl's room, an older girl who'd plastered the walls with posters of Serge Gainsbourg, R.E.M., and In Excess. Gainsbourg's picture had a black ribbon pinned to it. Not bad taste, except for the one of Madonna. Perhaps it was a joke.*

The bed linens smelled faintly of her perfume. He closed his eyes and undid the buttons on his fly. He slipped his hand into his pants. Soon pulsating rhythms beat steadily across his consciousness and silent lyrics came to his lips. He exploded and sank back. Maybe he did think too much about sex, but in any case, this was the best sex he'd ever had. He bid his phantom lover good night and crept back down the fire escape with her jewels.

Benjamin had wandered into the closet after Faith, and his "What are you doing, Mommy?" startled her into action. If she left the strands of hair, they might be removed. If she took them all, the *flics,* as she was now calling those known to her on the force, would no doubt imagine she had dyed some of her own locks or plucked them from a hairpiece on display at the wig shop around the corner from the apartment. She had to assume that she could get back here with Chief Inspector Ravier before anyone else tampered with them, but she carefully placed two of them in the envelope from her mother's recent letter, which she had been carrying around, trying to find a moment to answer. The door to the tunnel was still locked, but it looked to be one of those antique safeguards similar to the one on the door to her hallway that could be opened with any number of keys.

"Come on, let's go get our cakes," she told Ben, who had been watching the whole operation in utter fascination. She hustled him down the stairs and into the information bureau, where she displayed her dark glasses triumphantly and thanked the exceptionally nice *fonctionnaire* for his help. Then it was out the door before he could wonder why madame would have been wearing dark *lunettes* on such a rainy, gray day as yesterday and before Ben could start to tell him about the hide-and-seek game Mommy had been playing in the closet upstairs, both risks being about equal.

Exhausted, she sank into a delicate chair at La Minaudiére and ordered cakes, coffee, and milk. They arrived and the sight of the assortment of bite-sized cakes—miniature éclairs, cream puffs, fruit tarts, and dark chocolate truffles—momentarily distracted her from the envelope burning a hole in her purse. Ben was reciting "eeny, meeny, mini, mo" over the cake plate, getting mixed up and starting from the beginning again—and again.

"Just take one," Faith snapped, quickly adding an apologetic "sweetheart." She decided they'd better eat their cakes and go back to the apartment for some quality time before the recent events in her life turned her into the mother from hell.

On the way up the stairs—was this only the third *étage?*—they met Madame Vincent tripping effortlessly down the flights in her Chanel pumps, with Pippo eagerly following along. Faith suddenly remembered the invitation to tea and started to try to make some sort of excuse for not calling.

"Don't worry, *chérie,* you have much on your mind these days. I think I will have a little party on Friday instead with Mesdames d'Ambert and Joliet. Would you care to meet them again, say at four o'clock, and we can have tea or whatever the ladies prefer?"

"That would be lovely," Faith replied. "I always enjoy seeing all of you and our time here is going so quickly."

"See you Friday then, if not before," and Madame Vincent was off in a puff of Shalimar.

Faith would have to ask Solange if one of her brood could play with Ben. The problem was that children in France had such a long school day. There might not be anyone around at four and it would be no fun to have Ben there, a constant menace to the bibelots no matter how many Legos Faith brought to distract him.

As she got her elaborate dinner ready, which was making her feel better, Faith kept trying Michel Ravier's home number. She had called the work number immediately and left a message. Then she had tried his home. No one answered, not even his mother, and Faith was forced to assume he was still in Marseille.

Tom was thrilled with the dinner and in between delightedly crunching the little quail bones to extract every last morsel, he told her he was further ahead in his research than he thought and they could take a long weekend.

"Where would you like to go? Paris? Provence? Beaujolais? Except we'll be going there soon for the Veaux's niece's wedding. How about leaving France? We could easily make it to Switzerland," he said.

"I'd like to go somewhere we've never been before, either of us. Is there anyplace the Albigensians used to hang out that you'd like to see?" Faith felt it was important for a wife to occasionally take an interest in her husband's work. The problem was that having had a grandfather and father in the trade, it was hard to drum up much enthusiasm for prayerbook battles or the rewording of certain hymns. The Albigensians were something new to her, though, and she could listen intelligently without resorting to internal list making or dreaming up yet another creative use for phyllo dough.

Tom's face shone. "Well, I'd love to go to Carcassonne. It was one of the centers of Albigensianism and, while I wouldn't say this to Paul, we can thank Viollet-le-Duc for saving it. Maybe he did restore it a bit too neatly, but it's supposed to be wonderful. Very romantic, too. The citadel and walls are illuminated at night. We could stay in the old city—and it's in the Southwest, so that means great food."

His enthusiasm was catching and the idea of getting out of Lyon very appealing.

"When do we leave?"

"We could get an early start on Saturday and I wouldn't have to be back until Tuesday morning, so it gives us almost three full days."

"Great, and you can tell me all about who lived there on the way."

"More like who died there. Poor, noble Raymond-Roger Trencavel—what chance did he have against all those Northerners? And believe me, it was no religious crusade; they wanted his land, pure and simple."

Once he got going, Tom could talk about the wrongs done to the Albigensians for hours, and Faith was getting sleepy. She stifled a yawn and got up from the table.

"You're quite a lovely nobleman yourself. Now why don't we clean this up and go to bed."

"The sooner the better, milady."

Absorbed in hearkening back to the strife of the Middle Ages, Faith had almost forgotten the present turmoil, but on the way to the *garderie* the next morning she was still startled by innocent events: a dog racing across her path as she walked down the street, a sudden squeal of brakes, or raised voices from a doorway. She was definitely getting too schizy, she told herself, and longed for Michel Ravier's return or their trip to Carcassonne—whichever came first.

Ben was going to his beloved friend Léonard's house for lunch and an afternoon of blissful play. Léonard, at four, was a year older and Ben worshipped him. Léonard's mother, Chantal, lovingly referred to the young *amis* as the "two naughty boys" of the *garderie* and seemed more than able to cope with them, despite her diminutive size. There was no question that Chantal could have taken on tigers in the zoo or anywhere else—staring them down like Madeleine, her compatriot, and saying, "Pooh pooh."

This left Faith with a large block of time and she decided to get all their clothes in order for the trip, which meant the real thing—a visit to the *lavomatique,* the laundromat—and not a tub wash.

Laundromats were as scarce as peanut butter in Lyon, neither having captured the French imagination, unlike microwave popcorn, nor did they promise an elevation in a quality of life that placed pâté de foie gras well within the reach of the average citizen. After consulting the telephone directory and asking friends in vain, Faith had finally spied behind a storefront a telltale row of washers and dryers on rue Chapeaux, not far from the Place des Jacobins. The laundromat was usually deserted except for some of the prostitutes who frequented the area and squeezed in a load of wash between clients. The first time Faith had ventured in, she had not brought nearly enough one-franc pieces—it took almost a laundry bagful to pay for the washer and dryer—and after unsuccessfully asking at the bar/*tabac* next door, solicited help from some of the girls, who were only too happy to oblige. It seemed to be her lot in Lyon to frequent the same neighborhoods as her otherwise-employed sisters. She had also made the mistake of trying to obtain some *monnaie,* change, from a man passing by. At first, he could not believe the low price she was offering, then once the mistake was explained, he did not know whether to be angry or amused. He chose the latter and Faith had the distinct impression he would be dining out on the story for months—the *belle Américaine* who wanted *monnaie* to keep her clothes clean but would do nothing for the favor. There were also a number of *clochards* in the area and Faith could see they had plenty of change, yet she was loath to approach one.

The *faux clochard* had disappeared from the front of the Eglise St. Nizier and apparently no one else wanted to take his place too soon. Remembering the violence of his temper, she didn't blame them. But then, that had been the real one, she reminded herself.

As she sorted her clothes into the washers and added detergent, she was lulled by the familiarity of the routine and settled down to watch the garments spin about through the glass doors. She was feeling better—if not exactly ready to whip her weight in those tigers, at least able to go a few rounds with their cubs.

She opened an ancient Tauchnitz edition of Trollope's *The Small House at Allington.* Her quest for English books at the *bouquinistes* on the Quai de Pecherie near the apartment had turned up an astonishing number of books by Stephen King, Pearl Buck's *The Good Earth,* ancient Fodor's to everywhere, and this. She was up to chapter three and the radical contrast with her life at present—or any other present—was entertaining. She was soon engrossed until the lines "Let her who is forty call herself forty; but if she can be young in spirit at forty, let her show that she is so" leaped from the page. Faith didn't intend to call herself forty for at least two decades, and when appearances did force the matter, her youthful spirit with some help from Canyon Ranch would show it without any advice from Mr. Trollope. Somewhat disgruntled with the intimations, she shut the book and decided to take a walk. The doors on the washers locked until the cycle ended and it had another thirty minutes to run. She could get a coffee.

It was a beautiful day, warm and filled with what Faith thought of as a Mediterranean light—clear, sharp, and bright—catching the strong colors of the stone buildings. Everybody in Lyon is always looking at something, she observed as she walked along. Shop windows, something in the street, and often you suddenly become aware that everybody is staring in the same direction. You stare, too, and it is a car being towed, garbage collected, a minor car accident, a helicopter—but it all has the feel of an event because everybody watches.

And the light: She was constantly amazed at the beauty it imparted to the city, masking its flaws and, especially in the late afternoon, bathing vastly disparate neighborhoods in the same long, soft glow.

She passed the large Beaux-Arts Prisunic department store building and a few *clochards* who were leaning up against its walls, sunning themselves like cats, their faces turned upward. One was asleep. An old lady sat with her knitting. It seemed to be some sort of scarf. Faith saw her at this spot frequently. She always seemed to be at the same stage and she always had a different color yarn. In front of the group a young man was drawing an elaborate chalk portrait of the Last Supper on the pavement. His *casquette,* seeded with a few coins, was placed next to his chalks. He had written, "I am hungry. I am German. I want to go home" in several languages on a small card. Faith dropped some coins in the cap.

She bought a newspaper and settled down at a table facing the rue de la République. It wasn't long before people-watching became more engrossing than the news. She was surprised to see Christophe walk by. It was early for lunch and he should have been in school, she supposed. He walked directly over to one of the *clochards* by Prisunic and soon the two were in deep conversation.

She finished her coffee and went over to them, intending to ask Christophe if he or one of his siblings could stay with Ben the next day. Her arrival sent a look of panic into the *clochard*'s eyes, and surprisingly, Christophe's. His "Madame Fairsheeld, how are you?" lacked a certain warmth.

Faith was intrigued. From the tone of the boy's voice as she approached, this did not seem like the acolyte at the feet of the master. It seemed like business, but what possible business could Christophe have with a *clochard?* The man appeared younger than most and, if cleaned up, quite presentable. He was not as far gone as some and although his hair was in tangles, his face covered with some kind of rash, and his clothes filthy, there was the look of earlier prosperity about him. He was wearing a camel's hair coat cut like a bathrobe, even though the weather was very warm. Possibly, there wasn't much underneath. The coat had been a good one and she wondered how he had come by it. He sat without moving and kept his eyes on the ground. Beyond the initial greeting, Christophe had said nothing and was plainly waiting for Faith to leave. Instead, she asked the man where he was from. She wondered whether he was French or, like the sidewalk artist, from someplace else. This openly irritated Christophe.

"It is not advisable to speak to these people, especially for someone not from France. The *clochards* can sometimes be quite crude and even violent."

"But your mother has told me they are harmless," Faith protested.

"Oh, my mother," Christophe answered, the words speaking for themselves. Faith realized she had to get back to her clothes and reached for a coin. As she put it in the still immobilized *clochard*'s outstretched hand, she noticed he wore a ring on his right hand. It was a heavy silver one, and when he put the coin into a small box by his side, she saw that it was a signet ring with a crest—three small birds against a background of diamondlike shapes. It might have been stolen, but he would have been more apt to sell it than wear it. The mighty fallen or the black sheep of a noble family? The whole thing was odd. She said good-bye to Christophe, noted the relief in his eyes, and went back to the laundromat.

She transferred her wash to the dryer. What was the relationship between Christophe and the *clochard*? And the ring. If slipped off, it would leave a mark.

And the nails on both hands had been bitten until bloody—just like the nails of the *faux clochard*.

She struggled up the stairs with her clean wash and was

glad they were going out for dinner. She'd made reservations at Café des Fédérations—a *bouchon,* that Lyonnais institution not exactly a bistro and not a restaurant, either. A *bouchon*—literally a cork—where Tom would drink deeply of Monsieur Fulchiron's Morgon and they would eat quennelles in Nantua sauce—those delicate, lighter-than-air fish dumplings floating in lobster sauce—or maybe *andouillette,* the Rolls-Royce of chitterlings.

Feeling virtuous, she put away the wash and went back down the stairs to get Ben. It was still sunny and beautiful and she decided to walk to the Croix Rousse plateau, where Léonard lived. The exercise would be good for her. She knew she must be gaining too much weight, and even if Baby Fairchild was getting unheard-of nutrients, Faith had better keep herself in shape.

The tour of the *traboules* and *montées* of the Croix Rousse was something she had meant to do since she'd arrived, but she hadn't had the time. She took her guidebook and set out. As she crossed the Place des Terreaux, the spray cascading from the horses at the Bartholdi fountain fell in a mist on her face. The afternoon had grown warmer and it felt lovely.

Faith began to make her way slowly up the incline, passing through the *traboules,* to emerge blinking into the daylight of the courtyards that were bordered by a series of long staircases crawling up the hill. Sometimes the steep stairs were set in long zigzags against the crumbling walls of the old buildings, which seemed ill suited to shore up the *colline.* Other staircases ran straight up to the next level in hundreds of small steps. Several times, she had to stop to catch her breath. It was like a labyrinth and she hadn't thought to bring any string. The Royalists had used these pathways and, more recently, the Resistance during the Second World War. It was said a man could live in the *traboules* indefinitely, always keeping one step ahead of his pursuers—able to duck into the apartment window of a sympathizer, then to emerge from another into a further series of stairways and tunnels on the other side. As she followed the route suggested by the guide, the images of these desperate men and women became increasingly vivid in Faith's imagination. She began to worry about getting lost. Suddenly, she thought she heard the cries and running footsteps of those long-ago fugitives.

There *were* cries, and she froze against the wall for a moment, before smiling in relief as a group of schoolchildren came racing around the corner. She emerged into the daylight at Place Colbert, noted an interesting-looking *fromagerie,* and sternly reminded herself she was there to get Ben, not Brie.

Chantal greeted her at the apartment door and said the boys had had a wonderful time playing cowboys. Judging from the state of the kitchen, which was also Léonard's playroom, they had been riding the range hard. Faith collected Ben, stifled his cries of protest with a firm "If you cannot leave nicely, you cannot come back," which—amazingly—worked, and thanked Chantal, arranging for Léonard to come to them on Tuesday.

She put Ben into his stroller—Chantal had used it to take him from the *garderie*—and pushed him to the metro. It was one thing for Faith to do the circuit of the *traboules* and *montées,* but she shuddered to think of Ben on all those stairs. They arrived home quickly and Faith was folding the *poussette* up to put in the closet when Jean-François d'Ambert came down the stairs, carrying his briefcase.

"Bonjour, Faith." He kissed her soundly on both cheeks. "Let me do that for you." He flourished a massive key ring that suggested either a life of crime or extensive holdings. He saw her glance.

"It's ridiculous, isn't it, but I need them all—for the apartment, our small *maison secondaire* in the country, my office, the *cave* for the wine, of course, and *voilà,* this little, so very convenient *placard.*" He opened the closet door and carefully placed the stroller inside.

"*Bouf,* it stinks. They really must do a better job of keeping this place clean. I will speak to the *régie* tomorrow."

"The *régie?*" Faith asked.

"Yes, the—how do you say?—agents."

She was quickly thinking of some way to extend the conversation, for as soon as he had taken his keys from his pocket, she'd noticed his hand and wanted a longer look.

"Will you be going to the country this weekend?" she asked, moving closer to him with what she hoped was unobtrusive scrutiny.

"No, it's too far for just a weekend trip and nothing is prepared. We will wait until the children are out of school. Now, you must forgive me, I am late for an appointment."

It was all right. She had seen enough. The heavy silver ring he wore on his left hand was not a wedding band. It was the twin of the one the *clochard* she'd seen talking with Christophe had been wearing. Three small birds couchant against a field of diamonds. What did it mean? And whom was Jean-François going to meet? A business appointment so late in the day?

"*Merci,* madame, I would love another cup," Faith said the following afternoon as Madame Vincent proffered the elegant Sèvres, or perhaps Limoges, pot of steaming tea. The day had been another warm and sunny one. The rainy spell was broken. But it was not too warm for the tea and it seemed exactly right to be sitting on one of Yvette Vincent's velvet and gilt chairs, drinking cup after cup in companionable conversation. Solange and Valentina, obviously old friends, were making madame laugh hilariously with their gossip.

"*Tiens!* I shouldn't laugh. You two are terrible. And

what do you say of this poor old woman when her back is turned?"

"That she makes the best macaroons in Lyon," answered Solange, taking another from the cake stand.

"A recipe of my grandmother. A tyrant in the kitchen, she was. 'The eggs must be lighter, Yvette,' she'd say, 'keep beating.'"

Faith thought she saw an opening in the conversation.

"Speaking of ancestors, is that ring Jean-François wears from his family?" It was clumsy, but it would have to do.

"Ring?" For a moment, Solange looked puzzled. "Oh yes, of course. It is not his marriage ring. That"—she paused to roll her eyes at Valentina—"I can never get him to wear. But the ring of his family he does wear sometimes. It was his father's. All the men of the family have the same."

So the *clochard* was a d'Ambert. A d'Ambert probably not on the *A* list of Lyon society and a d'Ambert certainly not frequenting these d'Amberts' Sunday dinners, Faith suspected. Curiouser and curiouser. The *clochard* with the ring, posing as the dead *clochard*, connected to the d'Ambert family. The pieces of the puzzle were all on the table, but there was still a lot of sky to fit together.

"Your face looks so odd, Faith. You have wrinkles in your forehead. What is troubling you?" asked Valentina.

"Nothing really, though I suppose I am bothered by some of the things that have happened this week. You know—the *clochard* and that poor girl's suicide."

Madame Vincent looked at her sharply. "I have heard of your *clochard*. Do you think the two had anything to do with one another?"

Things were going much too fast.

"Oh, no," Faith protested. "How could they be?"

"Well, they are both gone now," said Solange, "so it's best to put it out of your mind and enjoy being here."

"Which is exactly what I intend."

117

The talk moved on to babies. Solange's sister had just had a sixth—obviously a prolific family. Faith was happy to hear all three women were convinced she would have a girl from the way she was carrying. It wasn't that she didn't adore Ben, but a girl would be a set. Like bookends or salt and pepper shakers or . . . Her mind was wandering and she reined it in to listen to the next conversational turn.

"They broke into the de Roulets last night. Jean-François is nervous about going away and says we must find someone to stay in the apartment this summer. And you, madame, aren't you worried here by yourself?"

"But I have Pippo, who I assure you can be very fierce." Faith looked at the fat little pug curled up on the Aubusson carpet and doubted it. Wave a hunk of filet mignon at him and he'd help carry the furniture. "Besides, I am seldom away and I doubt anyone could get into the apartment."

"This is true," Valentina said. "They come in from the fire escapes or the balconies and Madame Vincent has neither so far up in the clouds here. I think she is quite safe. I worry for my pictures, you can imagine, yet so far they seem interested only in jewels. I will have to ask Michel if there are any changes in what they have been taking. Of course, the newspapers are allowed to say nothing."

"He's away. I have been trying to reach him," Faith said before thinking better of it, but having called his house virtually every hour on the hour, the mere mention of his name caused this reflex response.

"Michel is away?" Valentina asked.

"Is this Michel Ravier you are speaking of?" Solange asked.

"Yes," Faith answered, glad to take the conversation into other waters. "Do you know him also?"

Solange laughed and reached inside her pretty Longchamps bag for her cigarettes. "Everyone knows Michel and many wish they did better." After the laughter died down, she said to Faith, "He was at school with my husband and we have known him for many years."

"Sometimes I think all the men in Lyon were at the Marists together," Faith commented.

"Ah, so you are acquainted with the Marists. Yes, it does seem that way. Jean-François was very disappointed when Christophe left the school. He wanted to go to this one on the Croix Rousse that is so popular these days. But since the Marists are taking girls, all the other children are with them and I pray they stay there for their father's sake. Amélie has been talking of Lycée du Parc; I am not listening."

"Children will do what they want," Madame Vincent said emphatically. "We wished for them so long, but now I think maybe it was a good thing. Pippo is far more obedient and life has been simpler."

Faith looked at Valentina, wondering whether she, too, would attest to the benefits of the childless state, but she was looking very pensive and perhaps her flippant answer about Georges being enough was not the true key to her feelings.

"Well," said Solange, "I speak as an authority. Children are nice, especially when they are babies, but it is a frightening thought to have five teenagers. Perhaps if he had known, Jean-François would not have been so eager." She stood up and picked a crumb from her bright blue Sonia Rykiel outfit, looking very beautiful and very complacent. If anyone's children were going to frighten their mother, it wasn't going to be Solange's. Faith was reminded that she wanted to get the name of Solange's hairdresser.

"I like the way your hair is cut so much, Solange. Where do you have it done?"

"A wonderful man, Italian, of course—they are the best coiffeurs—named Giovanni. He works at the Quick Coupe in the Place Sathonay, not far from here. Just at the foot of the Croix Rousse."

"I know where it is, behind Ben's school and near the covered market at Place Rambaud."

Valentina laughed. "You know the markets of Lyon better than we do."

Faith was thinking out loud. "I'd love to get my hair cut before we go to Carcassonne."

"Oh, Carcassonne. My husband and I went there often. It is so beautiful," rhapsodized Madame Vincent.

"When do you go?" Solange asked.

"Tomorrow morning," Faith answered. "Just until Monday."

"If you like, I can call Giovanni and see if he can take you early before you leave, or perhaps you would prefer to wait until you get back?"

Faith was filled with a great longing to have her hair done. She'd go this instant if she could. There was nothing quite like the feeling of all that pampering and the resultant new look.

"Could you call? I can be there when they open."

Madame Vincent waved Solange to her telephone, which nestled behind a line of leather-covered, gold-embossed classics of French literature on a marble-topped chest. It was quickly done and Faith was signed up for a *coupe* and *brosse* at eight o'clock. She was amazed they opened so early.

"At Carcassonne, you must search out what is left of a bust of Lady Carcas," Valentina instructed Faith. "It is not so interesting artistically as historically. She was a Spaniard, a Saracen, who outsmarted the great Charlemagne himself. The town had been under siege for five years and the entire garrison dead of hunger. Lady Carcas made some dummies and arranged them on the ramparts, then went from one to another, shooting arrows at the enemy. Finally, she took the last remaining pig, let it eat all the grain left, and threw it from the top of the tower. Of course when Charlemagne split the belly open and saw it was filled with grain, he gave in and left. Some say the town is called Carcassonne because when she sounded trumpets to call him back to reveal what she had done, satisfied with the glory of it, he didn't hear. But an equerry did and said to him, 'Sire, Carcas te sonne.' Personally, I doubt whether a woman like that would have called her enemy back, unless she could gloat over him in some way."

"What a wonderful story. I'll tell Tom and we'll be sure to pay homage to Lady Carcas," Faith said, thinking at the same time that the whole thing was very like something Valentina might do. She pictured her running along the battlements taking aim, much as she sized up prospects at her gallery.

"Now, *chéries,* this has been such a nice time with all these stories and so forth, but I must go. Next time, you come to me," Solange announced, and moved toward the door.

Faith stood up also. "It has been lovely. Thank you so much, Madame Vincent."

Solange looked surprised. "But you do not have to leave yet, Faith. Amélie is so happy to play with Benjamin."

"Do stay," Madame Vincent said as it became apparent that Valentina was also leaving.

"Only for one more cup," Faith agreed, realizing how lonely Yvette Vincent must be up among the chimneys.

The others left and as Faith sipped her tea, Yvette reminisced about her husband and all the traveling they had done together. "But we never got to your country, *malheureusement,*" she said.

"Perhaps you will come yourself," Faith said, getting up this time in earnest. It was almost six o'clock.

"My travels are finished. A short trip to my sister in Narbonne, occasionally. It is enough. And sometimes a few days in Paris. That is always necessary."

Faith totally agreed.

At the door, madame kissed her on both cheeks with

a heartiness that surprised Faith. As Faith returned the salutation on Yvette's velvety soft, wrinkled skin, she realized madame was whispering something to her.

"Go to Carcassonne with your lovely husband, *chérie,* then do not stay in Lyon long. It is not a place for everyone."

As she went down the stairs to her apartment, Faith wasn't sure whether she had imagined the warning or not.

Like the body in the trash, it would disappear if mentioned aloud.

When he got to the bottom of the fire escape, he took off his gloves and shoved them in his pocket together with the black knit hat that had covered his hair. He knotted a red bandanna casually about his neck before strolling out to the street. It was late and there weren't too many people out. He passed a young couple, entwined together, with their hands in the back pockets of each other's jeans. They didn't even glance his way. Lovesick fools, he thought. What did they know of life? For an instant, he thought of emptying the shopping bag he was carrying with such apparent nonchalance in front of them. He could hardly stop himself from laughing out loud as he pictured their astonished faces when they saw what was wrapped in rags under the old clothes.

He was almost there. He crossed the avenue Maréchal de Saxe to Place Quinet and placed the bag in the trash basket closest to the entrance to the playground. Then he slipped into the darkened doorway of the Lycée Edouard Herriot, on the opposite side of the square, and waited. It wasn't long before he saw a lone figure shuffle into sight and take the bag from the trash, adding it to others grasped in his hands. The clochard *paused, reached into one of the bags, and took a long pull from a bottle he'd found there, then moved slowly off again.*

Benoît's part was over. He ran down rue Bossuet toward the river as fast as he could, his heart pumping and every nerve stretched. It felt glorious. He continued to sprint toward the pedestrian bridge arching and swaying in the night breeze before him. He wanted to get home. He was starving.

Seven

The Café des Fédérations was as crowded as usual and the Fairchilds were obliged to share a table with a happy group of wine merchants from Beaune. The men were teasing Monsieur Fulchiron, the *patron,* about his Morgon, *only* a Beaujolais. He was retorting that all that mustard from Dijon had seared their palates. During the course of her meal, Faith learned more about the growing conditions in various parts of Burgundy and the relative merits of the resulting vintages than she'd ever thought possible. The Burgundians' criticisms did not impede their consumption, and Françoise, the pretty blond waitress who had told Tom and Faith she had been there forever—in which case she must have started at age four—was kept busy replacing empty *pots,* the old, thick-bottomed wine bottles that were standard in Lyon's *bouchons*. The meal ended with a large slab of *tarte aux pommes,* thick slices of juicy apples piled onto a shortbread crust.

"It's heaven," Faith said to Tom with a sigh. "Literally. I'm sure this is what it will be—good bread, cheese, lots of happy people, and no frozen foods."

"At the moment, I agree with you," he responded, and called for the check. They said good-bye to their *amis* for life from Beaune as business cards and invitations to stay were pressed upon them, marveling once more at all those silly people who insist the French aren't friendly.

Back at the apartment, Tom had finished packing for the weekend quickly and was in bed reading. "But you're not packing for two," Faith pointed out. Although packing for Ben was easy. You took everything. The problem was finding space in the bag for one's own modest requirements.

She looked at Tom. He'd fallen asleep over the Michelin guide. She gently took the green bible from his hands, turned out the light, and kissed him. He mumbled something she interpreted as an endearment and was down for the count.

Faith, however, was wide awake. After she finished packing, she went into the kitchen and made herself a *tisane*—camomile. At home, she now drank Sleepy Time tea, which was much the same but, with a bear in a night shirt on the box, lacked some of the *éclat* of the French brew.

She sat down at the dining room table and looked out the long windows across the narrow side street into the school opposite. It was completely dark. The windows were arranged in rows as tidily as the desks within. Tomorrow the scene would be filled with the children and teachers she had become used to watching every day except Sunday. It was like a play and she had their routines down pat. When they would stop for *goûter*—a snack—when they would go outside to the blacktop next to the car park by the river, which served as their playground, and when they would finally get to go home. If she looked out the front windows of the apartment, she saw different productions—weddings, funerals at the church, an occasional *manifestation* in the street, with marchers protesting the latest indignity toward the Algerian-French community or demanding a stop to the importation of foreign cabbages or some such things. She would like to be able to sit by the windows for an entire year and watch the events and changes each month brought. She took a sip of the hot tea. Of course, one change had already taken place. The *clochard* was gone.

She took another sip.

Who could have murdered him?

She had been assuming that it had to have been someone associated with *le milieu,* because of the way Marie had worded her warning, but the three women stood on the corner and observed everyone in the neighborhood. It could just as well have been locals. Faith sketched out a possible scenario. The *clochard* is lured into the vestibule by the promise of a drink or whatever, killed for some reason as yet unknown to her, and placed in the dumpster for safekeeping while whoever goes to get transport or waits until it's late enough to take the body out to the river undetected and throw it in. *Clochards* were pulled out of the Saône and Rhône with some frequency, and the police wouldn't bother with an autopsy. Which, it suddenly occurred to her, they may not have done with Marie, either. Knowing her profession, they probably assumed it a suicide and decided to save a few francs. The policemen, Martin and Pollet, had mentioned an autopsy, but she didn't put much stock in what they said. Just placate Madame Lunatique any way possible. She wished for the thousandth time that Ravier were back. She'd tried again when she'd returned from the tea party. And she could try again now.

Faith went to the phone and, after dialing, listened to ring after ring with a growing feeling of helplessness. But, she thought, she could write a letter and leave it at his

126

apartment on the way to Carcassonne, after she got her hair cut. This way, if he came back before she did, he could start things moving. She especially had to tell him what she suspected in case an autopsy had not been performed.

She got some writing paper, an envelope, and a pen and sat down again. What to say? The most important things were her discovery that the man posing as the *clochard* was a fake—her discovery of the corpse had apparently made it necessary—and that Marie had been killed. She started to write. The whole thing sounded incredible, but she kept going. After she mentioned finding the hair at the *hôtel de ville*—she enclosed the strands—and wrote, "I'm very much concerned that an autopsy was not done, or perhaps just a cursory examination made. Even if they did do one and found water in her lungs, she could have been drugged before being pushed down the tunnel—to make it look like drowning." She was on her third sheet of paper.

What else? Her suspicion that the man playing the *clochard* was a relative of the d'Ambert's? No, best keep to the two main points and she'd tell him more when they could speak in person—not an unpleasant prospect. She gave him the name of the hotel where they would be staying in Carcassonne—the Hôtel du Donjon, which the guide-book had praised for cassoulet and comfort, despite the suggestions to the contrary implied by the name—and signed the letter "Sincerely, Faith." The standard French closure for friends, *embrassons,* seemed a bit too—well, what? Intimate? Maybe honest? She smiled at herself, sealed the envelope, and put it in her purse.

Tumbling into bed, she drifted off to sleep with images of Carcassonne drifting through her mind: bright pennons flapping in the breeze, the sound of trumpets, rough cobble-stones, and high fortress walls overlooking the plain where the enemy was fleeing in disarray.

* * *

At eight o'clock sharp, Faith was leaning back in a chair, luxuriating in the sensation of the warm spray of water on her hair as Giovanni rinsed out the shampoo he had vigorously massaged into her scalp. He squirted some conditioner on and it felt cold, then more of those magic fingers and her hair was rinsed again. He put a towel around her head and motioned her to another chair. It wasn't a particularly elegant shop, and Giovanni and his receptionist seemed to be the only people working today, but it did sport an espresso machine. She sipped some as he combed her wet hair and stared at her in the mirror with intense concentration. She set the cup down and he went to work. More hair than she thought she had on her head fell to the floor as he snipped away. She had a moment of panic, then remembered how Solange looked—and also that hair grew back, eventually. So far, Giovanni had not said a single word to her after asking whether she wanted coffee. Now, he stood back, apparently satisfied with his labors, and reached for the blow-dryer. She followed his every move in the mirror so she could try to duplicate the style later. There was no question. It looked great. She thanked Giovanni profusely and went to the door.

"Madame Fairsheeld?" It was the receptionist, whose black dress had a high neck but barely covered her thighs. She wore a long strand of oversized pearls and had neatly coiffed bright orange hair with one white streak down the side. There was something feline about the whole effect.

"Yes?" Faith replied.

"Your husband has called with a message. He is going to get gas and will pick you up in front of the art museum at Place des Terreaux, since it is so hard to park here."

Faith thanked her. That made sense. They should have arranged it in the beginning. She hoped Ben was cooperating; the prospect of a long car trip in his beloved Deux Chevaux probably had him hastening Tom along. Normally, getting the three-year-old to dress himself was prac-

128

tice for sainthood. He'd get one sock on, then sit and hold the other, gazing at something, anything, nothing in total concentration. "Your sock, Ben," she'd remind him gently, or not so gently if they were in a hurry. He'd look at the odd bit of clothing in his hand as if seeing it for the first time. "Sock?" It was Tom's turn today, Faith thought happily as she left the salon.

Out on the sidewalk, she walked quickly toward the museum, aware that the sun was shining down on her own shiny coif. She passed a window and admired the way her hair moved when she tipped her head. Ah, vanity, vanity, thy name is . . . She hoped Tom liked it. Husbands tended not to like any changes in their wives' appearance. "But I liked you the way you were!" In addition, Tom fell under the Rapunzel rubric and would have Faith's tresses falling in golden waves to the floor if it were left to him.

She crossed the street and walked down rue Terme, past a toy store whose windows never failed to fascinate both mother and child on their way home from school. There was a new display of small, brightly painted knights in armor. Ben would love it—a large castle with some knights manning the towers and others on horseback in front of the drawbridge. It seemed appropriate and auspicious. She could hardly wait to get to Carcassonne.

A car pulled over to the curb, someone wanting directions. It had happened before. It was easy to get lost in Lyon. Faith walked over, starting to tell them apologetically that boy, did they have the wrong person, when the back door opened, a man in a ski mask jumped out, grabbed her, and pulled her into the car.

She wasn't the wrong person at all.

After a second of shocked disbelief, Faith started to struggle. The car was speeding up toward the Croix Rousse and her assailant had a firm grasp on her wrist. She started to scream and banged on the window with her fist, hoping to attract attention. The driver hadn't turned around. As the car slowed slightly for an intersection, she dove down and bit her captor on the wrist with all the force she had. He cried out and instinctively pulled his hand away. She already had her other hand on the door handle; the moment she was free, she pushed it open and ran down the street. He was after her in seconds, but she had sprinted ahead, getting a good lead. As she ran, Faith looked wildly around. The street was empty. It was also familiar. She'd been here on Thursday when she'd gone to get Ben at Léonard's. She remembered it from the tour in the guidebook, rue Burdeau, and there was a *traboule* somewhere. If only she could find it, she could lose her pursuer, she was sure. Her heart pounded madly. How long could she run this fast?

Up ahead, she saw the entrance to the covered passageway on the left. She plunged into the dark tunnel and ran on, stumbling until her eyes got used to the dim light. The *traboule* would take her to the next street and there had to be someone there, or she would be enough ahead to find a place to hide.

Faith could hear the footsteps following her. She realized she couldn't wait. She had to hide *now*. At the next bend, the *traboule* branched in two directions and she went to the right. Soon she saw there was a stairway at the end. She threw herself underneath and crouched down, hoping whoever was after her would assume she had gone up it or that he would go the other way.

He did take the other way. She heard the footsteps stop for an instant as he considered, then get fainter and fainter until she couldn't hear them anymore. He was gone.

She took several deep breaths but stayed where she was. It was only then that Faith allowed the image of the hand that had grasped her wrist in the car to rise to consciousness. It was his right hand. The fingernails were bitten and bloody. The fourth finger was bare except for a band of white where a ring had been. A family ring.

It was the d'Ambert *clochard*.

She'd never have been able to get away from anyone else so easily, she reflected. The *clochard*. She had drawn blood when she bit him and was aware that she had been spitting out the bitter, filthy taste as she ran. She took a tissue from her pocket and wiped her mouth.

And what about the message from Tom? She felt in a muddle. It was obviously a fake. The receptionist wouldn't have known his voice. But how had they known where Faith was? Unless they'd been watching her. Watching her for days, just waiting for the chance to grab her. She felt cramped and queasy. It was all too obvious what the main use of her hiding place was and she cautiously crept out.

She went up the staircase, which led to another *traboule*. It was silent. The only sound was her own footsteps. She could see the daylight ahead and moved toward it slowly. She looked out. No cars in sight. No people, either. This was the wholesale garment district, bustling with activity during the week and deserted on the weekend. Weak with relief, she saw there was a phone booth at the corner. Seventeen, the police emergency number. That was all she had to do. One seven. Push the buttons and the nightmare would be over. She began to walk quickly down the uneven cobblestones, afraid she might trip if she ran. She put one hand on her rounded belly. It would be all right. It *had* to be all right.

A few yards away, a man stepped from the alley. Before she could make a sound, the blow came and she was in darkness again.

"But I don't understand. There must be some mistake," Tom Fairchild said in bewilderment to the young woman whose bizarre orange hair seemed only too appropriate to the strangeness of the situation.

"I'm sorry, monsieur. I can just tell you what madame said. That she preferred the train to a long drive and would

131

meet you in Avignon for apéritifs opposite the Palais des Papes."

"But we hadn't even planned to stop at Avignon."

The young woman shrugged. "Sometimes when like this, women can get sudden impulses. She called for a cab and left for Perrache."

"Where's Mommy? I want Mommy!" Ben began to cry.

Tom picked him up. "Hush, sweetheart. Don't worry. Let's go to the train station and see if we can find her." He thanked the woman and left. As he strapped Ben into his car seat, he thought, "This just isn't like Faith. Or is it?"

The young woman watched the proceedings from the shop window. Tom had been able to park right in front. Giovanni would be coming back soon from the café down the street, where he'd gone for the first of his morning *mâchons* and the accompanying glass or two. She waited. She wasn't about to leave the store wide open. That would be a crime.

He arrived a few minutes later. "Ciao, I have to leave now," she told him, and did.

The Reverend Fairchild stood overlooking the platform at the station in despair. He had just missed the train for Avignon, which had pulled out only a few minutes before. He returned to the main part of the station and asked at the appropriate *guichet* if the ticket agent remembered a young woman with blond hair—newly cut—blue eyes, of average height, who had purchased a ticket for Avignon about thirty minutes ago.

"Maybe ten looked like that, monsieur. Now where is it you want to go?"

"I don't want to buy a ticket. I'm looking for my wife."

"Well, I cannot help you there. I am selling tickets. If there is some problem, you must go to the office."

"Are you sure you did not see her? She's an American. Her French is not very good."

"This is not unusual. If monsieur will please move—there are others here to buy tickets."

Ben tugged at Tom's hand. "Mommy, where's Mommy?"

"I don't know, but don't worry. We'll find her." And Tom strode across the station to get help.

Faith opened her eyes. Where was she? She tried to sit up and discovered that she was tied at the ankles and wrists like a fatted calf. She was in the back seat of a rapidly moving car, completely covered by a blanket. Tipping her head back and away from the rough wool, she could see nothing out the window but blue sky. The movement made her dizzy. Her head felt like it was splitting open. The blanket felt very warm—safe almost. She closed her eyes again and drifted back into unconsciousness.

Tom had no luck with the stationmaster, who suggested he call the police. Stopping only to buy the increasingly frightened Ben a package of Gummi Bears, Tom called the Leblancs instead. They arrived in what seemed like minutes.

Ghislaine took charge. "I will take Ben home with me while Paul goes to the police. They can arrange for the police in Avignon to meet the train. Obviously, Faith has become upset at this whole *clochard* business and has had some sort of *fugue*. She was talking about it on Sunday and I should have paid more attention to how upset she was."

"No, I should have. It's been going on all week. She even had some idea that the *clochard* outside the church was an imposter. My God, what if she was right! We have to tell the police everything. Can you get a hold of your friend Ravier?"

"Tom, *mon ami,* you must be calm. The best thing is for you to go to Avignon to be there after she arrives. You must take our car. It is faster. Go straight to the police and I know she will be waiting there for you." Paul tried to reassure him. "Meanwhile, I will call Michel and, yes, tell him everything. Now, Benjamin, would you like to play with Pierre? He has some new cars to show you."

Ben had been clutching Tom with hands sticky from the rapid consumption of the whole package of candies. He looked up at his father, unsure what to do. The cars would be nice to see, but one parent had vanished today and he wasn't about to let go of the one remaining.

"Sweetie, you go with Paul and Ghislaine and have fun this afternoon. I'm going to go bring Mommy back. We'll all have supper together. How would that be?"

Ben was reluctant, but he did not protest at being swung up onto Paul's shoulders, and they all left the station for their various destinations.

The car door opened with a jerk. An arm reached in and roughly shook Faith on the shoulder, yanking the blanket off, which she realized had not been draped over her out of kindness, but for concealment. She raised her heavy eyelids, aware that she had been on the edge of consciousness for some time, loath to leave her unknowing state. Her bonds were being cut and she rubbed her painful wrists. She sat up slowly.

Her captor was wearing a black ski mask. She could tell nothing about him. In the dim light, she could see the car had been driven into some kind of shed. It looked like an old farm building. *"Venez!"* the figure demanded, pulling her from the seat. Faith thought she would pass out again when she stood up and fell heavily upon the figure next to her, who immediately shoved her against the car. After a few minutes, she found she could stand. No sooner had she done so than she was pushed forward and made her way, staggering in pain, out into—what?

Where was she? And what time was it? It was dark, but

Faith had no idea how many hours or days had passed since she had been abducted. Had she been drugged? The cool air hit her and she shivered. She wished she had thought to wrap the blanket around her shoulders. She was wearing a thin T-shirt and short skirt, donned in the expectation of southern sunshine.

Across the yard, she could make out a small stone house surrounded by trees. The night air was still and it was quiet except for some faint stirrings—the flight of birds, a nocturnal creature, a slight breeze, soft sounds accompanied by two others—the rapid breathing and insistent footsteps a few inches behind her. The idea of escape was impossible without some knowledge of the terrain. Besides, there was a gun to her back.

After the door was unlocked, they entered the house. A gloved hand closed hard upon her wrist and he pushed her into a chair while he quickly lit an oil lamp on the mantel, producing a dim light. It was very cold inside and the room had a musty smell, as if it had been closed up for a long time. The shutters of the windows had not been opened and a thick layer of dust covered a long table in front of the fireplace.

If he was going to kill her, why was he waiting? Was she being held for ransom? She doubted it. If she'd been kidnapped because of what she knew about Marie and the *clochard,* it was her silence, not money, they wanted. These thoughts were rapidly supplanted by one other and she turned and spoke. "Please. I must go to the bathroom." She tried to convey her urgency, aware from her slightly damp pants that in her previous state she'd already had one accident. It was horrible enough to be in the position she was without adding total loss of dignity.

He motioned her out the door again to an outhouse at the edge of the yard, beyond some large evergreens. The moon had risen and she could see mountains not too far away. The house seemed to be at the bottom of a gorge.

When she got closer to the trees, she could hear a stream.

The privy was very clean and there were cartoons by Sempé clipped from magazines taped to the walls. Hard to imagine gangsters with such a well-developed sense of humor and housekeeping. What they didn't have was toilet paper, and as Faith searched through her pocketbook for tissues, she found the letter she'd written to Michel Ravier. She could use it now, for all the good it would do her, she thought, before finding a packet of paper *mouchoirs* at the bottom. Holding the letter in her hand, she finally broke down and began to cry. She was all alone in a French outhouse, about to die.

Chief Inspector Michel Ravier had returned from Marseille at nine o'clock on Saturday night, looking forward to nothing more—or less—than a very good meal and a good night's sleep. But he'd dutifully called headquarters to report his return and that was why he was in his office drinking abominable coffee from a paper cup, reading with mounting exasperation the brief reports Louis Martin and Didier Pollet had filed on Faith, instead of consuming warm *saucisson* with plenty of mustard at La Mère Vittet. He grabbed the phone and demanded the two men's presence immediately. He also told the sergeant on duty to get him some food, preferably edible, but even a burger from FreeTime—though it pained him to think of comforting his hunger pangs so inadequately.

Michel had spoken to Paul, and he and Tom were on their way in. Ravier closed his eyes and thought back to the week before when he'd met Faith at Valentina Joliet's gallery. Madame Fairsheeld had seemed delightfully unserious, bright, and very pretty—all the things he liked in a woman. There had been no suggestion of instability, apart from the *clochard* story, which was a bit odd but could no doubt have been explained if they'd questioned the man the next day. Or it may have been true. In any case, Martin and

Pollet's conclusions that her pregnant state was causing her to fantasize were absurd. Although this represented sophisticated thinking for the team. He would have thought the two, with a combined chronological age near Michel's own and combined mental age near Stéphanie Leblanc's, still believed in the *"bébé* under the *chou* leaf" theory.

There was a knock on the door and it opened almost simultaneously. Tom Fairchild walked over to the desk, grabbed a chair, sat down, and started talking. Paul was not far behind.

"You've heard, of course, the whole story from Paul. What can possibly be going on, damn it! Where can she be!"

Tom was angry and frightened. He'd driven to Avignon and gone straight to police headquarters. There they'd told him that they'd met the train from Lyon and Faith hadn't been on it. They'd questioned the servers at the buffet and the conductor and shown them Faith's picture, which had been faxed from Lyon. The Leblancs had given it to the police. It had been taken the Sunday before—a laughing, smiling Faith sitting in a lawn chair next to Paul's father. No one remembered seeing anyone resembling her. Avignon was the first stop after Lyon, so there was no way she could have gotten off the train. They were continuing to meet the trains coming from Lyon, but Tom had left quickly after reporting back to Paul.

When he'd arrived at the Leblanc's house, Ben had greeted him tearfully. Tom had told him Mommy was visiting some friends and would be back soon, yet Ben knew something was wrong. Soon after, Pierre had tucked him into his own bed and stayed with him until he fell asleep. The call from the police telling them Inspector Ravier had returned came soon after.

Ravier was as puzzled as Tom. He'd gotten the name of the owner of the hair salon where Faith had been seen last, but it was Saturday night and Giovanni Cavelli was out on the town. Michel had sent a team to search the various bars and bistros in Giovanni's neighborhood. Until they found him, they couldn't get in touch with the receptionist, who might be able to add something. Tom had called Solange d'Ambert; however, she did not recall the young woman. "Of course I might know her. They change their hair so often, but the last time I was there, the girl helping was short and a bit heavy." She had not heard Faith say anything about going to Avignon at tea on Friday and could add nothing to what they already knew.

"First," Michel said, "let me reassure you that a description and picture of your wife have been circulated all over the country and the newspapers will also carry the information tomorrow morning. Now, let's go back to the beginning, Reverend Fairsheeld."

"Tom, please call me Tom."

"Thank you. Well, Tom, what has happened obviously must have an explanation in something that has occurred since your arrival. I am assuming she has never done anything like this before?"

"Never," Tom answered.

"Then try, if you can, to relax a moment and tell me everything your wife has been doing and how she has been feeling since coming to Lyon. Has she made any friends? Become involved in any activities? Paul, perhaps you can help."

Tom was suddenly so tired, it seemed almost impossible to talk. Friends, involvements? This was what Faith lived for. Slowly, he began to list what he knew. When he got to Faith's experiences the night of the dinner party, Michel interrupted him. "She told me about this the following evening and we have the report of the two men responding to your call. What has been plaguing me all night is that she may, in fact, have found a corpse. But then how did he come to be outside the church the next morning? I am waiting for the men who responded to her calls. According to their report, she seemed to think it might not be the same *clochard.*"

"Faith definitely thought he was a fake. Sunday night, she told me she thought the body of the *clochard* she found on Saturday had a scratch on the back of the hand. The man outside St. Nizier the next day didn't." Tom stood up and walked up and down the room. When he next spoke, his voice was thick. "I suggested it might have been a piece of string or something from the trash. I didn't want to believe it. Everything has been so wonderful. He looked the same to me. And she accepted that, but I know Faith. She must have kept poking around and now . . ." He couldn't finish.

"Vite!" and a loud banging on the outhouse door startled Faith from her misery and she quickly finished. Descending outside, she took a good look at her captor before the figure, all in black, still masked and gloved, moved behind her and jammed the barrel of his gun into the small of her back. He was certainly dressed for the weather, she thought enviously as she began to shiver again. Her spirits had lifted slightly and she took it as a good sign that he retained the mask. If she was to be killed soon, it wouldn't matter if she saw him. And the wool, though warm, must feel scratchy on his face. He was taller than Faith but slight and moved with agility. They walked back to the house and once they were inside, he motioned her back to the chair, locked the door, and started to build a fire. After he got it going, he opened the shutters covering the windows. Was he watching for someone?

Things had gone far enough.

"I am an American citizen and I demand to know what is happening. I think you have mistaken me for some-one—" she said, cut off abruptly by his *"Ferme-la!"* She did, and after he poked at the fire some more, he collapsed in a chair opposite her, with the gun trained somewhere on the vicinity of her womb. She didn't open her mouth. Neither did he.

Ravier sent Tom home with Paul. There was nothing more he could do and so Michel urged Tom to try to get some sleep. It had been a long drive to Avignon and back. "Sleep?" Tom had repeated, and Michel realized what a ridiculous suggestion it had been. "Then pray, *mon brave.* I know *le bon Dieu* will not let anything happen to Faith."

A trace of a smile had crossed Tom's weary face. "I have been doing nothing else since this morning."

After they left, Michel sat with the files in front of him. It wasn't simply the business with the *clochard.* There was Faith's second call reporting that she had information regarding the suicide of the prostitute, Marie. Michel had been on vice not too many years ago and he remembered Marie well. An intelligent girl from the Midi. She would be away from the city on occasion and told him once she used to go to visit her family. He wondered what she told them— that she worked in a boutique, perhaps. Her *carte d'identité* listed her full name as Marie-Claude Laval, and he sensed she came from a decent family. Like her two friends, she was addicted to various things, but in the last year, she had told him she was straight and hoping to get off the streets. He had wished her well, yet knew it would not be so easy to accomplish. She probably owed her pimp money and he would see she continued to work off her debt until she no longer served his purpose. Then she'd be left with nothing. He felt the angry frustration that had never left him since his first days in the district, talking to the girls. The pimps, working from Italy, Switzerland—and now South America—grew rich. Parasites. The only consolation was that when they did get caught on French soil, they faced long sentences and stiff fines.

So Faith had come to know Marie, too. But how? What would they have in common? The French women he knew did not chat with the *filles de joie* on the corner but walked quickly past, perhaps a nod of the head to indicate they were *sympa*.

Faith had told Martin and Pollet that Marie was supposed to meet her at the *hôtel de ville,* and earlier Marie had given her some sort of warning. Faith was convinced Marie had been murdered before they could meet. The notes were disgracefully vague and his conversation with the two officers, while making him feel better for letting off steam, didn't garner much more information. They thought her scatty and hadn't paid much attention to what they clearly thought was an overactive imagination, the product of too much American television. The inspector from the *police judiciaire,* Ravier's own division, had not thought it worth his time to go up the stairs to speak with Faith when they found the trash bin empty, but had sent the two *gardiens de la paix* as a formality. Probably also wanted to stick them with the paperwork. Michel had let off some steam on him, too.

Marie's body had already been released to her parents. There had been what Michel suspected was a perfunctory autopsy, as was usual in this type of case. He looked at the few lines in front of him. She did have water in her lungs, indicating drowning. Still, there were ways to do this—if she had been alive but drugged when she entered the water, for example. Even if the autopsy indicated the presence of drugs, it would be assumed she had gone back to her old ways—or never left.

Michel didn't think Faith was scatty. If she thought Marie had been murdered, there must have been a reason—even if Madame Fairsheeld *had* cried murder once before. But how would Marie have tied in with the *clochard?* In the morning, he'd go to the Place St. Nizier and talk with Marie's friends. It would be pointless to try to find them tonight. *Clochards* and whores, both on the street and both knowing what went on in those streets better than anyone.

It was possible this knowledge had gotten the two of them killed, which left Faith trying to tie the threads together.

His phone rang. Giovanni Cavelli had been located. Faith had not said anything to him about Avignon—or anywhere else, for that matter. He didn't like to talk with his clients, he told the officers. It distracted him from his work. The receptionist was new. She'd only been there a month and was Italian also. He'd liked having someone around who spoke his language. Her name was Gina Martignetti. She was from Rome and he had an address in Lyon for her on the Croix Rousse. She'd left about eleven that morning and never come back. He was prepared to take her back, but not until he'd said a thing or two, and judging from the rehearsal the police were forced to listen to, it would be a wonder if the woman would continue to work for him. After they finished talking to Cavelli, they'd gone to the address he'd supplied for Gina. It was a rooming house. They proceeded to rouse the owner, who was displeased at being awakened and obviously cherished little affection for the *flics*. She told them Mademoiselle Martignetti had stopped by her apartment at noon, given her what she owed, said good-bye, and left. She didn't know where Gina was going. That was the girl's business, not hers. She'd been a good tenant, paid on time, wasn't around much.

Ravier ordered them to circulate a description of Gina Martignetti, particularly at the Italian border, and he had had a call put through to the police in Rome. Her disappearance at the same time as Faith's and after having delivered what was obviously a phony message to Tom, was no coincidence. He also had Giovanni put under surveillance. He'd already been told not to leave Lyon.

The inspector's phone rang again. It was his mother. Did he want to speak with her? He glanced at his watch. She was up late, but then she slept very little. Of course he would take the call. Since his father's death, she had moved into the city and she missed her old friends and neighbors.

"You had a good trip, *mon fils?*"

"*Oui, Maman,* and you? Keeping busy?"

"But of course. All the things an old lady does. A little walk. Mass in the morning. And I cleaned your apartment. It was disgusting, Michel. That woman is not worth what you pay her."

His mother had a running battle with the woman who cleaned and, when told, left dinner for him. Neither thought the other adequate for his needs. "Oh, *Maman,* really you mustn't do this."

"It's no trouble. Oh, and while I was there, a very nice foreign lady called. Her name was Madame Fairsheeld. I told her you were away and she said you must call her as soon as you get back, so please do. I promised you would."

"Madame Fairsheeld! When was this?"

"It must have been Wednesday. I remember I went to your apartment after confession."

"You are sure?"

"About my confession, *bien sûr!*"

"No, *chérie,* about what day Madame Fairsheeld called," he said patiently, wondering not for the first time what his mother could possibly have to confess. Impure thoughts? He hoped so.

"Yes, yes, I am sure. Is it important?"

"Perhaps. Now, I must say good night. Go to sleep. I will call you tomorrow."

"*À demain,*" she agreed in her soft, slightly chirping voice.

He picked up the file on Marie. Her body had been discovered on Wednesday. It had been on Wednesday that Martin and Pollet had responded to Faith's call. Obviously, she'd called him first. But she hadn't disappeared until two days later. What had happened in between? He looked at the notes he had taken while Tom talked. The lavomatique, the *marché,* a tea party, dinner at a *bouchon.*

It would not be light for some hours and he was eager to start questioning everyone Faith had come in contact with during those days—and the days preceding. She'd visited one of the shelters for the *clochards* on Monday, Tom had said. To learn what the French were doing about the problem, she'd told her husband. Yet, Faith had not struck Michel as a woman who told her husband everything as it happened. Not that she lied, but perhaps there was more than one reason for her visit.

He stretched out on his couch to get some sleep. Soup kitchens, the *hôtel de ville,* the prostitutes on the corner, and at the beginning—the *clochard* of St. Nizier in the *poubelle.* The answer had to be somewhere among them.

Faith Fairchild had gotten to know Lyon very well indeed.

Faith was getting restless. She wasn't tired. She'd slept enough for a month and the silence was beginning to drive her crazy. Maybe that was the idea. She wasn't going to be killed outright, merely driven insane.

"Do you speak English?" she asked.

There was no reply. She knew her French wasn't that bad. He'd understood her other question. She wondered what would happen if she stood up and calmly walked out the door. Whoever it was seemed passive enough. Still, she didn't want to chance a sudden spurt of energy that might lodge a bullet somewhere about her person. Looking around the room, she'd noted there was another door and, to the right of it, a stone stairway. The stairs probably led to bedrooms or a loft of some sort and the other door no doubt to the kitchen. Kitchen! She was starving. She hadn't had anything since her hasty breakfast. She thought longingly of the picnic she'd packed for the trip to Carcassonne. A huge *marguerite*—crusty rolls joined together in the shape of the flower. Instead of "he loves me, he loves me not," you pulled a hunk of bread off and, in today's case, slathered it with Normandy butter, pâté, or cheese. She'd also packed some salads—tiny vegetables in vinaigrette and hearts of palm with endive. Faith firmly ordered her mind to turn off before she got to dessert, but the chocolate cake with a hint of orange from Tourtillier pushed through insistently.

"This is ridiculous. I am hungry and cold. I am going to have a baby and I must have some food." The sentences were non sequiturs, but she didn't care.

She accomplished one thing. The immobile figure leapt out of the chair, causing her to draw her breath in sharply in fear. Was it the end?

But he simply proceeded to pace up and down the small room, pausing only to throw some more logs on the fire. He appeared to be muttering under his breath. After what seemed like ages, he stopped abruptly in front of her and pulled off the mask.

"What can I do? *Merde!* This is a hopeless situation!"

Faith gasped—not at his words. At his face.

It was Christophe d'Ambert.

Eight

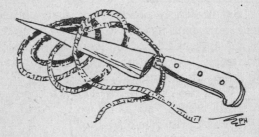

"Christophe! Is this some kind of joke!"

"No, I assure you it is not a joke at all."

Faith had felt a wave of relief sweep over her when she realized who was behind the mask. It was absurd to think that the teenager—the boy next door—would harm her in any way. But the relief was short-lived, and the possibility of her own reduced life span more distinct, when she heard the tone in his voice. This was not the nonchalant, slightly teasing adolescent of their encounters on the apartment staircase. This was a deadly serious, possibly crazy man.

Keep them talking. Wasn't that what all the books, not to mention Geraldo and Oprah, advised?

"Can you tell me where we are?" A neutral topic, a logical question for a tourist to ask.

He seemed surprised. "We are in the Cévennes. This is the country house of some friends of mine. They are in Canada for the year and asked me to check on it occasionally. They worry since it is so far away from any other houses or a village," he added pointedly.

"Oh, I thought perhaps it might be your family's house." She'd had a thought that if Christophe was gone, the d'Amberts might think to look for him at the *maison secondaire*. Jean-François had said it was closed up, as this place had obviously been. Christophe could be lying about whose house it was. He'd never struck her as Eagle Scout material and now she was beginning to think he could walk into a role in *Bad Boys* without any rehearsal at all.

Her comment had produced a smile—not a nice one. "I'm afraid my mother would find the Cévennes a bit boring." He ran his knuckles across his cheek in a shaving gesture, *rasant,* which Faith had observed was the way to express ultimate ennui. "Our house is closer to St. Trop."

Unfortunately, it made too much sense. But if Christophe was taking care of the house, the d'Amberts would know.

"So, this belongs to friends of your family. It looks very old." Act casual. Try to get more information. Stall.

"Friends of *mine,* Madame Fairsheeld, and yes, a very old house, but I do not think this is the time to tell you the history of the region, interesting as it is," he said sarcastically.

What a prick, Faith thought, a few tears starting to burn. She wasn't sure whether they were due to fury or fear. The whole thing had been a stupid idea to start with. It was obvious Christophe kept his own hours and own company. The fact that he was away when she was missing would mean nothing. She imagined the search that must have begun. Everyone would be so busy trying to find her, they'd forget Christophe even existed.

Christophe was talking to himself out loud. "It's all *tonton's* fault."

"Tonton?" Faith asked. It sounded like a pet: Ron Ton Ton, the wonder dog.

"It means 'uncle,' " he explained impatiently, "in this case, my father's youngest brother. The one most d'Amberts don't like to talk about."

"You mean the *clochard?"*

"I mean he chooses to live his life as he pleases without being weighed down by bourgeois ideas and possessions." He'd raised his voice and each word was dripping with scorn.

Faith gave a passing thought to Christophe's wardrobe—the Tissot watch she could see between the end of his sleeve and the band of his glove, the Girbaud jeans he wore.

"I am not criticizing him," she placated.

"Well, I am." Christophe suddenly became a teenager again. "The dumb fuck. *He* was supposed to finish the job, then what does he do but get cold feet and jump out of the car. Next time I see him, he's going to hear about this. I took care of Bernard and he was going to take care of you. That was the deal." He was almost whining.

Nausea and what was certainly now fear threatened to overwhelm Faith. I mustn't start screaming. I mustn't throw up. I mustn't upset him. She repeated the sentences over and over like a mantra.

Bernard. Bernard was the *clochard*'s name, Lucien at the shelter had told her.

Which meant Christophe was the murderer.

It was too much to suppose otherwise. Christophe lived in the building and was rapidly displaying the tendencies necessary for the crime—means, personality—but what could the motive possibly have been?

Faith was reeling. He'd "taken care of" the *clochard*. His uncle was supposed to do the same for her, but had fled, leaving . . . Christophe. A funny thing about murder: Everything was out of focus until the end.

He was pacing again. Faith watched him cautiously, waiting for him to spring. His eyes were directed away from her for the moment, considering some inner view. She could make a move, but the front door was locked and if the kitchen had a door to the outside, that would be locked, too—if she even made it that far. There was no way out.

Keep him talking.

"Christophe, I'm sure there is a logical explanation for all this and if you will just take me back to Lyon, we can straighten everything out. I'll say I bumped into you after I got my hair cut and decided on a whim to come with you while you checked on your friends' house. Women in my condition are supposed to be a little erratic." That sounded good.

He laughed disagreeably. "You think we can go back and I will get a little slap on the hand. No, *chérie,* I think not. And as for being thought 'erratic,' we have counted on this. It's possible the hunt for you has started already, but I doubt it. You took the train for Avignon, and remember, the police think you are crazy to begin with."

Faith was truly startled. What was he talking about? Avignon? And his use of *chérie* had more in common with Cagney's *sweetheart* than Solange's and Madame Vincent's use of the endearment.

"Why would I go to Avignon? Everyone knew we were going to Carcassonne."

"But you left a message for your husband at the salon that you preferred to shorten the long car trip by taking the train as far as Avignon. I believe you were to meet in front of the Palais des Papes for drinks. *Malheureusement,* you do not show up, but then *les femmes,* especially attractive ones such as yourself, often disappear. There are a lot of nasty people around." He was obviously enjoying this, definitely a nasty piece of goods himself.

His words made it sickeningly clear. He and his uncle had worked it all out. Tom would go to Avignon, and even if he did get in touch with the police, they'd assume it was another one of her "fancies." By now, Tom knew she wasn't in Avignon, but would the incredible idea that she had been kidnapped occur to him? Yet what else? That she had simply run away? Women did it all the time, and sure, she'd had her moments when driving alone in the car. How easy it would be to just keep on going to, say, sunny California instead of Shop and Save.

Still, Tom would know she hadn't run away. And Tom would start moving heaven and earth to find her.

Now what next? Christophe's uncle had botched it, so here they were, Plan B, in a cold, drafty farmhouse somewhere in the Cévennes, which she knew was considerably southwest of Lyon and very sparsely inhabited. She didn't need a lecture from d'Ambert the younger. The Leblancs had already related the rise and fall of the area. It had been a prosperous center of the silk industry in the eighteenth century, then in the nineteenth and twentieth had become an empty landscape. First the silkworm disease attacked, and when that crisis had passed, competition from foreign silk and artificial textiles finished the job. Phylloxera destroyed the grapevines and a fungus killed the chestnut trees. Not exactly the luckiest place to live in France. People left in droves. Christophe couldn't have picked a better place to take her. Now the question was, what did he intend to do with her?

It was as if she had spoken aloud.

"You present a curious problem," he said, pulling a chair uncomfortably close to hers and lovingly stroking the gun with his left hand. "I do not mind to eliminate an adult. You have had a taste of life, although madame is not such an old lady, *bien sûr.*" So polite, these French teenagers, even when engaged in major crime.

He looked straight into her eyes. His own were puddles

of amoral sincerity. "The problem is the baby. I cannot in good conscience kill him. Who knows what he may accomplish? A cure for SIDA? Overthrow the Republic?" If Faith had had any doubts about the basic immaturity of Christophe's level of moral development, they vanished as quickly as socks in the wash.

He stood up. "Yet it is difficult to imagine how I can keep you here for, how long? Five, six months?" He directed a studied and impersonal look at her body. She could just have easily been a car he was considering buying, a piece of *saucisse,* or a painting in Valentina Joliet's gallery. She was amazed at the accuracy of his appraisal, then remembered all the little d'Amberts and *accouchements* he would have observed. She didn't say anything. There was nothing to say.

"It just needs some thought. I will keep you alive until your time comes, then kill you and take the baby to a priest. These details can be worked out." He sounded very definite. Still, he wasn't going to do anything immediately and the relief she felt was genuine at last. Four and a half months was a long time. She ought to be able to get away by then. She had a sudden vision of her delivery on some lonely Cévennes mountaintop with the maniacal Christophe waiting to cut the cord and her throat. She placed her hand on her abdomen to reassure the baby—and herself. It wasn't going to happen. The boy had to go to school, for goodness sake. He couldn't disappear to play midwife for the next few months.

"Fortunately, I will be taking the *bac* soon and then school will be over. Until then, I'll think of something." Faith was horribly afraid he would. "And, of course, if you try to escape or do anything else so very foolish, I will have to forget about the child and you both will die."

He seemed genuinely sorry. It was chilling. All this concern for the unborn. His early years with the Marist fathers, an unconscious desire for his own rebirth, the stirrings of paternity? She'd hate to be the one to spoil the two or three good apples left in the barrel, but there were limits.

He seemed almost cheerful, having gotten the unpleasantness out of the way, and turned in a typically French manner to the demands of the flesh. "I am very hungry, and tired, as you must be also. First, I think food. Then sleep. Tomorrow, we will take a trip to get provisions and I must find a phone. I am afraid you will not be in a position to see the beauty of the countryside, however. Now, *s'il vous plaît,* the kitchen."

Bearing the lamp aloft in one hand, he nudged her toward the door with the gun firmly clenched in the other. The kitchen was large and when they entered, the light was reflected in the soft copper burnishings of the pots hanging on one wall. Like the other room, it had a stone floor, and without the fire, it was very cold. There was a gas stove next to the sink, stone also. It appeared that the early inhabitants of the region had simply walked into their backyards and constructed whatever they needed from the mountains of rock there. She dismally noted the tap over the sink. There was running water. So she could rule out giving Christophe a quick shove at a well.

"Open the closet over there. I think it is where Danielle keeps supplies."

The closet was full of baskets and boxes that once contained potatoes, onions, and other vegetables, judging from the shriveled evidence. The shelves were stacked with brightly colored pottery and, in one corner, they found a few dusty cans of what turned out to be corn kernels.

"Ah, *maïs.* My friend Benoît was sent last summer to practice his English with a family in Iowa, do you know it? All he ate was *maïs.* It was some kind of farm and he did not go well there. His parents are *cochons.*"

Faith doubted that Benoît was descended from porkers, but she got the message. All this farm talk was increasing her hunger and the corn in the can was calling to her as succulently as a fresh cob plucked from the stalk, raced to a pot of rapidly boiling water, cooked for four minutes, and consumed immediately, dripping with butter, salt, and, in Faith's case, pepper. She was salivating.

"They must have a can opener. I'm sure it's safe to eat if they were here last summer." She tried to steer him away from a potential diatribe on the inevitable shortcomings of the older generation and back to the matter at hand.

"Bien sûr, and here is a packet of *pâtes.* I understand you are a good cook. See what you can do with this."

She couldn't do much, but shortly after, when she dug into the macaroni and corn, she decided it was one of the best meals she'd ever tasted.

Christophe had lighted some more lamps and a pair of candles that were on the kitchen table. He'd found a bottle of wine and sat holding a full glass up to the flame, regarding it intently. The light cast ruby flickers on the gun by his plate. Maybe he'd get drunk. Faith took a sip of the water. The situation was very intimate—and unreal.

It didn't seem the moment to ask why he had killed the *clochard* in the first place—the question that was at the front of her mind. Was it for kicks? If so, then what was Marie talking about and how did his uncle figure in all this? Obviously *tonton* had been the person impersonating poor Bernard. Did Marie know? She wasn't going to mention Marie, though. Faith didn't want to let Christophe know how much she knew, which, after she'd learned he'd murdered the *clochard,* was not much.

She ate some more *pâtes à la* Fairsheeld. Even after assuaging the initial sharp pangs of starvation, the mixture tasted surprisingly good. All she had to do was add some pieces of slightly charred red peppers, a hint of garlic, some summer savory, and maybe a round of warm fresh chèvre on top. . . .

She opened her mouth to speak. After all, what could it hurt?

"Christophe, I don't understand. I know the *clochard* was a violent man." She recalled the scene she'd seen only a week or so ago from the apartment window. "Had he been threatening you in some way?"

"Bernard? No. Do you think an old drunk like that could frighten me? *Crétin!* He was stupid and nosy."

Not what she would categorize as the best possible defense for justifiable homicide. She decided to *ferme-la*. Her colloquial French was increasing by leaps and bounds and she desperately hoped she'd be able to display it for Tom.

Time went by. Christophe poured himself another glass of wine. It was producing no discernable effect. He lit a cigarette and Faith noticed the pack was almost empty. She hoped he had more. She didn't want him to be forced to quit now, however beneficial that might be to his health and hers. Irritability from nicotine withdrawal might just send him over the edge. But at the moment, lazily blowing smoke toward the ceiling and sipping his wine, he seemed at peace with the world—the world that appeared to owe him a living. She regarded him for some time in silence.

But there were simply too many questions.

"So, where were you when I came downstairs and how did you get him away so quickly?"

He laughed reminiscently. "You can imagine that I was surprised to see my neighbor come to dispose of her garbage at such an hour. But my father's office is just there, you know, and I have a key. It was very fortunate. Then when you left, I returned and put old Bernard in that small closet by the stairs. We got rid of him later."

The *placard,* of course. That extremely convenient place for Ben's stroller—or a dead body.

"It was no easy job getting him in the *poubelle,"* Christophe bragged. "They were late and I could not take the chance to leave him in the vestibule. Then, because of you, I had to lift him out again and up the stairs by myself. *Ouf!"*

"Eh bien." He wolfed the rest of his food down. "Now, bed."

Bed. And all that suggested. Maybe there was a way out of this.

Back in the main room, he bent down to pick up something at the door, then said, "Upstairs. *Allez!* I'm *très fatigué.*"

Thoughts of seducing her way out of the situation were quickly dispelled in the bedroom when he tied her wrists and ankles together again in the same way as before with the ropes he'd brought in from the car. As a final touch, he looped another length around her, securing her to the bed. Unless he was into bondage, her vague plan to charm him into submission would have to be scrapped.

"Bonne nuit, Madame Fairsheeld. Sleep well."

Faith did not wish him the same. She was thinking of Sartre's famous remark: "Hell is other people."

A bird cried sharply in the night and Faith opened her eyes in sudden panic. Where was she? She remembered and the panic did not subside. Christophe had spoken of the *clochard* as a mere encumbrance, something to get out of the way, a fly buzzing on the wall. Yet it had to be more than that for him to take such a risk, and she still didn't know why he had killed the tramp. It was a point she hadn't wanted to press. It was dangerous to know too much. Although how she could be in more peril than she already was with what she'd learned was a moot point.

Christophe, acting with his uncle and some others— those references to "we" and "they"—had murdered the *clochard* in the vestibule. Something put in the tramp's beloved bottle, since there were no marks or blood on the man, apart from the scratch on his hand. Then, when she arrived on the scene, Christophe had repaired to his father's office, more than likely made a call or two about what had happened, then reappeared to spirit away the evidence as soon as she went back upstairs.

In the old Cévennes farmhouse, it had become very quiet. The door was open, but she could not hear anything from the room across the hall where her captor lay soundlessly in a deep and dreamless sleep. Soon she did the same.

The early morning sun streamed in the *chambre*'s one small window. Faith opened her eyes. The room was charming. There was a large rustic armoire against one of the whitewashed walls and next to the bed, a round table covered with bright Provençal fabric was stacked with books. Across the room, a comfortable-looking chair draped in the same fabric sat next to an old marble-topped nightstand holding an arrangement of dried flowers in a turquoise vase. The door in the nightstand gave an urgency to her needs. Damn these ropes. She needed to get over there and see if there was a chamber pot behind the marquetry.

"Christophe! Christophe!" she called, waited, then tried again. He came stumbling into the room after her fourth attempt. His hair was rumpled and he was rubbing his eyes. The gun was shoved in the waistband of his jeans.

"What do you want?" he asked angrily. Christophe was obviously not a morning person. Neither was Faith under ordinary circumstances, whatever those had been in the past—a past that had receded so swiftly in the last twenty-four hours, it was beginning to take on a medieval character. Her immediate present contained but two thoughts: I am tired and I have to get out of bed.

"I need to go to the bathroom."

He grunted and untied the knots. She stood up stiffly. The baby gave a little flutter. The sensation did not bring the joy of previous days. She took the blanket and wrapped it around herself. She had no intention of answering nature's call under the scrutiny of this eighteen-year-old. Let him take her to the outhouse.

To his credit, Christophe had piled blankets and a down comforter on Faith's immobilized body the previous night—out of concern for the future luminary she was carrying, no doubt. Without that drift of warmth, she was shivering. Her two thoughts were joined by a third, which she said out loud. "It's so cold. Do you think there are any jackets or sweaters in the house?"

"Perhaps in the armoire. It is always cold in the country in the mornings. You had better become used to it."

So whatever plan he had hit upon involved keeping her here. She didn't know whether to be glad or sorry.

She opened the doors to the armoire and was rewarded by the sight of what was obviously the country wardrobe. She took a heavy Irish fisherman's sweater and some corduroy pants. Christophe grabbed a well-worn shearling jacket. Faith was annoyed she hadn't spotted it first. She put the sweater on and immediately felt more optimistic than she had since arriving. It was lovely to be warm again.

They did the Siamese-twin walk across the yard to the trees. It was beginning to become a familiar routine, but Faith would rather not have been joined by a gun. She slipped on the pants before leaving the privy. They were too long, so she turned up the cuffs, but otherwise they fit fairly well. She couldn't do up the button on the waistband, but the sweater hid the fact, and besides, she wasn't exactly worried about making a fashion statement at the moment. Now only her feet, clad in a thin pair of Bennis/Edwards flats, needed attention. Socks and boots of some sort were what she had in mind. Also a toothbrush.

As they walked back across the yard, she looked around her. It was beautiful. The house had been built on one of a number of deep terraces she could see covering the mountain. The others were marked by low, crumbling stone walls. Once they had been filled with rows of carefully tended green vines. Now they were yellow and purple with spring wildflowers. Below the house, the land continued to slope sharply, ending in the stream she had heard the night before. Evergreens and deciduous trees stretched out on either side of the small area marked by civilization.

"It's beautiful here," she said to the air.

Behind her, Christophe agreed. "I like the Cévennes very much. It has not been spoiled like the rest of France."

A nature lover. Go figure.

"It's Sunday, so we must wait for the old woman who keeps the shop to say her mass and come home. Say ten o'clock."

Christophe did not appear to be in the mood for conversation and sat stolidly in the chair across from her. He'd tied her wrists together behind her back again in preparation for the car trip. The fact that he wasn't in a chatty mood didn't bother Faith. She was preoccupied with trying to decide whether it made sense for her to kick the gun out of his hand as he bound her ankles together, but the odds did not seem good. Given that she aimed accurately and accomplished the first part, she still might not be able to grab the gun with her hands tied. Could she hold it in her mouth? It wasn't a large gun. But how would she fire it? It was more likely that he would get to it before she did and shoot her. Such an attempt would certainly fall under the rubric of one of the "so very foolish" things he'd mentioned. Yet there had to be some way out of this and the trip to the store offered the first real opportunity. She continued to devise alternatives.

The time dragged like school in June and she tried not to think how hungry she was. She thought instead of Tom and what he might be doing. He'd enlist the help of the Leblancs immediately and they might think to call Ravier—if he was back. She sighed. Christophe stood up.

"It's time. We can go now. If we wait too long, all the bread will be gone."

This was serious.

As they were about to open the door, they heard a car coming up the drive.

"*Merde!* Who can be coming! Into the kitchen. *Vite!*" He grabbed the ropes. Faith was desperately praying he might forget, but he was very efficient. He'd trussed her up, pulled a bandanna from his pocket to gag her, and pushed her into the kitchen closet just as a car door slammed. Then another. So it was more than one arrival. The closet door opened again and he threw her pocketbook in after her. "Your *sac!*" Dreadfully efficient.

But not infallible. He'd neglected to close the closet door completely the second time. Faith was able to wiggle closer and, by wedging her foot in the crack, succeeded in opening it. The door to the other room was firmly shut. She lay still, listening.

It wasn't hard to hear what was going on, even through the closed door. Two people in addition to Christophe, and all three were shouting at the tops of their lungs.

"You *salaud!* You are not fit to wipe my ass! And you thought we would never find out! *Imbécile!*" It was a female voice, an extremely enraged female.

"How could you possibly think Dominique wouldn't tell me! Or didn't you care!"

Christophe was just as furious. "How did you know I was here and what business is it of yours what I do! We live our own lives and I can fuck anyone I want!"

"Yes—and tell her she's the only one!" The girl started to cry.

"Come on. Let's go get something to eat. There's nothing left in the house. You both need to calm down."

Faith could have told him these were the words most known to have the opposite effect on women in any language, and the explosion almost shook the beams of the kitchen ceiling. They would not calm down. They were not hungry and they were not leaving.

"And why are you so eager to get rid of us? You know,

159

Berthille, I think the little shit is waiting for someone. *Zut!* He certainly brought me here enough times last fall."

"And *moi.* I am sure you are right. Look at how scared he looks."

Berthille and Dominique—Ghislaine's niece. The one whose mother was so worried about her, and now, it appeared, with good cause. The two girls Faith had seen at the gallery. And Christophe had been sleeping with them both. Another thing women tend to frown upon—one's boyfriend cheating with one's best friend. Christophe had a lot to learn.

But, Faith told herself, this was no time to get caught up in the adolescent intrigues going on in the next room, however interesting they might be. She had to decide whether to make her way across the floor and bang on the door or try to get the ropes untied, escaping out the back door. That was the best plan. She didn't think Christophe would do away with her while the others watched—or kill all three of them—but she didn't want to find out.

And maybe the girls, in their rage, had left the keys in the car's ignition.

The closet was narrow and she was finding it hard to get to her feet. Finally, she succeeded in rolling to her knees and stood up, bent over because of the rope that was strung from her ankles to her wrists. She looked at her purse on the floor. There was nothing much inside to help her. It was a small summer shoulder bag, not the capacious Coach saddlebag she carried at other times, which contained everything from toys for Ben to sustenance for them both—and a handy Swiss army knife. The only thing remotely resembling a tool in this one was an emery board. But, she thought, as she hopped awkwardly out of the closet and, having kicked off her shoes, silently into the room, she was in a kitchen! And kitchens, especially French ones, had sharp knives.

The fight in the next room had not abated. Christophe

had apparently decided the best defense was offense and he continued to yell at both the girls. They had been lucky to be with him at all was the gist of it.

Faith tried to spit the uncomfortable gag from her mouth, but it was too tight. She hopped from drawer to drawer, turned around to open them, and, after locating where madame kept her dishcloths, odd bits of string, flashlight batteries, and coffee filters, hit pay dirt—three Sabatier knives in graduated sizes. She gripped the black handle and worked the blade back and forth on the rope binding her wrists. It wasn't exactly making carrot-flower decorations for sushi or deboning a turkey, yet it required the same precision if she wasn't going to open a vein inadvertently. She was almost free when a sentence came through the door that made her stop in amazement.

"And if you think we're breaking into any more apartments with you, you're crazy. I don't care about the *clochards.* They could get jobs, my father says. They are just too lazy and drunk."

Breaking into apartments! The apartments of their own friends and relatives! But who better? Inside knowledge of not merely who had what but who was where. Have a nice time skiing at Val D'Isère, *ma tante,* and by the way, why don't you leave that too-heavy and inconvenient gold necklace at home?

And what was she saying about the *clochards?* Faith would have to think about that one later. At the moment, she didn't plan to stick around to hear anymore. Maybe sweet Dominique and Berthille were only part of the break-in scheme—and maybe not. At the moment, she didn't trust any of them.

Faith cut through the last of the rope, quickly freed her ankles, and untied the gag. Just as she was moving across the room to retrieve her purse from the closet, she heard Christophe's voice.

"I want some water."

She didn't wait to watch the latch on the door move, but heard it as she raced to the closet, pulling the door shut behind her. Obviously, he was coming to check on her and obviously he wasn't going to find her as he had left her. She stuffed the gag in her mouth again, lay on the floor, quickly wound the ropes approximately back in place, and held tightly to the knife. If it came to that, she'd have the element of surprise. A nick just to get the gun; she hoped it wouldn't have to be anything else. She rolled on her back, so he wouldn't see the ropes had been cut, and started praying. She was in the middle of "Our Father" when she remembered.

Her shoes.

Sitting side by side on the kitchen floor right outside the closet. She quickly switched to "Please, God, don't let him see my shoes" and held her breath. She was so frightened, her heart seemed to stop beating.

"Water! Since when do you drink water? No, my boy, you sit here. We haven't finished with you, have we, Berthille? Maybe the thing to do is to leave him here for a nice long vacation. You take his car while I drive mine. How would you like that, you *fumier!*"

The kitchen door was slammed shut.

Faith was out of the closet and into her shoes instantly. She exchanged the paring knife she'd been using for the largest one in the set, placed it in her bag, and slung the bag around her neck to leave her arms free.

She'd already noted the door to the outside. It was covered with a long curtain of brightly colored plastic strips that were supposed to keep winged pests out of the kitchen when the door was open on hot summer days. She unlocked the door, noiselessly pushed aside the fluttering screen, and stepped into the backyard. There was a small lawn, bordered by a flat court for *pétanque,* then the rest of the property dropped precipitously down to the stream. There was a well-worn almost vertical path to its banks.

However, that was not the way she planned to go. Somehow she must get to the front of the house and check out the car. It was a risk she had to take.

There were two windows on either side of the front door and a smaller one to the left of the fireplace. This was the one she had to worry about, since it overlooked the drive where the car was probably parked. But by crawling along the ground, she might avoid detection. Besides, she was fairly certain no one was looking out the windows at the moment.

Faith crept along the side of the house, careful to stay in the shadow. When she got to the chimney, she dropped down as flat as her body allowed and pulled herself along on her belly. She could see the car ahead of her. A shiny new red VW Golf convertible, number one on the most-stolen list. But *Papa* would have plenty of insurance.

The earth was still damp and had the rich smell spring brings. The promise of growing things. It was not unpleasant. She was almost to the car. Her knees were starting to get sore. She was really out of shape. Of course, Christophe's rope tricks hadn't helped. She reached up and cracked the driver's side door open. She was breathing more rapidly in anticipation.

No keys.

She was so disappointed, she almost collapsed. She'd been counting on finding them there. It appeared even in the country, Dominique reflexively pocketed her keys. A girl who didn't take chances—chances of this sort. Now there was only one thing to do. Go back and make for the woods on the other side of the stream, away from the road.

Easing the car door shut, Faith crawled back across the yard. She'd almost made it to the corner when the front door banged open.

Nine

Berthille came running out the door, dragging Dominique by the wrist behind her. She'd obviously reached a decision.

"I did not think it was possible to insult us even more! If you wanted to get rid of us, this was the way! You are lower than a snake. Your bed! We wouldn't even stay in the same room with you! Breathe the same air—" She stopped abruptly as she saw Faith's fleeing figure.

"He *did* have a woman here! I knew it! Who is the bitch?"

Christophe pushed them aside and started to run after Faith, who looked over her shoulder to make sure he hadn't pulled the gun from his pocket. It was an incredible scene. Christophe's face was contorted with rage—and fear. He was rapidly gaining on her. The two girls, both dressed more for a night of jazz at Lyon's Le Hot Club than Sunday in the country, were at his heels, screaming.

Suddenly, Berthille kicked off her high-heeled platform shoes, put on a burst of speed, and threw herself forward, tackling him. He fell heavily to the ground face first and Dominique piled on them both.

"So, you thought you could join your whore and get away from us!" Both girls began to laugh triumphantly, as astride they pummeled his back. Swearing continuously, he was trying to get up, but it was hopeless.

Thank God there were some things you could depend on in life, Faith thought as she reached the top of the path at the rear of the house and started down toward the stream. The wrath of a woman scorned—fortunately complicated in this instance by there being two women.

The path was very steep and she was forced to go slowly. The *jeunes filles,* weighing in at about ninety pounds each and with arms and legs like elegant pipe cleaners, wouldn't keep Christophe pinned for long. But Faith was afraid to go faster and fall. It wasn't just the baby. Twisting an ankle at this point would be fatal.

She could see the path continued into the woods on the opposite side of the stream, but the logs that had been fashioned into a crude bridge had been pulled apart by the ravages of winter, so only one remained completely in place. Grateful for at least this means to cross, Faith gingerly stepped up onto it. It had been soaked by the melting snow and felt spongy. She hoped it wouldn't give way in the middle. The water wasn't deep. She wouldn't drown, but she'd get very wet and the rocks below the surface looked slippery. It would be hard to get a footing in the swift current.

The commotion up at the house sounded closer and she half expected the three dervishes to come whirling down the hill.

She made it safely to the other side of the brook and

reached down to toss the log into the water. Under her weight, it had already started to break and might go completely when the next person trip-trapped across, but she wanted to make certain. Anything she could do to slow Christophe's pursuit.

Running down the path into the dense forest, she was glad for the training she'd done in the last weeks walking up and down the stairs at St. Nizier several times a day, usually as burdened as a pack mule.

The path ended in a large clearing. It was obviously the family's picnic area. A crudely fashioned brick barbecue was surrounded by logs, dragged from the surrounding forest to provide seating. The undergrowth had been cleared and it was a beautiful spot. Beyond the tall trees, Faith could see the pink and gray granite crests of the mountains surrounding the plateau.

She still wasn't that far from the house and the shot she heard propelled her from the clearing. What did he think he was doing? If he was trying to frighten her, it was working, but how were the two girls reacting to Christophe's Jekyll and Hyde transformation? Another shot rang out and she could hear his voice. He wasn't looking for partridges.

She struck out in what she judged to be the same direction as the driveway, which she assumed led to a larger road. She didn't want to get too close to it. Christophe would soon give up tracking her—she hoped—and take to the roads. But she didn't want to get too far away, either, and roam deeper and deeper into the woods. From the isolation he'd stressed, she'd figured she must be in or near the huge Parc des Cévennes, occupied by hikers in the summer; at this time of year, virtually uninhabited.

She was beginning to get winded, but at least the exercise was keeping her warm. She didn't even want to think about nightfall and how cold she would be.

A shaft of sunlight caught the shimmering mica in a large granite rock and Faith gratefully went over to it and sat down to catch her breath. The sounds of pursuit had ceased. She was safe. She and the baby would live to tell the tale. She just wished there were some way she could communicate this to Tom and Ben. Their ordeal was as bad as hers. She felt almost sleepy sitting in the sunshine and wondered if she dared take a quick nap. She'd need all the energy she could get for the walk that was beginning to loom in her imagination as only slightly less arduous than Hannibal's stroll across the Alps. But no, a nap would be foolhardy, however tempting the oblivion from her hunger pangs.

A voice, not close, but not far enough away, either, startled her out of her ridiculous woolgathering. It was Christophe! She could hear her name.

There were more rocks on either side of the slight clearing she'd been sitting in and she climbed on top of the largest group to find another ledge, then more rocks. Her best bet was to get as high and as far away as possible. Her thin shoes didn't offer much traction and she briefly considered going barefoot, but her feet would be cut to ribbons before she'd gone very far. She used her hands to grip the rugged stone and pulled herself up. At the next leveling off, she was rewarded by the sight of a series of openings, more vertical than horizontal, that she could see were marked caves. The Cévennes was famous for these strange and abundant configurations. Spelunking was a major vacation activity for the Leblancs. They'd bemoaned the fact that Tom and Faith would not be in France long enough to join them.

Trying not to think who might still be finishing a long winter's nap inside, Faith eased her way into one and cautiously took a step or two into the darkness. She opened her purse, which had hung awkwardly around her neck, for the matches she always carried after having been locked in someone's preserves closet a few years ago—not by mistake. These were from the Copley Plaza in Boston and she wished she were in some fairy tale and they'd take her there as she struck a light. She lit a match, remained firmly in place, stunned at how large the cave was. Limestone stalactites descended from the ceiling, meeting the stalagmites that spiraled up from the floor. The air was cool and damp. There were no bears or other monsters. Merely one closing in on her. She hid behind a large rock as far away from the opening as she could get, blew out the second match she'd lighted, and waited.

Christophe's voice was more audible. It sounded as though he was right outside one of the caves.

"Madame Fairsheeld, Faith," he called. "Please. You will never survive in these woods. We will return to Lyon as you suggested and try to straighten things out. I promise. I have been a bit mad and you must let me take care of you now. Think of the baby, madame! Please answer me. I swear you will not be hurt."

Faith closed her eyes even in the darkness and strained for the sound of his footsteps entering the cave. She took the knife from her purse and held it ready.

"Faith, believe me. You must. You are in great danger here. You will be lost and there are many wild animals in this area. Please come out and we will go back to the car."

He sounded so sincere. There was a hint of tears in his voice.

Faith didn't buy it for a minute.

She was ready to spring out at him. He would have to light a match to find her. Maybe he would go into one of the other caves. Maybe he was claustrophobic. Maybe she could kill him before he killed her.

The voice was starting to drift away until at last she heard only an occasional "Fairsheeld." She pulled the cuffs of the sweater down over her hands and tucked her feet beneath her. She wasn't moving. Not for a very long time. "Think of the baby," he'd implored. Well she was. Constantly. And very glad of the company.

* * *

It was four o'clock on Sunday afternoon. Michel Ravier and Tom Fairchild sat and looked at each other. Neither man had slept or shaved since Faith's disappearance, and Ravier's office matched their disorderly mien. Half-eaten containers of food and cups of coffee, some still filled and cold, were strewn about the room. Michel was not a smoker, but had made plenteous use of his snuffbox. Black grains decorated the papers scattered across his desk.

Faith had been spotted all over the country—especially after the reward was announced. Michel had just hung up after speaking with the police in Lourdes. A man and a woman had come dashing into the *gendarmerie,* swearing that the missing *Américaine* was one of a group of suppliants immersing themselves in the waters at that very moment. The Lourdes police had called Ravier and gone to check it out. Now they were filing their report. It was an American woman, all right—sixty-five and on crutches.

"She's got to be somewhere. All the borders, airports have been under constant surveillance. Her face has been on the front page of every paper in Europe. How can it be that no one has seen her?"

Tom stared bleakly across the desk at the inspector. "You know why, Michel."

"No, my friend. It's not the time for this. Have faith."

It produced a wan smile. "I hope to."

Faith was not wearing a watch and swore that she would never be without one from now on. She had no idea how much time had passed since she'd last heard Christophe's voice, but judging from the stiffness of her body, it had been some hours. She had been too frightened to sleep. She crept cautiously to the front of the cave. The sun was lower in the sky. It was late afternoon. She didn't want to be in these woods in the dark. Christophe had threatened wild animals, and while she was sure he was lying, she didn't want to put it to a test. She'd have to try to find the road and follow it until she came to some sort of dwelling or village. Before her ascent, she'd noted that the clearing she'd been in seemed to offer the best passageway and she started to climb back down to it, carefully fitting her feet in the crevices of the rocks. There were plenty of short bushes to hold on to and it wasn't difficult, just scratchy. Vivid images of Christophe lying in wait for her at the bottom filled her with terror, but she couldn't continue to climb. There would be no road.

The forest at one end of the clearing was as she remembered—a dense carpet of pine needles and mosses with little low undergrowth or fallen trees. It was blessedly empty.

As she walked, she looked about at the wide variety of plant life. She'd never been a Girl Scout and her family had tended toward vacations where her father could do research on Thomas Hardy's theological metaphors and her mother could hole up in an English country inn with a stack of Agatha Christies. Faith and her sister, Hope, explored on foot and bicycle but never learned much about flora and fauna—or any survival tips other than the advisability of avoiding British railway food.

Faith knew there were plenty of things to eat in the woods—mushrooms, probably truffles right below her feet; however, the only thing she would have trusted not to poison her at the moment would have been a slice of crusty bread spread with butter, and there didn't seem to be a tree of those.

She plodded on. Her shoes had become part of her foot, adhering like a second skin more tightly with each step. How far could these woods possibly extend? The answer, she knew, could well be miles and miles in this part of France.

After what she judged to be an hour, she saw a break in the trees and what looked like a road, certainly flat, open land, on the other side. She picked up the pace. Her shoes, so comfortably a part of her body earlier, had now turned traitor and were rubbing blisters on her heels. She took some tissues and tried to make a little cushion, which helped marginally.

Faith stepped through the trees. The land was flat as far as the eye could see. The plateau was covered with low ground covers, and as she stepped forward, she smelled the strong fragance of wild thyme and rosemary. She was dizzy with hunger. There was no road in sight. Nothing in sight at all, except what looked like a pile of stones in the distance. For no other reason than that it was there, she headed for it. As she walked toward it, Faith felt a breeze that she did not doubt would become a strong wind by nightfall. Up above her, birds circled. Hawks. Birds of prey.

"Not me, you vultures," she yelled at them, and felt better.

As she approached the pile of rocks, she was disappointed to discover it was not a shepherd's hut where she might have bedded down for the night, but a dolmen, a burial chamber from megalithic days. Whoever had occupied it thousands of years ago had become one with the plateau, yet even if she could have squeezed into the chamber, Faith was uneasy with the implications. Besides, it was still daylight and she needed to press on.

How fascinated Tom would be with all this, she thought as she picked a few wildflowers, then looked at them slightly dazed, dropped them, and pinched herself. Keep walking. Keep moving. Don't stop. She started to say it out loud. It wasn't a desert, though it felt like one. Everything was so flat. She wasn't thirsty—there had been a stream in the woods—but mirages seemed to beckon. She thought she saw a cross ahead of her. She was hallucinating.

"Don't waste my time!" Michel slammed the receiver down. He'd sent Tom back to the Leblancs ostensibly to check on Benjamin, but in reality to keep him from hearing too much of what was going on. Now Faith had been sighted in the chorus at the Folies Bergère in Paris.

Gina Martignetti had disappeared into thin air. There was no record of anyone of that name and age living in Rome. Giovanni had been grilled but apparently knew nothing at all. The other two prostitutes, Marilyn and Monique, had also gone underground—and Michel hoped not literally. Everybody was missing and he was at a loss to figure out what it all meant.

It *was* a cross. Intricately carved and standing straight up. Cared for. No lichen. Which meant someone came here sometimes. Faith took it as the good sign it was and continued to walk. She was slowing down and she saw her shadow lengthen. It would be dark soon.

Where was Christophe now? she wondered. Far, far away. Having failed to find her, she assumed he would have made for the nearest border. Spain? Poor Solange and Jean-François. A child like that wasn't just sowing wild oats, but bad seeds. She'd feel a whole lot sorrier for them if she hadn't been the victim, or one of them.

The two girls must have heard the shots or maybe they'd left by then. She couldn't figure out where they fit in or what the business with the *clochards* and the break-ins meant. She certainly had plenty of time to try now. She matched her steps to her mental gymnastics. The kids figure out who's going to be out of town and one of them robs the apartment—or maybe a pair of them. More than that would be too risky. She wondered how many kids were involved. Could there be a giant ring of adolescent *cambrioleurs* in Lyon? Christophe, Dominique, Berthille, and the other boy, Benoît, had seemed so tight at the gallery—a little world unto themselves. She wouldn't be surprised if it was just the four of them. So they robbed the apartments and what did they do with the stuff? Hard to explain to

Maman where the new diamond and emerald choker had come from.

"I don't care about the *clochards,*" Dominique had said, and something about their being lazy and drunk, that they could get jobs. Was it some sort of nouveau Robin Hood enterprise? Steal from the bourgeoisie and give to the poor? Passing the loot to Christophe's uncle to hand out to his friends? But the first time one of them tried to buy a bottle of wine at Monoprix with a gold medallion of the Sun King, the smiling lady at the register would be more likely to call the police than say *"Merci beaucoup. Bonne journée,"* as she invariably did. So polite—like everyone else in other stores.

And what about Faith's own *clochard*? The dead one. Bernard. Had he wanted too many goodies? No, the whole thing didn't make any sense at all, she thought wearily. And how did Marie connect with the kids? She wouldn't have been afraid of them. She'd have told their parents.

Faith realized the land was sloping down again and decided to follow it. Nothing except sheep or goats could live on such a plateau. She might not know a great deal about animal husbandry, but this much was clear. She wouldn't mind encountering a sheep or two about now. They'd make cozy companions for the cold night ahead, plus she did have a very serviceable knife and a few matches. There was plenty of rosemary around. She began to salivate. Bo Peep would have done the same thing in Faith's place, she was sure.

But there were no sheep and she started down the slope that soon became a steep incline. She had to walk sideways to keep from tumbling forward on the loose stones. The sun set slowly. It was glorious, streaking vivid pinks and oranges across the sky until they faded to deep violet. Another night alone. Yet, she was still alive, she'd saved her baby's life, and in the morning, she was sure she would come across a road and find help. She had faith, she told herself—both.

Before long it was pitch-dark, but soon the moon rose, a bright golden half, joined by more stars than she had ever realized existed in the firmament. She noticed she was now following a rough track that showed an occasional tire mark in the ruts. Faith didn't think any find could excite her more than the Missoni sweater dress marked 50 percent off that she'd unearthed at Bergdorf's last January, but it paled in comparison with the exquisite pattern of these tires—proof that civilization and help were at hand. This track couldn't be called a road, yet it was bound to lead somewhere.

It did. Straight down again.

Standing at the top, Faith thought she detected the glimmer of a light far off in the distance. Without hesitating, she eagerly followed the trail down toward the speck and was rewarded to find it steadily enlarge as she moved closer. The way leveled off again, but the light did not disappear, and after about a half hour, she stood looking at a large, two-story stone house with a variety of outbuildings. An old Citroën truck was parked outside and she felt like kissing its fenders. The light was coming from the ground-floor front windows and she summoned all the energy she had left to go to the door and lift the heavy iron knocker. It fell with a thunderous bang. She was weeping in relief.

The door opened wide immediately and a dramatic figure filled the frame. It was a very large man in his late forties, dressed like a farmer, but under his beret, his graying hair reached almost to his shoulders, where it mixed with a long beard, creating confusion as to where one left off and the other began. His bushy eyebrows rose slightly in mild surprise and he said in an incongruously soft voice, *"Vous êtes perdue, mademoiselle?"*

Very, very *perdue. Très, très* lost, Faith reflected as she answered, *"Oui."*

A woman's voice called something out and the man stepped back, telling Faith to come in. It was a farmhouse, not unlike the one she had left but larger, and a different decorator had been employed—or rather, it was a matter of self-employment and frozen in time at some point during the late sixties. Batik wall hangings, pots of geraniums swinging in macramé planters, and furniture that had been scrounged and/or made from scratch. She'd entered a time warp—a sensation heightened by the immediate appearance of the lady of the house, who wore her salt and pepper hair parted in the middle and down to her waist. She was clothed in multiple layers constructed, surely by her own hands, from bright, well-worn India-print cottons. Sandals with several pairs of wool socks completed the look—a look that identified the individual as belonging not so much to a particular nation as to the whole world—in 1968.

"Pauvre petite!" the apparition exclaimed, and quickly pushed a chair stacked with pillows toward Faith. Faith let herself sink gratefully into their softness. She'd made it. She was safe.

The man and woman began to speak at once, quickly. It was impossible.

"Parlez-vous anglais?" Faith asked. She was so tired and speaking French took so much concentration.

"You are English!" The man was thunderstruck. There might be some logical reason for a Frenchwoman to be wandering around what Faith would soon learn were the Causses Méjean in the dark, but English? To be sure, they could be eccentric . . .

"No, I am an American and I hope you will be able to help me."

"American! *Sacrebleu!*" Faith hoped he would not go into orgies over Route 66 or the Large Apple, or, judging from the posters of Ché, Lennon, Roman Polanski's *A Knife in the Water* and the like, American foreign policy for the last twenty-five years.

There were wonderful smells coming from the kitchen and she wanted to eat, but first she had to call Tom. Maybe call Tom while she was eating. She had to have something, anything, even a crust of yesterday's baguette.

"American," he repeated in amazement. "But what are you doing here? Have you been with some kind of hiking group? At this time of year, it is not advisable, you know."

How to explain it.

"My name is Faith Fairchild and my husband, child, and I are visiting in Lyon. . . ."

"Lyon! But that is two hundred kilometers away at least!"

"Yes, I know. Do you think perhaps I could have something to eat and some water while I explain? I'd also like to make a phone call. Then, if you could take me to the nearest police station, I'm sure they will arrange for me to get back to my husband."

Faith didn't think she had made a joke, but her queries seemed to cause both her hosts great amusement.

"Madame, the food is no problem, but you understand you are not in the *centre ville* of Lyon here. We have no phone, no electricity at all, and the nearest police station is in Meyrueis—fourteen kilometers away," explained the woman.

"We would be happy to take you there," her husband continued, "but our fine old truck has at last refused all our attempts to start it and at the moment we are dependent on others to get our things to market. Tomorrow a friend will be here early to take us to Meyrueis and you can come, too."

Tomorrow! As pleasant as these people seemed—Faith was already planning on sending them an extremely nice bread-and-butter gift, shoes perhaps, or a new truck, which it was a shame someone hadn't thought of earlier—the idea of another night away from Tom and Ben when they still didn't know she was safe was too much. She put her head in her hands and began to sob.

Mama and Papa Bear, as Faith had begun to regard them, were galvanized into action. He thrust a large glass of what smelled like pure alcohol into her hand, while his wife set a steaming bowl of thick vegetable soup on a low table next to Faith's chair. Faith sniffed mightily and wiped her eyes on the rough sleeve of the sweater she was wearing. Hard to know how to go about returning it, she thought disconnectedly as she set the glass down and grabbed the soup.

"Thank you. *Merci,* you are so kind. It's just that no one knows where I am. I was kidnapped yesterday morning and only succeeded in escaping this morning."

"Kidnapped! Terrorists! Here in the Cévennes!"

"No, no, it was a neighbor in Lyon. You see he killed a *clochard* and I found the body, then he hid the body again and had his uncle pretend to be the *clochard*—" Faith stopped. Both their faces had "escaped madwoman" written in Bodoni bold type straight across their granny glasses. She hastily slurped down the rest of the soup. It was delicious.

"I am not crazy, although I admit the story sounds bizarre. I should start from the beginning and tell you the whole thing."

"But of course, madame. Let us sit in the kitchen. We were about to have our meal. If you sip some of this"—he indicated the glass Faith had set aside—"you will feel warm and perhaps calmer. It is my own *eau de vie.* I make it from the plums."

"I'm sure it's wonderful, but I am pregnant and avoiding alcohol."

This was the last straw, as far as madame was concerned. Lost, kidnapped, pregnant. She virtually carried Faith out to the kitchen, tenderly installed her in a chair near the hot cast-iron stove, and began to assemble the meal rapidly.

When it was ready, Faith had the distinct impression it was more than what had originally been planned.

"I hope you like French food. Ours is very simple. We make everything here. It is not Paul Bocuse, but Clotilde," monsieur said proudly, with a sweeping gesture. Faith was amused that the chef's fame had spread to this tiny corner of the world, yet why not when his well-fed, smiling face appeared in restaurants and on products from Tokyo to Disney World.

Clotilde was not Bocuse, but she was right up there. Dish after dish appeared on the round kitchen table: a fluffy omelet oozing with sautéed mushrooms, crisp pan-fried new potatoes, and thick slices of *tripoux,* which Faith recognized as a regional speciality—round sacks of tripe stuffed with an assortment of the chopped tripe, vegetables, and aromatic herbs. It was all sublime. This was followed by salad, picked moments ago, and fresh goat cheese made by madame herself, *fromage fermière.* Throughout the meal, Faith devoured slice after slice of bread, a dense, chewy combination of white and whole wheat, *pain de campagne,* made in the oven sending out such comforting waves of warmth. She was just beginning to feel well and truly fed for the first time in days when her hostess produced a jar of apricots, spooning the succulent-looking fruit into large bowls and liberally dousing them with cream. The coffee appeared and Faith started her tale.

By the time she had reached her escape from the kitchen closet, Clotilde and Frédéric, first names having been urged at the same time as seconds of the omelet, were in tears—hers of sorrow and his of anger.

Frédéric exploded. He jumped out of his chair and pounded his fist on the table. "If only I could get my hands on this boy! *Boy!* He does not deserve to be called anything human. And what is even worse is that he is not alone. It is the majority of youth today. They have no morals to speak of, live solely for the sensation of the moment. They have nothing to fight for. They do not care. It is total anomie. They cannot make love without thinking of SIDA. They believe a nuclear war will occur. And look at us with all our potential Chernobyls and Three Mile Islands waiting to happen. We are in the last stages of the degeneracy of the capitalist state. They are the offspring of our failure."

Clotilde took up the chant. "They drift with nothing to do, nothing to believe in. At least we had a cause to cling to and it kept us alive. We have tried to live the rest of our life according to those ideals. That was why we came here to the Cévennes. We believe this is the real France, rural areas as yet unspoiled. We could be self-sufficient and live simply. It was very hard at first and many have left, but here, away from everything, we could bring up our children without the omnipresence of the world military-industrial complex and the corruption of a materialistic society."

Faith looked around. She didn't see evidence of any children. Perhaps there hadn't been any little pattering feet.

"You did not have children?" she asked.

"But of course we have children. Two—to replace ourselves. More would have been selfish. They are called Honoré and Verité. Actually, Verité is legally called Valérie, because Verité is not on the list."

"List?"

"Yes, in France you must name your child an accepted French name. We wanted to name her 'truth,' but had to register her as Valérie. We have always called her Verité and I am happy to say she prefers it herself."

So, no little Moonflowers, Ringos, or Vladimir Ilyiches as a legacy of the times of turmoil in France. Faith often wondered how many of these had changed to Susan, William, or other common monikers upon entering junior high, that great leveler where blending in takes precedence over such mundane things as individual beliefs.

"Where are your children now?" Faith wondered aloud. Surely it was too early for them to be upstairs tucked in their wee trundle beds. Although these children would be older.

"Our daughter is studying to be a lawyer and is in Marseille. She is hoping to change the system from within. We have some interesting discussions about it. And our son works in a garage in Narbonne."

This didn't sound very revolutionary—within or without—or an occupation that would give rise to interesting conversations, but Faith refrained from comment.

Honoré's mother explained, "We believe each child must be what he or she wants to be. We only hope we have taught them to be honest and hard-working, and perhaps a bit of our philosophy of brotherhood, sisterhood, and peace. Honoré was never a student and he didn't want to stay on the farm. He loves to work with engines, so this was a good job for him. And he comes home often to help us."

Too bad he hadn't made a trip home recently to tinker with Old Faithful out in front of the house, Faith thought ruefully.

They had gotten far afield of Christophe, yet Faith didn't mind. She was pleasantly full and getting sleepy. Clotilde and Frédéric's life intrigued her. Did not beckon—not at all—but definitely intrigued.

"Don't you get lonely here, and how did your children get to school?"

"We are not so remote as you may imagine. We go to the market each week to sell what we grow and make. There we see our friends and also we all help each other when it is time to shear the sheep or repair a barn. It seems we are always going to parties, too. True, there are few of us here, but we know each other well. In the summer, we take guests and we've met many friends that way. One couple from England comes every year for two weeks in August to walk across the *causses,* the plateaus, and go into the *avens,* caves—Aven Armand, a wonderful one, is not too far. It is a shame you cannot stay longer."

"She doesn't want to sightsee, Frédéric! She only wants to get back to her husband and small boy."

Frédéric was a bit chagrined.

"I hope to come back with them someday and then we will see all these places," Faith hastened to assure him. He seemed so proud of the region. "Did you grow up here?"

This time, they did laugh out loud.

"Frédéric grew up in the eighth *arrondissement* in Paris and his only hikes were in the Parc Monceau. I fared a little better. I grew up in a suburb of Paris, but my grandparents had a house in Brittany and the best part of my childhood was going there.

"You asked about our children. We taught them here. You can do this by mail. The government sent the lessons and we followed them with some revisions and additions of our own." Faith could well imagine. "Then when they were old enough for *lycée,* they went to live with Frédéric's parents. It was quite a different life, but it did not spoil them and they were happy to come back here for all the *vacances.*" Her pride was evident.

Faith knew the area around the Parc Monceau well— the beautiful homes, nurses keeping a close eye on their privileged charges in the carefully manicured park with the ubiquitous KEEP OFF THE GRASS signs. If Frédéric appeared there in his present state, he'd be told to move on.

The contrast was enormous and her head was aching with all that had happened that day. Fatigue was causing things to blur. This much was clear: She had escaped, made her way across the rugged Cévennes landscape to the door of the local chapter of the Scott and Helen Nearing fan club, and now she wanted to find a bed, collapse, wake up, and go home.

She must have murmured the request out loud, for in a few minutes, she was in Baby Bear's bed, burrowing down under an avalanche of quilts and wrapped in a thick flannel nightgown that might have belonged to Clotilde's grandmother. First, there had been the unavoidable trip to the outhouse, fortunately attached to the main house by a small covered porch and complete with all the necessaries. It was clean and free of the usual heavy lime odor. She'd been amused to notice the stack of reading material—old copies of *Libération* and *Rolling Stone* magazine.

The quilts were so warm. Faith was so warm. And so to sleep.

Clotilde roused Faith the next morning. It was still dark and the air was cool, but Faith jumped from the bed with alacrity and threw on her clothes. Tom! Ben! In a few hours, they would be together. The baby stirred. It was as if he or she understood. The movement was so slight, like the flicker of a feather, Faith had almost missed it. She was thrilled.

Clotilde had left the oil lamp and Faith pulled the covers back over the bed before leaving the room. While tucking her in the night before, Clotilde had told Faith the building had originally housed silkworms. All day long, women would sit and unwind silk from the softened cocoons spun by worms, satiated by the leaves of the abundant mulberry trees that grew on the terraces. Years after all this had come to an end, the young Parisians had been able to buy the decrepit structure and surrounding acres for very little, slowly converting it into a home. The last thing Faith had remembered before falling asleep in her own cocoon was complimenting Clotilde on her, and her husband's, excellent English. Clotilde had thanked her. "We were both studying languages at the university before May of '68 and have enjoyed teaching several to our children." Then she added mischievously, "But, Faith, we are what we French call the 'children of '68.' Frédéric and I are not married. There is no need and it goes against all we believe."

Faith wasn't surprised. Pure was pure. Now in the

dim new day, she hastened down to her new friends and hoped their neighbor with the truck wouldn't forget to pick them up.

He was already there, the twin of Faith's lettuce man at *le marché* St. Antoine. Genial, red-faced, a dusty old beret pulled down over his ears, but not sufficient to hide the bristling tufts of hair shooting out from them. It was hard to believe that some manufacturer was turning out the standard blue cotton overalls large enough for his girth. He held a cigarette in his nicotine-stained fingers and was talking nonstop as Clotilde and Frédéric scurried about the kitchen packing their cheeses for market. It was all Faith could do to stop herself from throwing her arms around him and kissing his unshaven cheek.

It was he who kissed hers, striding over to her with outstretched arms, "Madame, madame. Soon your ordeal will be over! We will go directly to the *gendarmerie* in Meyrueis." He had obviously been filled in.

"Merci, monsieur," Faith replied wholeheartedly, and then offered to help with the packing.

"No, no, *chérie*. Eat something quickly and we will soon be going. It is almost dawn." Clotilde set a steaming bowl of café au lait on the table next to a loaf of bread, a jar of what looked like strawberry preserves, and a dish of butter. Faith set to her task eagerly, and by the time she had finished eating, they were ready to go. Besides the cheese they made from their herd of goats, Clotilde and Frédéric also sold honey from their bees, a variety of preserves, batik lamp shades, and sundry articles forged from iron—hooks, fireplace tools, drawer pulls.

Clotilde gave Faith a heavy loden-green wool cape, probably of local origin, considering the style and texture. It seemed to weigh about ten pounds and Faith found it a little difficult to navigate at first, but when she stepped out the front door into the cold, she was glad for every ounce. Monsieur Radis—Félix, he insisted—was already in the driver's seat, pumping the gas pedal, producing reassuring automotive noises. His truck was the same pedigree as the one that sat forlornly to the side of the house. Faith hoped this one would make it to Meyrueis.

Félix motioned her into the cab. Clotilde and Frédéric jumped into the back and happily settled into each other's arms amidst the crates. Faith noted their devotion but soon had cause to wonder how much was still-crazy-about-each-other-after-all-these-years and how much was common sense as the truck bounced its way over the rough track. She was grasping a strap that hung from the ceiling for dear life while Félix kept up a running commentary, presumably on the landscape they were passing and the history of the region, in such rapid French that Faith soon abandoned any pretense of comprehension, simply nodding and smiling at what she hoped were appropriate moments. She didn't catch anything about the death of a family member or the silkworm blight, so her responses seemed right so far. Félix appeared to regard personal hygiene with considerably less interest than his brother and sister of '68, if he was one of their group and not indigenous. Faith suspected these particular overalls had had many close encounters with his livestock, and between trying to stay upwind of him and trying to hold on, the time was passing rapidly.

Soon they were on an actual road, careening down the mountain, and as Faith caught glimpses of the precipitous drop and what she presumed was a river—a thin blue-green ribbon—below, she began to realize her ordeal was not yet over. Félix, either determined to get her to the police station as quickly as possible or because it was his habitual driving style—and Faith suspected the latter—was proceeding at breakneck speed in apparent disregard for any vehicle foolish enough to be coming around the narrow bend from the opposite direction. To his credit, he did lean on the horn from time to time with startling results. There was also his disconcerting habit of driving with one hand while he gestured with the other. After several repetitions, Faith understood that they were at the top of the Gorges du Tarn, the Tarn being the river, and would soon plummet into Meyrueis.

The truck was descending almost vertically, and just when Faith was about to cross the line from fear to abject terror, she caught sight of a village nestled at the bottom of two crevices. "Meyrueis," Félix announced with a flourish. The whole town was decked with red, white, and blue bunting gathered up with bunches of red silk poppies, cornflowers, and daisies. The tricolor flew from every building and there was an air of great festivity. How did they know? Faith wondered, then remembered that it was Victoire 1945, the celebration of the end of WWII and the reason Tom was able to take the long weekend. Well, it had been a long weekend.

Félix brought the truck to a screeching halt outside the *gendarmerie*. The oddly assorted party disembarked and prepared to go inside. Faith, her legs stiff after having spent most of the trip pressing an imaginary brake pedal to the floor, flung the woolen cloak about her and led the way.

She walked up to the counter, but before she could speak, the man on duty gasped, *"Mon Dieu!"* and raced around to the front.

"Madame Fairsheeld!" He kissed her ecstatically. "France is looking for you!"

Ten

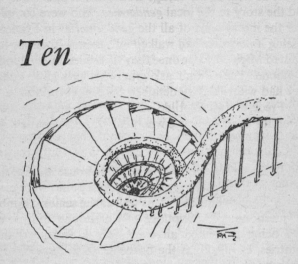

Faith Sibley Fairchild's eyes flew open in complete panic. Where the hell was she? The sight of the huge clock face of the Eglise St. Nizier filling the bedroom window slowed her heart rate and she took several deep breaths. She was home, or what passed for home these days. She was back in Lyon and the small boy curled up next to her sound asleep, snoring slightly and radiating heat, was her own Benjamin. Her Benjamin—who had not left her side since the whole family had rushed madly toward one another in Chief Inspector Ravier's office a few hours ago.

As she lay on the big double bed, so quaintly called the *lit matrimonial* even for those non-espoused, she felt a deep sense of peace. It was over. It wasn't that the horror of the events had left her. This had grown even more intense now when she thought of all the might-have-beens. The underlying peace came from knowing she was safe for sure.

The trip from Meyrueis to Lyon had seemed to take almost as long as her escape from Christophe. First, she'd told the story to the local *gendarmes,* who were completely over the moon—out of all the *gendarmeries* in France, the missing *Américaine* had walked into theirs—then she told it again to Michel Ravier once they succeeded in reaching him by phone. They didn't ask grandmother's shoe size, but they had wanted every detail of the last two days.

Frédéric and Clotilde were able to help narrow the search for the farmhouse where she'd been kept captive by their intimate knowledge of the surrounding terrain, especially after Faith described the series of caves. No one expected that Christophe would be at the house, but the police were anxious to check it out. The Lyon police were picking up the two girls and Benoît, as well as the senior d'Amberts, for questioning. Descriptions of Christophe and his uncle were being circulated all over France and surrounding countries, especially at the borders. Faith remembered to tell them about the gun, and he was being described as dangerous—an understatement, Frédéric avowed.

When the Meyrueis police had finally produced a car and driver to take her back to Lyon, Faith was numb with exhaustion and saddened to leave the two flower children going to seed, whom she now numbered among her closest friends. It was even hard to leave Félix. When she got into the police car, Clotilde and Frédéric had pressed not only the heavy cloak, already too warm in the morning sun, upon her but rounds of goat cheese, a lamp shade, and several iron implements of varying natures. Félix gave her a sack filled with radishes and lettuce.

Her driver had graduated from the same auto-training school as Félix and for a good part of the trip the words *déja vu* took on new and powerful meaning. Yet, even at many kilometers over the speed limit and with the siren blaring all the way, it had taken three hours to reach Lyon. As they entered the city on the A7, the Autoroute du Soleil, the sun had indeed been shining and Faith clutched the young *gendarme*'s arm in joy when she caught sight of the first bridge, the Pont Pasteur, then the train station and other familiar landmarks. The only thing that would have made her happier at that moment would have been a glimpse of the green in secure little Aleford, Massachusetts.

Michel Ravier had not wanted to keep her long, and after listening again to her story, had told her to get some rest and they'd get together later in the day. He was right. She was ready to drop, and when they'd emerged into the street, the throngs of reporters and photographers had overwhelmed her. Paul Leblanc offered a brief statement to the effect that Madame Fairchild was fine and the police were seeking her abductors. He referred them to Ravier and, like a devoted sheepdog, parted the crowd and shepherded them into the car, where Ghislaine was waiting at the wheel.

"You'll have to have some sort of press conference or they'll never leave you alone," she advised. Faith and Tom had agreed. But not until tomorrow. Paul had said he would take care of it.

"If I could have kept Dominique's name out of it, I would have," Faith started to say. Ghislaine interrupted her. "Absolutely not. It's obvious that she is deeply troubled and if not for you, who knows where she might have ended up." She gestured toward the street at two young women in high black boots, lace body stockings, and not much else. It reminded Faith of Marie. Michel told her a team had gone to the *hôtel de ville* after he had spoken with her and it did appear that Marie, or someone, had been dragged along the tunnel leading to the river. They planned to exhume the body to see if the evidence matched. Poor Marie, Faith had thought, she couldn't lie in peace even in death.

When they'd gotten back to the apartment, all Faith had wanted to do was sleep, and did almost immediately. Now, fully awake, she wondered where Tom was. She didn't hear any sounds of activity in the apartment. Like Benjamin, her husband had firmly attached himself to her with limpetlike devotion. All three had been napping together.

She got up cautiously so as not to disturb Ben. He'd been told she had been away visiting friends; and had greeted her with wails of "Why didn't you take me, Mommee? Ben would be good!" It almost broke her heart. The Leblancs had entertained him nonstop, Tom had told her—taking the little boy to the zoo at Parc de la Tête d'Or, the Roman ruins in Old Lyon, and to every playground in the area. Still, Ben had been aware of the tension around him and Faith was sure he hadn't been sleeping well, even with Pierre and the Leblanc's aging Irish setter, Lola, as comforting bedmates. She hoped Ben would make up for it now. When he awoke, she planned to be right before his eyes. But where was Tom?

She walked into the kitchen and found a note propped up against the sugar bowl.

Sweetheart, I know you're going to be hungry when you wake up, so I went out for a few provisions. Back soon. Before you're awake, I hope. Love you, Love you, Love—I could go on forever, Tom

He *was* a darling, Faith smiled to herself. And she *was* starving. Breakfast had been an awfully long time ago and she'd politely refused the Meyrueis *gendarme*'s offer to stop on the highway for le sandweech. She'd wanted to get back.

The refrigerator was vintage Mother Hubbard. Since they'd planned to be away, Faith had emptied it. All that remained was a jar of Amora béarnaise sauce, surprisingly good in a junk food kind of way; some juice; and a few bedraggled scallions. She poured herself a glass of juice and stood at the window. The people across the way had filled their window box with bright pink begonias during her absence. It was odd to think of life going on so normally while hers was being turned upside down. Hers and the d'Amberts.

She hadn't seen Solange and Jean-François but knew from Michael that they were in another part of the *commissariat*. What would she say to them? Or they to her? We're sorry our son planned to kill you? And from what Michel had said, it was not clear what role they, or perhaps only Jean-François, might have played. One of the large question marks that remained was what had happened to the stolen goods.

The girls and Benoît had told the police that they were stealing for the good of society. The idea had been Christophe's—of course. The people they knew had too many things. They did not need the jewelry, and other items they owned and it would help to feed, clothe, and house those who had nothing. The plan was always the same. The four would meet to draw straws to see whose turn it was to carry out the robbery, then afterward would place the stolen goods at the bottom of a shopping bag filled with old clothes and drop the bag in a trash can at a particular rendezvous. The place was the only thing that changed, depending on where the targeted apartment was. Then they were to watch from a distance to make sure a *clochard* picked up the bag. They presumed the *clochard* then took the bag to some shelter or agency. When pressed for more details, all three had exhibited a similar lack of interest. Christophe knew. He'd arranged it. They trusted him. They were still protecting him, and it was not until Ravier told Berthille and Dominique that it had been Faith at the farmhouse, kidnapped by their friend, that they had broken down and cried. They had both been in love with him and he had treated them miserably. He was horrible. They hoped he would spend the rest of his life in prison. None of them had admitted to knowing his uncle or the *clochard* Bernard, except as mentioned by Christophe in passing as a character in his neighborhood.

It had been exhausting, Michel had told Tom and Faith. He'd far rather question adults, even hardened criminals. Less posing, fewer hormones. In the end, he was fairly certain all three had known nothing of the murder or kidnapping. And as for the robberies, he was pretty sure they deliberately chose not to think about what happened to the loot. So long as they told themselves they were performing a noble deed, they didn't have to admit to the fact that they were doing it for the thrill of it, and in Dominique's case, he suspected, to get back at her very proper parents.

Christophe. It all came back to this one young man, Faith thought as she finished the juice, which unfortunately had served to make her even hungrier. She went back into the hallway to go check on Ben. Her hand gently rubbed her abdomen—all serene there.

There was some mail from Saturday piled on the table and *mirabile dictu*—a *ballotin* of chocolates from Voisin. She opened the box and they proved to be those yummy *Coussins de Lyon,* little pillows of thin, crisp sugar, colored pale green, coating a stuffing of dark rich chocolate. She looked inside for a note to find out who they were from. It wasn't likely that Tom would have had the time or inclination to buy bonbons these last two days. She lifted up the layers of candies and there was a note at the bottom. Not a card from the shop but a piece of paper with jagged edges that appeared to have been hastily torn from a pad. It didn't do much to solve the mystery. All it said was:

Attention à ♡. C. et ♡.

M.

It made no sense at all. Faith immediately put the box down. No matter how strong her hunger pangs, eating these did not seem to be a wise move. *Attention,* "watch out"—she'd seen it on signs. Said it to Benjamin. Watch out for hearts? *C.* could be Christophe. Christophe and a heart, one of his girlfriends? One of the girls—or some other girl? And *M.* Another *M* had warned Faith and she hadn't understood how deadly the game was. The other two *M*'s undoubtedly had. The candies had to be from Marilyn or Monique, placed in the Fairchild's mailbox before they, too, disappeared.

She had to tell Michel right away, so she walked into the living room to the telephone. As she picked up the receiver, the doorbell rang. It must be Tom, too burdened by comestibles to fiddle with the keys.

She darted to the door, opened it quickly, and said, "Darling, I have to call—" Then she stopped short. It wasn't Tom. It was a neighbor. It was Valentina Joliet. Dressed to go out in high-heeled pumps and a large red felt hat.

"Faith, Faith, we have been sick with worry about you! Thank God you are safe. And Christophe, who would have thought it? Such a good family. Solange is a wreck."

♡ . Valentina. Christophe and Valentina. Hearts and flowers. Guns and hot bijoux. *Attention à* Valentina. Watch out for Valentina.

She'd solved the puzzle.

Hard to believe, but true. Christophe and Valentina, not your average class couple. She had assumed that with his euthanasia attitude toward anyone over thirty, Valentina would be out of the picture, yet here she was, where she'd always been, right in the foreground. A simple matter of focus.

And she knew immediately. Her glance leveled and there was no speculation in her eyes. "I came to take you upstairs for something to eat, *chérie*. I met Tom as he was leaving and he said there was nothing in the apartment."

"Thank you, but he'll be back soon and I'm not really very hungry." Especially for Eggs Arsenic or whatever else Valentina had in mind.

"I'm so sorry. It would have been much easier and you see I am in a bit of a hurry to leave. A long-overdue visit home."

Italy. Of course. And precocious little Christophe panting in anticipation, waiting on the doorstep. With tun-tun, tonton, or whomever, although he was probably still running.

Italy. Where Valentina so conveniently shipped artwork in great big packing cases.

Again Faith demurred. "I'm very tired, as you can imagine." As you *know* would be more accurate. "Perhaps I will see you when you get back."

But Valentina had come prepared for all eventualities. She reached in the pocket of her very smart navy blazer, pulled out a serviceable little revolver, a twin of Christophe's and said, "I think not."

It couldn't be happening again. Tom would come through the door at any moment.

"Valentina, you must be insane. You can't get away with this." They were lines from a thousand *B* movies, but they suited the moment.

"Au contraire, Faith, I will. Please open the door and walk ahead of me. It would be so traumatic for your small son to find his *Maman* dead in the hallway."

Faith opened the door and stepped outside. The sunlight was struggling to filter through the dusty windows. Someone would have to call the *régie* to have them washed.

"Now start walking down the stairs," Valentina commanded.

As Faith took the first step, it became clear what Madame Joliet had in mind. No bullets, no poison. Just an unfortunate accident. She grabbed Faith and deftly flung her up and almost over the railing. She'd have been successful if she hadn't teetered off balance in her high heels.

"No!" Faith screamed as she threw her body back away from the five-flight fall. She wrapped her leg around one of the upright iron rods that supported the banister and held tightly to another with both hands.

Valentina continued to push, using all her considerable strength. Faith took one hand away from the railing and slashed at her assailant's face with her nails. Blood streamed from the cuts, and while she tried to wipe her eye, Valentina dropped the gun, which fell to the vestibule below. Faith heard it strike the stone floor, and she clung more desperately. She'd be all right if only the whole banister didn't give way and send her over the edge. She wouldn't hear the sound of that landing. And there was an occasional missing rod, she'd noted in her travels with Ben, keeping him always away toward the wall. But she couldn't choose another place now and she willed herself to believe it was her own fears making the iron in her grip feel looser.

Valentina was trying for a firm grasp of Faith's short hair to turn her head around to get at her face. She brought her foot up, kicking at Faith's leg, which was locked into the railing. The pain was tremendous.

"Help!" Faith screamed again. "*Au secours! Au secours!*" There had to somebody in the building. But it was the holiday. The offices were empty and everyone else was out enjoying the sun.

If she let go right now, they would both go tumbling down the stairs. Valentina was both taller and heavier than Faith was, and if this happened, she'd most likely knock Faith out, then throw her over. Faith tightened her grip and tried to kick back with her free leg. It was impossible. The two women grappled in silence punctuated by oaths from Valentina and Faith's own breathing, which was fast and labored. She'd kept Valentina away from the baby so far.

She mustn't let her get an opportunity to kick her there. She bent over and screamed again.

She heard a sound from above. It was a door opening. Someone came to the railing and called down, *"Mon Dieu! What is happening! Mesdames!"* Valentina stopped her attack for a moment, surprised at the voice from above. She arched her head over the side to see who it was. Faith dredged up every ounce of strength in her body, reached for Valentina's ankles, and tipped her over.

It seemed to take a long time for the body to reach the bottom. The woman's screams rattled the windows as she passed each floor, making vain attempts to halt her progress by reaching for the iron bars. Her shoes fell off and her skirt ballooned up around her face. The *poubelle* lid was closed and she hit it dead center.

Faith sat down on the stair. Someone was next to her taking her hand and stroking her head. It was Madame Vincent. Faith started to try to explain. "Hush, *ma petite.* She was not a good woman."

Sirens were wailing outside, but in the building, all was quiet. They stood up and peered over the railing down the dizzying stairwell at the limp figure clad in navy and white with the chic splash of red resting on top of the trash bin. The hat, the *chapeau rouge,* had never budged. It must have been pinned on.

Eleven

French country weddings, Faith Fairchild decided, were either an endurance test or a question of habit. They'd set off for Beaujolais early Saturday morning for Act One—the civil ceremony at the *mairie* in the groom's small village, where the couple was officially wed in the eyes of the state and the mayor of the village. Then they adjourned to a church where the bride's mother and grandmother had been married, in the neighboring village of Matour, for the eyes of God. Coming down the aisle of the ancient Romanesque stone church on her father's arm to kneel at the side of her betrothed, Adèle, the Veaux's niece, looked as radiant as she was supposed to in a simple long ivory satin sheath, carrying one perfect calla lily and replacing the traditional veil with a short wisp of tulle that floated about her short dark curls. The groom, who worked for France Gas and Electric, seemed ill accustomed to his wedding finery and tugged at his cuffs nervously as if to make the suit fit better. His name was Jean-Jacques and he smiled so continuously that Faith wondered whether his jaw muscles would ever function normally again. The happy couple left the church in a hail of rice, accompanied by their *garçons et demoiselles d'honneur,* a dozen or so angelic-looking small children in bright, flowered frocks and long white Bermudas, which as the day advanced took on new and different hues. Wide-eyed and preternaturally solemn during the mass, the children exploded out of the church laughing, calling to the newlyweds, and scooping up the rice from the steps to hurl at each other. Quickly collected by mothers and fathers mindful of village opinion, they were hustled into cars to be tidied and transported to Act Three, the brioche and champagne reception for the entire village at the family farm.

The farm appeared as old as the church. Delphine took Faith and Benjamin into the house to use the *salle de bain* and explained that very little had been changed since Clément's great-grandfather had settled on the land. Portraits of sober-looking individuals peered down on her in the stiff company parlor where Faith had been placed to wait her turn for the amenities later Veaux had fortunately deemed essential. Meanwhile, out of sight of the ancestors, the village was toasting the bride and groom in mounting merriment, filling the courtyard that separated the house from the immense stone barn and other farm buildings.

Clément took Paul Leblanc away to the orchards as soon as decency allowed. He was eager to get Paul's advice about his experiments with hybrid peaches. The two men strolled companionably across the fields as if they had been friends from childhood. The Fairchilds and Ghislaine were left to make conversation with the locals. Tom was soon caught up in a discussion with one of Clément's brothers, who explained there had been six boys in the family. One stayed to farm, one became a priest, and the others split fifty-fifty—two going north to Paris to learn to be bakers and two going south to Lyon to train as butchers and *charcutiers,* sausage makers, which was the pattern for villages like this. Coming together for weddings, baptisms, even funerals was more than an old custom. It was a way to maintain their ties.

Faith wasn't sorry they'd brought Benjamin. He could have stayed with the Leblanc children and Paul's sister Michèle, but as she watched her son, in his own long Bermudas, blue seersucker ones, and a white polo shirt, climbing the gnarled old apple trees near the wisteria-draped house with the *garçons d'honneur,* she knew he was having an experience she, if not he, would remember all his life. Besides, she wanted him near and she had a strong feeling he felt the same.

She had taken him to school most of the week, not wanting him to miss the fun of playing with Léonard and the others, but had stayed, leaving only to go to the market. In the end, sitting at a low table at the *garderie* and helping to play a variety of *jouets éducatifs*—educational games like pasting beans in designs and of course Legos—turned out to be just what she needed to regain her own equilibrium. Looking at this gathering of well-wishers, happily sipping grape juice and eating the best brioche she'd ever tasted in her life, Faith resolutely turned her thoughts away from where she'd been a week ago. And it might have remained that way, except for the car just now pulling to a halt at the gates, scattering gravel and discharging none other than Chief Inspector Ravier.

Michel Ravier had cursed himself repeatedly all week for not having sent the guard to the Fairchild's apartment sooner. They knew Christophe had not been acting alone and it should have been obvious that another attempt would be made to keep Madame Fairchild from talking. Michel knew she didn't know who else was involved, but whoever they were did not. Now, it might or might not be over. Christophe had vanished, presumably to Italy. Valentina Joliet had miraculously survived her fall—much to Faith's relief, who, while not relishing the idea of joining the *clochard* in the *poubelle* coffin herself, did not want to be the cause of another human being's death, however justifiable. Also, knowing a bit about the French legal system, she realized she had been spared an endless amount of questions and paperwork that would have made grandmother's sister's husband's place of birth seem a mere bagatelle.

Valentina would be hospitalized for a long, long time and would never walk again, but after some days, she was able to talk. She just wouldn't. Meanwhile, Ravier had had Faith discreetly followed all week, deciding to take on today's duty himself. He loved country weddings and it wasn't often he had the chance to attend one, particularly since becoming a police officer. Besides, the Fairchilds were leaving on Monday and it would be his last chance to see Faith—and Tom—until the trial.

"Inspector Ravier, how nice to see you," Faith said in genuine delight, thinking what a stupid word *nice* was. "Friend of the bride or groom or both?"

"Neither, but they were gracious enough to allow me to come."

In fact, Adèle Picard née Veaux was looking upon her wedding as one of the events of the decade. The press had gotten wind of the missing *Américaine*'s attendance and reporters and photographers had surrounded them at the *mairie* and the church before the bride's father had ordered them off. All week, Faith had been having her fifteen minutes of fame over and over and now Adèle was having hers. It would be something to tell her grandchildren. When Chief Inspector Ravier asked to come to keep an eye on Madame Fairchild, they had not only agreed, they had been honored. Then there were those big boxes from Cambet in Lyon that arrived, expensive crystal and china underneath the shredded tissue. No, Adèle was not unhappy at all. All this and Jean-Jacques, too.

Ravier had arrived just as Act Four was about to commence. The wedding guests bid adieu to those from the village and jumped in their cars to report to a scenic spot for the photo. The cars pulled up to an open field, grass neatly mown, surrounded by Lombardy poplars. A small Renault truck roared to a stop and in the twinkling of an eye, two young men had pulled stacks of risers out of the rear and assembled them at the far end of the field. Then rapidly, they began to assemble the group for the wedding souvenir. It was like her eighth-grade class picture, Faith recalled, thankful that her braces were off. The children flanked the newlyweds in front on the first level, Ben included, and all the rest stood on the risers behind them. The photographer took a long look at the group and made a few adjustments. You there, you there. Madame, remove your hat. Then *click, click, click* and he was hurrying them off. They'd packed the gear and were gone in a cloud of dust before the wedding party had reached their cars for, at long last, the reception.

The *salle des fêtes* was indeed a room for parties, actually a hall with several rooms. There was a dance floor with a small stage overlooked by a large room with floor-to-ceiling windows on one side. This room was filled with long tables covered with white paper punctuated by small colorful bouquets of flowers at regular intervals, besides the requisite glassware, cutlery, and napkins. The kitchen was behind some doors on the left and the smells made Faith faint with hunger, not an unusual state for her these days. What a happy baby he or she was going to be! They'd located their place cards and she sat expectantly between Michel and Tom. Ben had joined the children again, twirling about madly on the dance floor to the lively music produced by an elderly but accomplished accordian player and an only slightly younger drummer.

"You won't hear any heavy metal here tonight," Paul said. "Maybe *'le canard,'* some tangos, walzes, an *apache* dance, if people really loosen up, and so forth. What was played at their parents' and even grandparents' weddings and all the village fêtes."

" *'Le canard'?"* Tom asked. "The duck?"

"Wait and see." Paul laughed.

After the *melon au porto* and the *saumon à l'oseille,* perfectly poached salmon with sorrel sauce, and while Tom, Michel, and Paul were proclaiming the Beaujolais Leynes the best Beaujolais ever to cross their lips, the music changed from stately Strauss to something more sprightly. Couples waddled onto the floor for *"le canard,"* which looked exactly like its name, performed with much enthusiasm and high spirits. Faith declined when approached by Clément, saying all too soon she would look like the dance. The others were also content to watch and wait for the next course. The whole affair reminded Faith a little of the dance she'd gone to on an island off the Maine coast the summer before. Grown-ups danced with children, women with women, men with men, as well as the more traditional pairing of men and women. There were all ages, all sizes, and all abilities. Watching the couples alternately glide and jump about below her in a series of remarkably athletic dances, Faith wished the evening could go on and on forever. Of course at that point relatively early in the evening, she didn't know that it would.

It was Ghislaine who first broached the subject on everyone's minds.

"Faith, *chérie,* be honest. We are here together and you are safe. Could we ask Michel some questions? There is still much I am unclear about. But if it brings back bad memories, we will watch the ducks and feed ourselves."

"I had actually been going to suggest something along those lines myself. Michel and his buddies have been asking me questions all week, but I have a few of my own." She raised an eyebrow in Ravier's direction in an attempt at a Gallic gesture. He replied in kind with a shrug. It sent a slight tingle up and down her spine.

"For myself, I don't mind. Tom?"

"I know my wife very well, my good inspector"—the ambience-inspiring phrases normally absent from the good reverend's speech, Faith noted—"And if you don't answer her questions, she'll try to find out some other way, and we know what happens then."

Faith was glad for the Beaujolais. Tom's glass was empty and she tipped some more in, though strictly speaking, it was impolite for women to pour wine in France. The stricture was loosening, yet she was fairly certain in the country, the last bastion of tradition, it still held.

"Shall I begin then?" Michel asked.

"Not until we are there," came Clément Veaux's voice from the dance floor, and he and Delphine, hardly out of breath, climbed the stairs, grabbed another bottle of the Beaujolais from an empty table, and settled down next to Ghislaine.

"There is no one else expected?" Michel asked

"I wish Madame Vincent were here," Faith said a bit wistfully. They'd been spending a great deal of time together during the week. "I think she suspected Valentina all along."

"I have spoken with that excellent lady and you are correct. She watches much of what happens in the building and had formed a very negative opinion of Madame Joliet. But all in good time, Faith. I think I will tell it as a story, because we are at a celebration and that is where stories get told—and where this one will be told for many years, I suspect." Ravier was clearly relishing his role.

"Your part of the story, *mon petit chou,* started perhaps with a bored young man, smart, yet not smart enough to do very well and be interested in his studies or applauded by the adults around him. But he is handsome and has a

202

great deal of charm. He has no trouble attracting girl-friends, particularly those like himself who are bored. His parents are busy and have little time for him. It is enough for them that he has grown up with a certain degree of politeness and intelligence. They suppose after his military service, he will study to be an *avocat* like his father or work in the bank of his uncle. Not the uncle who has disgraced the family, the d'Ambert upon whom all hopes once centered. The d'Ambert who was at ENA, the National School of Administration in Paris. The d'Ambert who was going to be, dare we say it out loud, perhaps President of the Republic. And eventually, the d'Ambert who discovered drugs and alcohol. We found this man, Guy d'Ambert, and that is how we know the story. He was trying to hide in a brothel in Marseille in the Old Port, although I do not think he has much sex drive left," Michel added reflectively.

"Does he know where Christophe is? And Valentina—did he know about them?" Faith asked.

"He does not know where Christophe is. Nor do we, unfortunately, but with all the police in Europe looking for him, it will not be long. I am convinced his parents had no knowledge of his activities. His mother has gone into seclusion with the younger children at her family house in Normandy and Monsieur d'Ambert is staying here to help us. He is as eager to find his son as we are and perhaps for some of the same reasons.

"Now getting back to Christophe's uncle. He vastly preferred being found by us to being found by his nephew and those he worked for. And yes, he knew about Valentina, has known for a long time. She and Christophe have been lovers for several years."

Ghislaine gasped. "My poor Dominique and little Berthille, the babies! The boy was completely wild!"

"I do not know who seduced whom. Apparently, it was a very satisfactory arrangement for both and helped Christophe to ease his boredom. He must have recognized quite soon that Madame Joliet was not the type of neighbor lady who gave you milk and a *biscuit*. Together, they hatched the plan. She because she wanted to give him something to do besides lie in her bed, so he would stay there, and he because he wanted the money. But I am sure Christophe also derived a great deal of pleasure in robbing his parents' friends and his own relatives, and involving their children. Out of luck or trickery, he almost never drew *la courte paille,* the short straw—I believe you, too, have this custom in the United States?"

"Yes," said Tom, "as well as spoiled and disaffected youth like Christophe."

"But he was more than that," Faith interjected. "He was a murderer."

"Yes." Ravier had been speaking in a light, almost humorous tone. His voice now became deadly serious. "Yes, as he revealed to you, he killed the *clochard* Bernard. We know from Guy d'Ambert that Bernard had discovered the jewelry in the bottom of the shopping bag one night. The others they chose were too far gone or too intent on collecting the hundred francs for delivery, if nothing had been touched, to look. Bernard smelled a rat, or rather something much more appetizing, thought he could get in on the action, and he got killed instead. If Faith had not served her pungent bouillabaisse to you all that night, but some veal, a few vegetables, they would have gotten away with it.

"Christophe enticed the *clochard* into the vestibule and poisoned him while his uncle, perhaps with Valentina, went to get Christophe's car. Guy had not the stomach to do the actual deed and part of why he is so terrified of his nephew is the exultation he observed on the young man's face after they dumped poor Bernard, almost naked and stone dead, in the Rhône.

"I'm sure they had some few moments of anxiety, but no one believed the crazy, although very-nice-to-look-at—

yes, this from Martin and Pollet—American. Guy posed as the *clochard* for a day or two, one *clochard* appearing much like another, and they thought they were in the clear.

"Your friend Madame Vincent, by the way, was not sure it was the same *clochard,* either, but unfortunately decided to keep an eye on things rather than go to the police with her suspicions. This is quite a widespread problem in France," he added sternly.

"I saw her speak to him shortly before I did. I thought it was odd, since she had made it so clear that she had no sympathy for these people. As to not going to the police, perhaps she wasn't sure they would believe an old lady." Martin and Pollet's dismissal of what were clear facts still rankled with Faith.

Ravier had the grace to look embarrassed.

"Then why did they kidnap Faith?" Paul asked. "If no one believed her and Madame Vincent had kept quiet?"

"Two reasons and again luck, bad luck, has played a role in all this. I was out of town. Valentina knew I would listen to the story and the story had changed now. She has learned that Madame Fairchild has been in touch with the police and believes the *clochard* who was currently in front of the church to be an imposter, *un faux clochard.* She also hears that Faith believes Marie has been murdered. Valentina takes a cup of tea with Faith and Faith herself reveals I am away and she is trying to get in touch with me. Madame Joliet realizes she must act fast. Again from this Mad Hatter tea party, she knows where Faith will be Saturday morning and sets the wheels in motion." Pleased with his joke, he turned to the group and grinned like the Cheshire Cat. "We police also read the classics, you know."

"But from what you have been saying, it sounds like Valentina has more resources than a few school kids," Clément commented, ignoring the allusion to English literature.

"I never liked her. You remember, *mon mari,* I have

often said that to you." Delphine shook her head vigorously, causing her glasses to rest slightly askew on her long acquiline nose. She pushed them straight with her finger and nudged her husband to pour her another glass of wine.

Faith looked at Michel. "This is where Marie and the others come in, right? They were afraid of Valentina. It was Valentina who was controlling their trade."

"Exactly—Valentina's brothers, to be more precise. They were happy to get their sister's little shipments of trinkets every once in a while and they were, in fact, making a good business legitimately selling paintings, but they liked Ferraris, not Fiats, and as pimps, they operated out of reach of French law, with their devoted sister on the spot to keep the girls in line. Valentina decided the *clochard* had to go; it was her brothers who decided Christophe had to do it, an initiation of sorts. The same with Faith. They wouldn't be bothered to come across the border for such small stuff, but they—or those in their pay here—did Marie. That was meant to be a warning to the women not just here in Lyon but also in Marseille, Avignon, on the Côte d'Azur, and in Paris."

"Poor Marie." Faith sighed. "She'd be alive if I hadn't come here."

"For a year or two, maybe. It was a question of what would get her first, the drugs, SIDA. I don't mean to sound cruel, Faith. Marie had no chance," Michel said.

Faith disagreed but thought he was probably trying to make her feel better, so kept quiet. Yet she knew what she felt and it would be with her forever.

"I remember now one time when the one with the dog came in for some scraps and Madame Joliet was there. The girl turned as pale as a ghost and left. Later, she returned and I asked her what was wrong and she said she had felt a bit ill. There was no one else in the shop except Delphine, and she does not have this effect on people," Clément related.

"We have strayed away from the story. You know all the rest. Marie was murdered at the *hôtel de ville* to prevent her meeting with Faith. Valentina was adept at getting information and no doubt knew all about the warnings. We do not know how she learned about Faith's calls to the police, but we are turning everything upside down to find out." Michel sounded grim.

Paul Leblanc spoke pensively. "We never could figure out why she married Georges. Georges, of course, was crazy for her—that long hair, those eyes. I'm sure she was the first woman he did not have to pay for and he was very proud of her gallery. But why did she want him? A respectable cover?"

"Perhaps she didn't mind being adored." Ghislaine smiled. "Few women do."

Paul grabbed his wife and gave her a lingering kiss that fully illustrated the technique made famous by the French. She emerged blushing furiously.

Michel gave them a long look. "If I may continue? *Bon.* Well, I always thought Valentina was overly ambitious and overly sexed. A good combination if you stay on the side of the law, but for her it wasn't as much fun and I suspect she enjoyed having so much power over others."

"What will Georges Joliet do now?" Delphine asked. "He seems to be trying to conduct his life as usual. He came into the store several times this week for some *steak haché.* Perhaps hamburgers are all he knows how to cook."

"He has been at work since Wednesday and we spoke briefly. He doesn't know what to say to Tom and Faith. I think he is writing a letter. I urged him to take a leave, go away for a bit. It hasn't simply been the shock of Valentina's illegal activities, enormous as it is, but that she was sleeping with the boy down the hall—and no doubt others."

Faith had a brilliant idea. "I have the perfect place for him to go. A political retreat to nature—Clotilde's and Frédéric's in the Cévennes! Clotilde will feed him wonderful meals and they can all sit around reminiscing about the glorious past. He can help them with their work and feel useful."

Tom laughed. "Then settle there himself, become the next mayor of the nearest village, marry one of the local farmers' daughters, have ten children, and live happily ever after."

"You've got it," she declared.

"Faith would be very useful here in France," Michel remarked.

"But you mention children and now Adèle will discover how many she will have with Jean-Jacques. Look at the head table; they are about to begin," Delphine said.

France and the French were associated with *l'amour* and romance, yet Faith had found what characterized the country best was pragmatism—a basic sensibility, besides that sensitivity. So, an eminently practical custom such as whatever she was about to observe did not surprise her.

A large stew pot was placed in front of the young couple and they dipped their forks in. "It's the *salmis de pintades,* the next course," Delphine explained. "They feed each other tidbits and we count the number of bites. That will be the number of babies."

"So simple," Tom murmured to Faith, and counted out loud with the rest of the room as the couple consumed the morsels of guinea hen in the rich sauce. *"Huit,* eight. Quite a family." He beamed.

"I know what you're thinking, Thomas Fairchild, and even if we'd had this at our nuptials, there is such a thing as shutting one's mouth." Tom was of the "more children the merrier" school and Faith of the "merry for whom" one.

Delphine had been listening to their conversation. "I don't think they plan to have eight, although who knows? They are making a joke that they have to stop, because the book you get from the priest when you marry only has a place to list eight and they would run out of room."

After this, courses kept arriving—platters of vegetables with a filet of Charolais beef, those pretty white animals that looked so perfect against the various shades of green and yellow in the French countryside—a Barbizon painting come to life.

The dancing became even more energetic, the music faster, the hall warmer. Couples continued to whirl below them, with the exception of the bride's mother, who danced the same slow, stately waltz step to everything, no matter who the partner or what the tempo. Her bright blue silk dress remained unwrinkled, not a drop of sweat on her brow. Between dances, she was everywhere—in and out of the kitchen, overseeing the preparations, and up and down the aisles between the tables, a smiling martinet making sure the troops were having a good time. And they were.

Faith couldn't eat another thing, but the next course, *"Le délice de l'escargot,"* the snail's delight, was intriguing. She turned to Michel Ravier. "Have you ever had this before?" She'd never seen it on any menu or in any of her cookbooks.

"Many times and so have you; however, only at functions like these do we find it done so well."

It was salad—of course.

Meanwhile, the entire party prepared to take a walk. They piled into any car available, drove to a nearby lake, strolled around the circumference, and returned for cheese, more wine, more dancing, and eventually the *pièces montées* displayed in all their glory on a table outside the kitchen. These were mountains of tiny cream puffs, stuck together with caramelized sugar, graced on each summit with sugared almonds and a tiny bride and groom—vintage 1940, by the style of dress.

The evening was wonderful. Tom made a lovely sentimental toast to the newlyweds, and almost everyone and everything else in France. Faith danced with her husband, her son, the bride's mother, and finally shared a tango with the good inspector that left her more than a little breathless. She was going to miss that man.

At two o'clock in the morning, just before the onion soup was served to tide the guests over to breakfast, Faith turned to Tom and said, "Let's go to bed."

"Great idea, but I may be too tired." He sighed.

The farewells took a long time and their cheeks were rosy from being kissed so heartily. They collected Ben from the pile of coats where he had been sleeping for some time under the watchful eyes of four very old ladies who had been supervising the dancing, tapping their toes in time to the beat of the music and their own conversation, which had continued without pause all evening.

To the Fairchilds' surprise, the car was not blocked in by others and they set out for the *auberge* a few miles away where they'd arranged to stay. It was a beautiful night, or rather, morning. The sky was clear and filled with stars.

"Happy, darling?" Faith asked her husband.

"Blissfully, now that you are back safe and sound. Don't do it again, Faith, okay?"

"You always say that." She leaned her head on his shoulder.

He kissed the top of her soft, fragrant hair. "And you never listen."

Just before dawn, there is a moment of total silence the French call "l'heure bleue"—the blue hour. It is not, strictly speaking, an hour, but a minute—a minute that seems to stretch far beyond sixty seconds.

It is the time when the night creatures have fallen asleep and those of the day are not yet awake.

If you are in the country away from the noise of a car or truck, you can feel the silence. It is palpable and, for the duration, even frightening. You stand in a large field and watch the sky begin to lighten, praying for the return of sound other than your own blood pounding in your ears. Praying for proof that the universe continues. You are tempted to call out—to no one.

Then the shrill peeps of the morning birds start and mount. They sound unnaturally loud. Only now—after the silence.

A rooster crows.

And far away from France, on this particular day, September sixteenth, a baby adds her first cries as l'heure bleue passes.

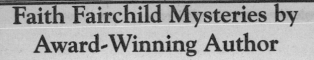